# Welcome to
# Fat Chance, Texas

To Doug '
Oh - the
places we've
Been'.

Love
Celia

Books by Celia Bonaduce

Fat Chance, Texas Series

*Welcome to Fat Chance, Texas*

Venice Beach Romances

*The Merchant of Venice Beach*

*A Comedy of Erinn*

*Much Ado About Mother*

# Welcome to Fat Chance, Texas

## Celia Bonaduce

LYRICAL PRESS
Kensington Publishing Corp.
www.kensingtonbooks.com

LYRICAL PRESS BOOKS are published by

Kensington Publishing Corp.
119 West 40th Street
New York, NY 10018

All Kensington titles, imprints, and distributed lines are available at special quantity discounts for bulk purchases for sales promotion, premiums, fund-raising, educational, or institutional use.

Special book excerpts or customized printings can also be created to fit specific needs. For details, write or phone the office of the Kensington Sales Manager: Kensington Publishing Corp., 119 West 40th Street, New York, NY 10018. Attn. Sales Department. Phone: 1-800-221-2647.

Lyrical and the L logo are trademarks of Kensington Publishing Corp.

First Electronic Edition: July 2015
eISBN-13: 978-1-60183-429-4
eISBN-10: 1-60183-429-2

First Print Edition: July 2015
ISBN-13: 978-1-60183-430-0
ISBN-10: 1-60183-430-6

Printed in the United States of America

*To my friend and mentor*
*Jodi Thomas*

Namasté

# ACKNOWLEDGMENTS

There are a lot of smart people in this world, and I ran across a bunch of them while researching this book. Thank you to those who shared their expertise. In no particular order, thank you: Koren Custer for sharing your knowledge of goats; Nancy Boerner, my go-to bloodhound expert; Patty Stith and Julie Murie for everything rabbit-related; Nancy Maxwell, for your love and support—and for introducing me to mules: Mack Kitchel for knowing about cell phones and their towers.

Rattlesnakes, air-cooled engines, how to use a straight razor, what berries grow in the Hill Country—no inquiry seemed too insignificant or far-fetched for the amazing Texans who miraculously appeared in my life. Thank you, Brandon Shuler, PhD; Ann R. Hawkins, PhD; and Miles A. Kimball, PhD. Texas *might* still be Texas without you, but Fat Chance would not exist.

They said it couldn't be done. A big thank-you to my brother-in-law, Kevin, for getting across the Mohave Desert without burning up your ancient Volkswagen bus. I would have lost an amazing story point without you.

Thanks for the inspiration, Kevin Bray, Taha Howze, Julia Townsend, Jimmy Hall, Rodney Leggett, Countess Bonaduce, Fe Cervoni, and Tiffany Galvez.

Lisa Ely, Mary Asanovich, Gene Asanovich, Laura Chambers, Dori Berman, and my beautiful mother, Elizabeth Bonaduce—the time you spent reading, rereading, researching, and prodding is appreciated beyond words.

Sharon Bowers, my agent, you are a blessing beyond measure! Martin Biro and all of Kensington/Lyrical Press, thank you for sticking with me through another series.

And always—

Even though he's from Southern California (not Texas): to my husband, Billy, who taught me how to Cowboy-Up.

The definition of insanity in Texas is so insane
that it's impossible to be insane in Texas.

—Malcolm McDowell

# PART ONE

# CHAPTER 1

"Please don't talk to anyone at the yoga stand," Erinn Wolf said. "Those people are dead to us."

"That's a bit harsh," Dymphna Pearl said.

"They threw down the gauntlet," Erinn replied. "Not us."

"I just don't want there to be any hurt feelings," Dymphna said, as she loaded two of her Angora rabbits into the hatchback of the car. Erinn, who was her best friend, landlady, and business partner, filled the backseat with knitwear—hats, scarves, bags, and gloves. When Erinn was upset, it was as if she lived in some medieval melodrama—or at least with the New York Mafia.

"Yes," Dymphna said, as she buckled herself into the passenger side of the car. "But we won. We have to see those people every Sunday. Don't you think it would be nicer to offer an olive branch?"

"By 'olive branch' I take it you mean 'carrot cake'?" Erinn asked as she pulled out of the driveway.

Dymphna winced. "How did you know?" she asked, eyes downcast.

"I could smell it as soon as I woke up!" Erinn said. "I could smell it *before* I woke up. I dreamt the gingerbread man was chasing me—until I realized it was the cinnamon and cloves coming from the guesthouse. I knew to what you were up."

Even when Erinn was in scolding mode, her grammar was perfect.

"I just think we could take the high road," Dymphna said. "I don't want to have enemies at the farmers' market."

"As Franklin Roosevelt once said, 'I ask you to judge me by the enemies I have made,'" Erinn said.

Dymphna thought that Erinn might want to rethink that particular philosophy. Did she really want to be judged by *these* enemies—people offering peace and spinal alignment?

Erinn drove down a deserted Ocean Avenue toward the Santa Monica Farmers' Market on Main Street, where Dymphna had a booth called Knit and Pearl. Dymphna was a bit of a celebrity, since she was the host of a video podcast—produced by Erinn—also called *Knit and Pearl*. The show fueled sales at the farmers' market and the clientele at the farmers' market created new viewers. Erinn, who knew what it took to get attention, insisted that a giant Angora rabbit would trump any display of yoga pants on the aisle, so Dymphna always brought at least two of her six angora yarn–producing rabbits. It seemed like a straightforward business plan, until the owners of the Midnight at the Mirage yoga stand complained the animals were disrupting the quiet zone that was imperative to the success of their business. Dymphna could see their point—people often came to her booth just to pet the fluffy fur of the animals that looked like an explosion in a cotton factory. It was anything but calm.

But Erinn would have none of it. She told the farmers' market board that Dymphna was using the rabbits as educational tools— teaching the public about the proper care of Angora rabbits and their fur. Knit and Pearl was every bit as *enlightening* as a chakra massage. Erinn won, but Dymphna got a stomachache every time the owners of Midnight at the Mirage looked over at a family squealing with delight over one of her rabbits. Dymphna didn't want to stir up Erinn's wrath, which was formidable no matter what the issue, but she thought maybe she'd sneak the carrot cake over to the yoga instructors when Erinn wasn't looking.

Dymphna understood all too well that sinking feeling when you thought your business was threatened. One of her greatest regrets was that she had never made a go of her shepherding business. She had tried to raise a small herd of sheep in Malibu, but when the land she was renting got sold out from under her it just proved to be too expensive. So she traded in her sheep for six Angora rabbits and moved out of the hills. Sometimes she felt guilty about trying to raise rabbits in Santa Monica. Dymphna wasn't sure city life was healthy for rabbits.

Erinn stopped the car near their allotted space and started to unload the collapsible tables and the knitted accessories, while Dymphna tended to Snow D'Winter and Spot, the two giant Angoras chosen to represent the show at the stall.

By midmorning, the farmers' market was humming. Once the booth was set up and everything was running smoothly, Erinn usually headed off to shop for produce. She offered to go shopping for Dymphna, who was stuck at the booth all day, but Dymphna could never gather up all her various scraps of paper on which she'd written reminders of what she needed. At one point, Erinn tried to relieve Dymphna at the booth so she could do her own shopping, but the customers all wanted to talk to Dymphna Pearl, designer of the knit creations, or they wanted to ask questions about the rabbits—questions to which only Dymphna had answers. Dymphna was perfectly content buying her groceries at an actual grocery store, but she knew better than to share that with Erinn.

Erinn started to gather her shopping bags and her detailed list. She turned to Dymphna and held out her palm. "Let me have it."

"Have what?" Dymphna asked.

"The carrot cake. I don't want you to have a weak moment."

Dymphna handed over the carrot cake and watched Erinn stride purposefully into the crowd. On one hand, Erinn could be exasperating, but on the other you had to hand it to her—she had amazing instincts.

Dymphna gave Spot and Snow D'Winter some fresh water. When she turned back toward the front of the booth, a tense-looking woman was standing in front of a display of knitted scarves. She didn't appear to be all that interested in them, though. Instead she was staring intently at Dymphna.

"May I help you?" Dymphna inquired.

The woman seemed startled that Dymphna was talking to her. Nothing about this woman suggested she resided in a casual beach neighborhood. Dymphna guessed the woman to be in her midfifties, her salon-highlighted hair glinting expensively in the sun. She extended a long French-manicured talon and snatched up a cream- and rust-colored scarf.

"Yes," the woman said. "I want to buy this." She thrust the scarf at Dymphna.

"Great!" Dymphna said, taking a charge card from the woman and sliding it through a contraption on her smartphone. She held her breath. She couldn't believe her phone could actually ring up sales.

Dymphna handed the card back to the shopper. The name on the credit card was C. J. Primb.

"Thank you, Ms. Primb," Dymphna said. "Would you like me to e-mail you a receipt?"

Ms. Primb looked startled. "No," she said. "Absolutely not!"

"All right," Dymphna said, handing over the knitwear. "I hope you'll enjoy the scarf."

As the woman took the scarf, Dymphna noticed a small gold band on C. J. Primb's left hand. It was sitting on the index finger, between the first and second knuckle joints. *Such odd placement*, Dymphna thought. She herself would never be able to get any real work done without losing a ring so precariously placed.

*Perhaps that's the point.*

Dymphna was happy to turn her attention to another shopper, who was scanning the hats. Ms. Primb was making her nervous. She couldn't put her finger on it, but there was just something about the woman that made her very uncomfortable.

The shopper wandered over to the booth and caressed a green-and-blue beret. She saluted Dymphna with her biodegradable cup of chai tea, purchased from a stall across the asphalt. "I love your TV show," she said.

"Podcast," Dymphna said in a breathy whisper. "It's just on the web. It isn't a real TV show."

The shopper held the hat up to the Southern California sky. The yarns sparkled, changing colors like a prism. She then expertly popped it on her head at a jaunty angle, studying herself in the mirror.

"Video, podcast, TV show, I don't care, I just love it all," the woman said, handing the hat to Dymphna with a smile. "This beret is just fabulous."

Dymphna stared down at the beret. Did the woman want to purchase it? Or was she just handing it back? There were more compliments than sales at the Santa Monica Farmers' Market. It was times like these when she wished she were a little more like Erinn—assertive and self-assured. Erinn would just come right out and ask the customer if she wanted to buy the hat. But Dymphna could never bring herself to be so blunt. She would just wait it out, until the woman made whatever decision she was going to make.

"Excuse me, ma'am, but are you going to buy that hat or not?"

Dymphna looked up. Sometimes people could get pushy and she

was not one for conflict. It was Ms. Primb. Why was she still here? What did she want?

"So," Ms. Primb said again to the shopper and pointed an accusing finger at the hat in Dymphna's hand. "Are you buying that or not? We don't have all day."

*We?*

"Yes," said the woman, handing over her charge card to Dymphna and blinking aggressively at C. J. Primb. "I am."

Dymphna hurriedly rang up the sale and started to put the hat in a paper bag. Whatever weirdness was going on with Ms. Primb, Dymphna didn't want to distress one of her customers.

The woman took her charge card back and put her fingertips on Dymphna's arm. "That's OK, sweetie," she said. "I don't need a bag. No need to kill a forest on my behalf."

"I wouldn't," Dymphna said.

"Pardon me?" the woman said as she adjusted her new hat in the mirror. "You wouldn't what?"

"I wouldn't kill a forest on your behalf."

The woman nodded quickly, first to Dymphna and then to C. J. Primb. Dymphna watched her as she drifted down the aisle to the vintage jewelry. Dymphna suddenly realized C. J. Primb was still studying the merchandise—or was she studying Dymphna? Their eyes met. Ms. Primb made no attempt to leave.

"May I show you anything else?" Dymphna asked.

"Not really. I just wanted to get a good look at you."

Dymphna tried not to show her surprise. Many people watched the show and felt as if they knew her—and could say anything they wanted.

"Well, feel free to look around," Dymphna said cautiously while looking around herself—mostly for something to do. She wished Erinn would come back. She started arranging embellished half gloves on a smooth manzanita branch that she used as a display rack. She tried to ignore the woman, who just stood, rooted, in front of her booth.

"Let me ask you something," Ms. Primb said.

"Yes?"

"If you had all the money in the world, what would you do with yourself?"

"I . . . I really don't know," Dymphna said. "I've never thought about having all the money in the world."

"Oh, really?" Ms. Primb practically snorted in disdain.

"What about you?" Dymphna asked. She had read somewhere that people loved to talk about themselves, and you could get out of practically any uncomfortable situation by asking your tormenters to talk about themselves. "What would *you* do if you had all the money in the world?"

"I *do* have all the money in the world," Ms. Primb said as she walked away.

# CHAPTER 2

On her return trip to Beverly Park Circle—arguably the most expensive avenue in Beverly Hills—Cleo took side streets all the way home. Having lived her entire fifty-two years on the swanky byways of the Westside of Los Angeles, Cleo could get almost anywhere—and, more amazingly, at almost any time—in L.A. without getting snarled in traffic.

Cleo Johnson-Primb had been determined to meet Dymphna Pearl. If that meant a road trip to Santa Monica, then so be it. As she drove, she fingered the scarf Dymphna had knitted. Cleo knew quality and fine workmanship, and this scarf reeked of both.

She turned her white Mercedes E350 onto her steep, quarter-mile, palm-lined driveway. Rolling down the window, she entered the code that would open the wrought-iron gates. She waited impatiently for them to swing far enough apart to permit the Mercedes to pass through. Cleo had misjudged the gates more than once. She always sent a case of beer during the holidays to the men at the Mercedes-Benz body shop who knew her—and her scratched Mercedes—on sight.

She turned into a well-manicured circular driveway at the top of the hill. There was a black Tesla baking picturesquely on the bricks. That meant her family's attorney had arrived. As she passed the electric car, it occurred to her that the automobile was probably just for show. God knows, Wesley Tensaw could afford a tank of gas on what the Johnson family paid him. But Beverly Hills did love all things environmental these days, and keeping Beverly Hills happy was what Wesley did best.

The front door suddenly swung open. A man in a blue suit and red tie stood placidly inside.

"Hello, Jeffries," Cleo said.

"Mr. Tensaw has arrived, ma'am," Jeffries replied. "He's waiting in the drawing room."

"Did he have anything interesting to say?" Cleo asked her butler as he held the door open. Cleo took her bag off her shoulder and dropped it behind her, confident that Jeffries would catch it.

"Not to me," Jeffries said, purse in hand, as he evaporated into the house.

Cleo walked through the marble-tiled foyer. A double staircase led up to the second floor and she really wanted nothing more than to go up one of them and take a nap. But Wesley was here. Hopefully, he would have some good news and she could put all the recent unpleasantness behind her.

She took a deep breath as she reached the drawing room. Putting on a cheerful, practiced smile, she swung open the doors. Wesley J. Tensaw was sitting on the sofa near the fireplace, sipping something amber from a cut-glass tumbler. He stood as she entered. She'd forgotten for the moment that it was Sunday and was surprised to see him out of uniform—a crisp Armani suit in a subdued color. He looked so less imposing in an open-neck polo shirt and khaki pants.

"Wesley, darling, good to see you," she said, offering her cheek. "I see Jeffries has gotten you a drink."

"I helped myself. I hope you don't mind." Wesley wagged the glass at her and settled back easily on the cream-colored sofa. "I can always count on you for good scotch."

"I'm happy you made yourself at home." Cleo tried to keep a pleasant expression on her face. She couldn't stand people who made themselves at home in her house. She took a seat in a winged-back chair opposite the attorney. She noticed his hair had more than a dusting of silver. He was somewhere around her age, but her father always referred to him as "the kid" and she always thought of him as one, too. Wesley had been a young associate when he first started working for Sebastian Pennyfeather—a high-powered Los Angeles lawyer with a reputation for being fearless in business affairs, the perfect attorney for her father. When Mr. Pennyfeather disappeared in a boating accident twenty-some years ago, the financial world had been stunned when her father decided to stay with Pennyfeather's protégé Wesley Tensaw. It was a high-risk move, but her father thrived on those. And it paid off. Over the years, Wesley had built himself a first-rate reputation around town.

"Where were you just now?" Wesley asked. "And please don't lie to me. It's a waste of time and just makes me drink more."

Cleo stared at him. He got up and poured himself another drink from the Waterford decanter.

"Fine," Cleo said, letting her fake smile crash to the Oriental rug. "I went to see Dymphna Pearl. She's—"

"Damn it, Cleo! I know who she is," he said, cutting her off. "I thought we agreed my office would contact everyone."

"But there are six of them . . . seven if we include my nephew."

"Which we do . . ."

"I just thought, at least this one is local. So I went to see her for myself."

"And did you learn anything?" he asked as he settled back on the couch.

"Not really," Cleo said, getting up and pouring herself a scotch. "I just can't understand what Daddy saw in her."

"Your father was ninety when he died," Wesley said, expertly swiping through the notes on his iPad. "This Dymphna Pearl is only twenty-eight. That this was a love connection seems . . . unlikely."

"This whole thing seems unlikely!"

"Yes, well, at least we agree on that." Wesley took a hefty swig. "Ready to go over this once again?"

"All right." Cleo returned to her chair, sat back, and closed her eyes. "Daddy died a month ago. He left specific instructions with you to contact seven people . . . six of whom no one in our family has ever heard of. They are all different ages and live all over the country. Some had no mailing addresses."

"No mailing addresses that we could easily discover, you mean," Wesley said.

Cleo opened her eyes. "That sounds promising."

"Let's not get ahead of ourselves," Wesley said. "Go on."

"Daddy said I . . . well, *we* . . . had to find them—*all* of them—or I wouldn't get my inheritance." Cleo's voice cracked slightly. "So, tell me—did you find them all?"

"In a word, yes."

"That's a relief," Cleo said, relaxing into the chair.

"I've followed your father's instructions. I've located them all. But I can't find any connective thread. Just a motley crew of random people."

He motioned for her to come sit next to him. She hesitated. What would Jeffries think if he came into the room and saw the two of them sitting side by side? She dismissed the thought. Clearly, Jeffries would know that someone with Cleo's breeding would never be interested in the family attorney. She glanced sideways at him. Admittedly, he was very handsome and had a certain charm. But Cleo tried never to mix business with pleasure, and this was definitely business. She got up, smoothed her skirt and sat next to him. She stared at the tablet screen as the image of an old woman appeared. The woman had gray hair pulled back into a bun and an equally severe expression.

"This is Bertha Belmont," Wesley said. "She's eighty years old. Retired, never married, no family to speak of. Worked as a secretary, a fast-food manager, that sort of thing. Ended up doing all right for herself as a bookkeeper for some entrepreneurs, but nothing earth-shattering. Seems she worked for one of your father's businesses in the nineteen fifties, but that's about it."

"My father was in his thirties then. He only had *one* business. And it wasn't even a proper company—it was a store."

"I stand corrected," Wesley said. "She worked for your father's *store*. Moving on?"

Cleo nodded. Wesley had been her father's attorney for more than two decades. Shouldn't he know this already? She realized that she was probably being unfair. Her father was not the type of man to discuss his personal life with the help—and he considered anyone he paid to be "the help."

Wesley flicked his finger over the iPad and the image of a young Japanese man came up on the screen.

"This is Wallace Watanabe. He's a fourth-generation Japanese-American. He's twenty years old. His gang calls him 'Wally Wasabi.'"

"His *gang*? Dear Lord!"

"Well, the good news is, he's been arrested a couple of times for petty theft, so he was pretty easy to track down."

"Fabulous," Cleo said grimly.

"His parole has ended, so he'll be able to get to Los Angeles for the big meeting, I suspect."

"Where is he now?"

"Up in the Bay Area."

*At least that's an inexpensive ticket.* Cleo let out a long, slow breath. She got up to stretch her legs and walked over to the large bay window. It was hard to absorb all this information at once, but time was running out. She had to get these oddballs *in* and then quickly *out* of her house. She had bills to pay. She needed her inheritance! What could her father possibly have been thinking? What did he want with them? What did he want from *her*?

"OK, that's two. And we know about Dymphna Pearl and my nephew Elwood," Cleo said, leaving her calming view and returning to Wesley "Wasn't there another woman's name on the list?"

"Yes. Polly Orchid."

Wesley scrolled to a picture of a young woman. She had long, bright red hair with the sides shaved. She wore thick kohl rimming her eyes that would have embarrassed Nefertiti. She had several piercings, including a nose ring and graduated-sized silver earrings marching from the tip of her ear to the lobe. Cleo stared at the girl, trying to make some sense of her fashion choices.

"She's twenty-two," Wesley offered.

"What was with my father and these young women?"

Wesley's eyebrows went up almost imperceptibly, but she caught it nonetheless.

"Forget I asked," she said. "Go on."

"Her father was a first responder on 9/11," Wesley said. "Fell through the floor during the World Trade Center rescue. Didn't make it. She apparently is a good kid, but aimless. Can't seem to follow through on anything."

"There's medication for that, you know," Cleo said.

Wesley ignored her. Cleo studied the picture of the willowy, long-limbed girl dressed in many layers of black. While Cleo would never sanction Polly's aggressive Goth style, she had to admit that the girl could carry it off.

"That leaves the body builder . . ." Cleo impatiently swiped the iPad herself. A well-muscled, oiled-up black man in a thong, striking a classic bodybuilder pose, stared back at her.

"Titan . . . real name Ray Darling. He's thirty-five." Wesley looked at Cleo. "Did your father take up bodybuilding late in life?"

"You know as well as I do. That would be no."

"This guy has an interesting past . . ."

"If it doesn't directly involve my father, I don't care. Anything else?"

"Not much. I mean, he's a disciplined guy. You'd have to be with all that bodybuilding. But he never really settled anywhere. Right now, he's a dresser in Vegas."

"A dresser?" Cleo's perfectly arched eyebrows shot up.

"Yeah," Wesley said. "You know, he does costumes."

"I know what a dresser does," Cleo said.

"He's working wardrobe at a gay burlesque show off the strip."

"Oh?" Cleo studied the iPad closely. "Do you think he's . . . ?"

"Gay?" Wesley ventured. "Possibly."

"Working at a gay burlesque show is kind of a clue, right?" Cleo asked.

"I'm not in the business of guessing," Wesley said.

Cleo found herself disconcerted by his smile. She looked down at the iPad, flicking through the pictures, stopping at each one and studying it—Titan, Polly, Dymphna, Elwood, Wally Wasabi, and Bertha.

"Do these people have *anything* in common?" Cleo asked.

"With you?"

"Dear God, no," she said. "Obviously, they have nothing in common with me. I meant—do they have anything in common with each other?"

"Nothing obvious, that's for sure," Wesley said, turning off the iPad display. "Except that none of them seem to have achieved much in life—at least by your father's yardstick. They're either lost, like Polly Orchid, screwed up, like Wally Wasabi, or, like Dymphna Pearl and Bertha, just don't seem very interested in money. Certainly none of them are in your father's league."

"What about my nephew, Elwood? He's a professor. Shouldn't that count for something?"

"You'd have to ask your dad," Wesley replied. "But he's not here."

# CHAPTER 3

Blanche and Earrings were Dymphna's least sociable rabbits. They had just hopped around the rabbit run—a large section of the yard given over to exercising the Angoras—when Erinn arrived with the mail. Because Dymphna lived in the guesthouse, she didn't have her own address, so they shared a mailbox. Dymphna had offered to get a post office box. It always made her slightly uncomfortable that Erinn, who owned the beautiful main house, always delivered Dymphna's mail to the backyard. But it was rarely an issue. She got very few deliveries, other than *Rabbits Quarterly*.

"You have a letter," Erinn said, walking across her own back porch and down the steps into the yard. "Very good stationery, too."

Dymphna finished locking the rabbits' pens and brushed her hands over her jeans before taking the envelope.

"How do you know it's good stationery?" Dymphna asked. "Is it like thread count?"

Dymphna's knowledge of fibers was often her gauge for comparison.

"All writers can instinctively rate stationery," Erinn said. "It's a gift."

Dymphna could never tell when Erinn was joking, so she nodded and took the letter. It was from "The Law Office of Wesley J. Tensaw." She stared down at it and frowned. "Why would I be getting a letter from a law office?"

"As Carl Jung once said, 'Often the hands will solve a problem that the intellect has struggled with in vain.'"

"Meaning?"

"Meaning . . . Open the letter."

Dymphna looked up and saw that Erinn had taken a seat on the top step of the porch.

"All writers instinctively want to know what's in someone else's mail," Erinn said. "It's a curse."

Dymphna opened the letter carefully. She didn't want Erinn to think she wasn't respectful of good stationery. She read every line over three times, trying to process it. Without a word, she handed the letter to Erinn.

The Law Office of Wesley J. Tensaw
43298 Avenue of the American Stars
Los Angeles, CA 90067
888-555-1212

Ms. Dymphna Pearl
612 Ocean Avenue
Santa Monica, CA 90402

Dear Ms. Pearl,

This office represents the executor of the Estate of a prominent, internationally known client. The testator instructed that his Will cannot be read unless you, among others, are present. Until the reading I am not at liberty to discuss either his identity or any other provision of the Will—except to note that it would be particularly against your interest to mention the reading or to show this letter to the press. Please call Ms. Rhonda Kimberly at the phone number above to confirm that you will attend the reading at 10:00 AM on Tuesday, August 12. Ms. Kimberly will give you the address (which must also remain confidential). I look forward to meeting you.

Very truly yours,

*Wesley J. Tensaw*
Wesley J. Tensaw

"Do you think it's real?" Dymphna asked when Erinn was finished reading.

"Well, Wesley Tensaw is definitely real. A heavy hitter in the legal community," Erinn replied. At Dymphna's astonished look, she confessed, "I Googled Tensaw when I saw the envelope. I told you, it's a curse."

Dymphna arrived at the Beverly Park Circle address at 9:48 on the appointed morning. Erinn was insistent that Dymphna attend the reading.

"Think of it as an adventure," Erinn said.

"I'm not really a huge fan of adventure," Dymphna had replied.

"Don't be silly," Erinn shot back. "Anybody who hates adventure does not raise rabbits for a living."

Erinn had a way of making Dymphna feel much more interesting than she found herself on a daily basis. So there she stood, across the street from the gates, behind which twisted a long driveway lined with palm trees. She'd parked across the street from the intimidating drive. She looked down at her brown skirt to make sure there was no rabbit hair sticking to it. She also wore a white blouse with billowy sleeves and a brown cloche hat she'd knitted the night before. She always felt more secure—more grounded—when she was wearing something she'd created from the fur of one of her rabbits. She wasn't sure how you dressed to meet anyone associated with a prominent, internationally known person, but these were the best clothes she had. Mr. Tensaw's secretary gave her no information other than the address and another warning not to speak to the press. Was she meeting his family? Why weren't they meeting in an office? The longer she stood, the more questions she had.

As she forced herself to approach the gates, an astonishingly muscular black man walked up to her.

"What a dump," he said, looking up the driveway.

"Do you think so?" Dymphna wondered if this gentleman was a billionaire as well.

"No, honey," the man said. "I'm teasing! I've never seen anything like this in my life. And I've been to a pool party at Siegfried and Roy's!"

"Oh! A joke," Dymphna said. "Sorry. Sometimes, when I'm nervous, I have no sense of humor."

"Well, you need to get over that right now. When you're nervous, that's when you need your sense of humor the most."

Dymphna was struck by the kind, mellifluous voice coming from this moving van–sized man. She looked back up the drive.

"I was wondering if I should drive up or walk. I couldn't remember what Mr. Tensaw's secretary told me to do. First I thought I would look too aggressive if I drove up. Then I thought I would look too passive if I parked down here and walked up."

"I know just what you mean," the man said, putting out his fist for a bump.

"So I've just been standing here," Dymphna replied, giving his fist a solid thwack. "And—"

"Don't tell me. You've been standing here watching car after car go in, and now you're afraid, even if you did drive in, there wouldn't be any room left in the driveway."

"How did you know that?"

"Great minds," the man said, beaming at her. "Well, let's do this." He pressed a meaty finger to the buzzer.

"May I help you?" came a disembodied voice from the speaker box.

"Yes, hi," the man said.

"Please push the red button to speak," the voice commanded.

"Oh my God," the man said to Dymphna, putting his massive hands to his temples. "I feel like I'm in Oz."

He pushed the buzzer and continued. "Hi. Uh . . . This is Ray Darling . . . um . . . I might be on the guest list as 'Titan' . . . and this is . . ."

Before Dymphna could open her mouth, the buzzer bleated at them. The gates opened with a quiet hum. Ray Darling stepped aside and let Dymphna precede him through the gate.

"Do you know why we're here?" he asked.

"No," Dymphna said, shaking her head. "And I'm really, really tense."

"Well, don't be. You've got Titan as a wingman, now."

"And you've got Dymphna Pearl," she said, staring up the drive. "I've never seen a driveway this long in Los Angeles."

"Come on, girl," Titan said, picking up the pace. "Power walk!"

Dymphna smiled. She felt much better knowing she had a wingman. By the time they reached the front door, both of them were glistening from exertion. Jeffries was waiting for them at the door with a tray of fluted goblets. He held it out to them. Dymphna was so thirsty, she thought she could down the whole tray-full.

"Orange juice, mimosa, or Bellini?" Jeffries offered, without a smile.

"Oh, I haven't had a Bellini in ages," Titan said, turning to Dymphna. "Would you like one?"

"I don't know what that is."

"Peach nectar and Italian sparkling wine, ma'am," Jeffries said.

"It's fab," added Titan.

"I think I'll stick to juice," she said, taking a glass.

She watched Titan daintily navigate the tray with its array of delicate stemware, before selecting a peach-tinged flute.

"You are expected in the library," Jeffries said. "If you would follow me, please."

Jeffries pivoted on his heels and led the way, still carrying his tray. He guided them under the double staircase and through a long hallway with modern artwork lining the walls. The recessed lighting highlighted each painting perfectly. Dymphna was dizzy as she took in the names of artists on the canvases. She didn't catch them all, but she was almost sure she saw a Salvador Dalí, a Louise Bourgeois, and an Arshile Gorky—all leaders in surrealism. Dymphna spent hours at the Los Angeles County Museum of Art, the Getty, the Norton Simon, and the Museum of Contemporary Art, getting inspiration for her own craft. She was open to all styles of painting, but found the twentieth-century avant-garde movement cold by its very nature. Give her the Impressionists any day. Art was about feelings and emotions, not an intellectual exercise. Dymphna and whoever picked the paintings for this household had very different ideas about art.

Before Jeffries disappeared down the hall, he indicated that they were to enter a room that was already studded with a few other people.

She felt Titan hesitate at the door. They each silently surveyed the room, taking in the odd mix. There were four other people who looked as out of place and uncomfortable as Dymphna felt. Besides Titan, there was a young Asian man Dymphna guessed to be about twenty years old. He glowered at everything and everybody. There was a young woman, probably younger than Dymphna, dressed in all black—except for her white lipstick—and an older woman, a senior citizen at the very least. With her steel-gray bun, ample middle, and wrinkled face, the older woman bore an uncanny resemblance to an apple doll. Finally, tucked into a wing-backed chair, looking most uncomfortable of all, was an older man with russet hair. He pushed back into his seat every time someone entered, as if he didn't want anyone to know he was there.

There were two other people in the room, but they looked like they belonged there. Although the man about her own age, wearing round glasses, was certainly not dressed particularly well in his Dockers and polyester no-iron shirt, which he had rolled to the elbow, he didn't wear the shell-shocked look of the other guests. His hair was thick and unruly. He looked the way she envisioned Harry Potter to have looked as a grown-up, until Daniel Radcliffe changed everyone's mind.

From her Internet research, she knew that the last man in the room, the one with the perfectly styled salt-and-pepper hair and understated suit was Wesley J. Tensaw himself.

Dymphna was momentarily distracted from her nervousness, taking in the mystifying assortment of people gathered together by a dead man. But Titan's voice brought her back.

"Now it's official," he said, taking Dymphna by the arm and guiding her into the room. "We are *not* in Kansas anymore."

Dymphna looked around the room. There was a sideboard with bagels, cream cheese, and assorted jams; a tray of perfectly presented pastries; pitchers of orange, grapefruit, and tomato juice alongside a silver tea and coffee service. There was also an array of purposefully mismatched teacups and crystal juice and water glasses. None of the food had been touched. If it weren't for the fact that a few of the teacups were absent from the lineup, there would be no indication that the library was already full of people.

Dymphna fleetingly thought of her friend Suzanna's teashop in Venice. Suzanna could give this household a tip or two about throwing a brunch. Suzanna, who was Erinn's sister, effortlessly made every day seem like a celebration at the Rollicking Bun . . . Home of the Epic Scone. Nothing was picture-perfect at the Bun, but everything was inviting. Everything in this room was picture-perfect, but nothing was inviting.

"Is this a party?" Titan whispered.

She shrugged. "I don't know *what* this is!"

Dymphna spotted two beautifully upholstered chairs on either side of a small table in a corner of the room. She pointed to them. Relief flooded over her when it became clear that Titan was content to stay with her rather than mingle. As they made their way to the chairs, it occurred to her that Titan didn't really look like the mingling type. Settling in one of the chairs, it startled her to realize that no one in the room appeared to be socializing at all. The room was completely quiet except for the attorney's shuffling of papers on an expensive looking desk and the occasional clink of a porcelain teacup making contact with its saucer.

Dymphna sipped her orange juice. She wanted it to last. She couldn't imagine anything worse than having to stand up and walk over to the buffet table at this mad tea party. She looked over at Titan, who was sitting as straight as a schoolboy, a tight smile on his face. She patted his knee and smiled. She felt his leg tense and she wondered if she had overstepped her bounds. She froze. She felt his leg twitch. She looked at him. He was biting hard on his knuckle.

*Oh no—is he about to cry?*

She removed her hand, appalled at herself for being so intrusive. She was just used to comforting skittish rabbits by petting them. She turned to him and reached out to touch his shoulder, then reconsidered. "Are you all right?" she asked, deciding on the direct approach.

Titan nodded. "This is so crazy. What am I doing here? I hate rich people."

Dymphna realized he wasn't about to cry—he was on the verge of laughing hysterically. She surveyed the room again, taking in the magnificent furniture, the priceless collection of books, the untouched buffet, the crazy-quilt assortment of guests. She felt the church-giggles welling up in her throat.

"Heeheeheeheehee," Dymphna croaked, staring at her shoes.

"Oh no, you don't," Titan said. "Don't *you* start!"

Dymphna tried to stifle her laughter, but as she took a deep breath, she snorted. For a brief instant, the two of them stared at each other, wild-eyed. They looked around the room, but no one was paying them any attention.

Their laughter, cathartic as it was, came to an abrupt halt as the library doors swung open. A woman entered with such authority that Dymphna knew instinctively that this was the Lady Of The House. She was wearing a white pantsuit with simple gold jewelry. Beige heels completed her outfit. Dymphna appreciated beautiful clothes and had to hand it to this woman—she knew how to pick an outfit for a grand entrance. Dymphna didn't want to stare at her, but she felt she knew this woman—or at least had met her before.

"Good morning, everyone," the woman said, tossing her custard-colored hair off her shoulders. "Welcome to my home. I'm Cleo Johnson-Primb. I know most of us have never met, but please make yourselves at home."

Dymphna watched the woman in the white suit go to the buffet table. She took the coffeepot and Dymphna could see a slight tremor in her hands. Dymphna could also see that the woman was barely in control of her emotions. When the well-manicured hand lifted the cup to her lips, Dymphna saw it. The ring sitting oddly on the index finger of her left hand. C. J. Primb, from the farmers' market! Cleo Johnson-Primb. A cold chill went up Dymphna's spine.

Those church-giggles were now over.

# CHAPTER 4

Cleo peered over her coffee cup, staring into middle space. Her father had taught her many lessons in life, but the ability to take in a room without actually looking at—or talking to—anyone was one of the most useful. She started clicking off the invitees—there was Dymphna Pearl; the bodybuilder with a name like some sort of metal. Alloy? Steel? Titanium? Yes, that was it—Titan; the old woman, Bertha; the Asian gangster, Wally; that other young woman, Something-or-other Orchid; and her late brother's son—her nephew—Professor Elwood Johnson.

Languidly sipping at her coffee, she studied the professor. He'd grown into a somber, good-looking man. Intelligent in his way, but he certainly didn't have his grandfather's head for business. And he militantly didn't have a taste for the finer things in life—what in God's name was he wearing? She felt a flash of annoyance as she realized he'd ignored the cashmere sweater-vest, merino wool trousers, French-cuffed shirt and Italian leather shoes she'd left for him in the guest room. Cleo could not understand his aversion to first-class cars, nice clothes, and good wine. Someone at the club had suggested that it might be a reaction to the fact that his parents died young and needlessly—the fast lane taking its toll. She dismissed that theory immediately. Hadn't she done her best for him—sending him to elite boarding schools around the world, and then spending scads of money at various universities—Yale for undergrad, Georgetown for his masters, Harvard for his PhD? She couldn't for the life of her remember what degrees he held—only that they were nothing sensible. If he wanted to spend so much time in school, at least he could have had the practicality to get a degree in business or law—something useful to the family.

*If you'd become a lawyer, Elwood,* she thought, *perhaps we wouldn't be at the mercy of this one.*

She looked over at Wesley. Weren't family lawyers supposed to protect the heirs of a man who had obviously been off his rocker? How could her father have gotten around Wesley and insisted on this crazy party? She tried to curb her annoyance. Wesley might be her only ally in the room, so perhaps she should cut him some slack.

She noticed someone she had missed during her initial survey of the room. He was sitting too far back in one of the wing chairs to get a good look at him. All she could see were his very long legs, which were crossed at the ankles. The heels of his boots were worn down—a sign of plain old slothfulness, if you asked her. Her father had specified only six people, and they were accounted for. So who could Daddy Long Legs be? She tried to catch Wesley's eye, but the attorney was busy pulling documents out of his briefcase and didn't seem to know she was trying to get his attention. On the other hand, maybe her father had also taught Wesley the valuable skill of keeping people invisible until you needed them.

As if Wesley had read her mind, he suddenly looked straight at her and gave her a brief nod. Cleo thrust her shoulders back and headed to the fireplace. She had decided that this was the perfect spot from which to greet her guests. Last night, she had practiced casually leaning one elbow on the mantel shelf, made of a smooth, dolomite white marble. As she walked to it, she realized that she was wearing all white and standing next to the snowy mantel would rob her of all authority—she would look like a talking head! Switching gears—and locations—she put her coffee cup on a tray and perched on the edge of the polished desk instead. She displaced Wesley, but so be it. Her father had left her in this uncomfortable position and she would handle it her way. She had a practiced speech and was about to ask Wesley to call everyone to attention, but realized that everyone was already quietly staring at her. She plastered on a smile.

"I suppose you are wondering why I called you all here," she began, warming up to her well-rehearsed icebreaker. "I'm wondering that myself!"

She waited for the titter of laughter she was expecting, but her guests continued to stare at her. Most stared blankly, but she noticed that Dymphna Pearl was wearing an encouraging half smile. That absolutely infuriated Cleo. How dare her father put her in the position of being pitied by a *knitter*!

She looked around the room and took in the curiosity on her guests' faces. They were as in the dark as she, that much was evident. She tried to get a peek at the man with the long legs and worn boots in the wing chair, but he was still hidden in shadow. Well, she had more urgent problems than identifying the strangest of the strangers in her library.

"Well, luckily for all of us, we're about to be enlightened," Cleo said. "I'm sure there is no need to introduce Mr. Wesley Tensaw. Wesley, I know we all look forward to hearing what you have to say."

Cleo stood up and stalked over to the French doors at the side of the library, in case she needed to make a quick escape.

"Everyone—" Wesley nodded to the assemblage as he gave the tiniest signal to Jeffries, who had magically reappeared. Jeffries used a remote control to trigger a large flat-screen, which lowered from the ceiling over the mantel. He then loaded a disc into the DVD drive. Jeffries passed the remote to Wesley much like a big spender would hand over a tip—almost by sleight of hand. As Wesley addressed the guests, Jeffries silently left the room.

"I have instructions to play a DVD for you," Wesley continued.

All eyes turned toward the screen as curtains were drawn and the lights were lowered. Cleo gasped as her father's gaunt face appeared on-screen. He was inches from the lens, obviously operating the camera himself. When he appeared to be satisfied, he wobbled to a chair strategically placed in front of the camera. Picking up some papers, he began to read.

"My name is Clarence Johnson. If you're watching this, it means I'm dead. There has probably been some celebration over this news—I made a few enemies in my day. And I make no apologies for that! I've always believed you have to have a tough hide to succeed."

Cleo glanced around the room as the identity of her father settled over the people in the room. She could hear whispers about "Cutthroat Clarence," the billionaire who always seemed to land on his feet, no matter what the stock market was doing.

"When I first heard that this cancer was inoperable, I refused to believe it. I know that sounds arrogant. It *was* arrogant! I was almost ninety, I had to die from something. But I had spent my life bending people and situations to my will and I was accustomed to winning. It took me a while to admit that I wasn't going to win this one. I have more money than anyone would know what to do with, but not enough money to buy even one more day of life for myself. Those five stages of grief? I've been through them, all right. Denial that my money wouldn't buy me more time, anger that my money couldn't buy me more time, bargaining that if I gave enough money to re-search I'd have more time, depression that my money was not going to extend my life. And then, finally, acceptance.

"Acceptance was the tough one. Because not only did I accept that my days are running out, I also accepted that I made some bad choices in my life. I would do anything, cheat anybody, to make more money. Did I need more money? I haven't needed more money in fifty years! I realized I was an addict. Not to drink or to sex, but to power. And so, I went through the addict's twelve-step program. Not officially. There isn't a support group for power mongers. But on my own. And, OK, some of those steps seemed like hogwash and I ig-nored them. I've always done things my own way. But, hey, that 'make amends' thing . . . that really hit home. I don't have time to make amends to everyone I've wronged in this life. Hell, I don't even know who most of them are."

Cleo was mesmerized. She forgot about everyone else in the li-brary and watched the screen as if he were talking only to her. On screen, her father put the papers on his lap and looked right into the lens.

"But I know who *you* are, and that's why I've asked my attorney to gather you all here today in my daughter's house. Cleo, you might be wondering why I put you to the trouble of hosting this little get-together."

Cleo gripped the doorknob. She didn't usually mind having all eyes on her, but even in the dark, she could feel the roomful of con-fused eyes turning in her direction.

"I was hoping that you'd start to see these people as just that—*people*," Cutthroat continued. "Instead of just a bunch of obstacles standing in the way of your inheritance. Did that happen, Cleo? Even for a minute?"

*No, actually.*

"Well, if that happened, I'm glad, but I suspect it didn't. You are my daughter, after all." Her father laughed, which sent him into a coughing fit. When his breathing settled down, he continued. "I know you're probably pretty steamed at your old man right now."

Cleo started to speak to the screen but caught herself in time. She tightened her grip on the door to the outside, not sure if it was to steady herself or force herself to stay inside.

Her father continued. "Cleo, I know I passed on to you my passion for getting what you want, so I have no doubt that all our guests are here. But for the seven of you gathered here . . ."

*Seven? Who is this seventh person?* Daddy had only told her to track down six.

The DVD continued. "Wesley has all my philanthropies covered and I won't bore you with details that don't concern you. I know you are all wondering what this meeting is about, so I'll get right to that."

There was a murmur spreading throughout the room like thick, hot lava. Cleo tried to see Wesley's face in the dark, but it was impossible. All she could see were his diamond cufflinks catching the light from between two of the drawn curtains.

"Here's the thing," Cutthroat continued. "I lived the American Dream. I'm not talking about just owning your own home. I own . . . well . . . I guess now that's 'owned,' since I'm dead . . . ten of them. After four, it just kind of bogs you down. No. I'm talking about the opportunity to make something of yourselves. I took that opportunity away from a lot of people. My gain was very often someone else's loss—either directly or indirectly. And that includes all of you in this room."

Cutthroat stopped speaking. Cleo stared at the screen. Her father appeared to be choked with emotion, but she couldn't say for sure. She'd never seen her father choked with emotion.

He continued. "I intend to give you people back your chance at the American Dream."

Cleo wondered, not for the first time, if her father had lost his mind before he died. What did any of this mean?

"Let's start with Wallace Watanabe. Wally, wave to everybody so they know who I'm talking about here."

Cleo could barely make out everyone turning to the sullen young man slumped on the sofa. Wally gave a flick of his index finger, which in the dark was easily missed.

"Wally," Cutthroat Clarence continued, "you are a disgrace to your family."

"This is bullshit," Wally said as he sprang from the couch and pointed at the screen.

Cleo was horrified by this raw display of temper in her home, but had no idea what to do. Luckily, her father kept talking.

"A disgrace! You should be ashamed of yourself. But I blame myself for that," Cutthroat said. "Please hear me out."

Cleo was relieved to see Wally sit back down.

"I don't know how much you know about your family's history," Cutthroat continued. "Many of the Japanese-Americans who were forced into internment camps during World War II never discussed it. I was always happy that many wanted to keep that part of their story under wraps, because I never wanted to face up to my part in it. You see, Wally, I bought your great-grandfather's store in Oakland, California, in 1942. I was sixteen and was friends with his son, your granddad. I couldn't believe that my friend and his family were going to be sent away. I lied about my age—the officials never questioned me—and I bought the little grocery store for a few dollars. I promised . . . I *promised* . . . that I would watch over it and return it as soon as that—craziness—was over. Well, I'm not here to give you a history lesson. Everybody knows that the war ended and the Japanese left the camps. Many of them returned to the lives they'd been leading previously, but many of them didn't. Couldn't. Your family, Wally, had nothing to return to, because I got an offer on the grocery store and sold it. I realized very young that money was easy to come by if you just didn't take people into account. I'm ashamed to say it, but I never gave another thought to your family from the day I took that check."

Cleo felt sick. Why was her father confessing now? What good was this going to do? The silence in the room was almost unbearable.

"Once I started making my list of people I needed to own up to, I thought about your great-grandfather. Well, I figured he was long dead, so I tried finding your grandfather instead. I was actually relieved that he was dead, too—I wasn't too keen on talking to him. Two old-timers slugging it out over an ancient injustice seemed a little pathetic. So that brought me to your dad, but he was off the radar. Figured he'd gotten it together and was leading a quiet life somewhere. Don't get me wrong—I could have found him. It just would have cost me a few more dollars. But then I found *you*. A police report full of petty crimes. You come from a good family and you're throwing that away. Would things have been different if I had kept my promise and returned the store? Maybe not. But...maybe. And that's why you're here."

Cleo's eyes had adjusted to the light. She thought she saw the young man flip off the screen with his middle finger. She looked back at the screen and saw her father was looking through his notes again.

"Next up," he said. "Old Bertha."

"Hey, dead man," the old woman with the gray hair said. "I'm still here, so don't 'Old Bertha' me."

"Now, Bertha, you...I can't say I never thought of *you* again."

Cleo watched a smile stretch across her father's face. He looked twenty years younger for a fleeting second, before returning to his notes.

"The year 1955 was a great one. America was at peace and the economy was going strong. I bought a hardware store and hired pretty Bertha Belmont to run the cash register. She was the prettiest girl in town. I was crazy about her. I couldn't believe my luck when I found out the feeling was mutual. In the evening, when I turned the sign in the window to Closed, Bertha would make us some tea, I'd put the radio on, and we'd dance to 'Only You' by the Platters. But one day, I got a lead on investing in a restaurant. I already had a nose for success and I smelled a winner. The only way to go for it was to sell the hardware store. I also had a little stash put away because I was planning on buying an engagement ring for you, Bertha."

Cleo heard a gasp in the dark.

"I knew this restaurant was going to take all my time and money and...well...I always figured I'd meet another girl," Cutthroat continued.

It was Cleo's turn to gasp. Did he mean he hadn't met another girl he loved as much? What about her own mother? Until her mother's death many years ago, her parents always seemed to have had a very respectful marriage. Cleo had always assumed that the fact that her father never remarried was a testament to their love. Perhaps their union could have had more passion—but who wants their parents to be passionate?

"Not the last time that I'd pick money over love. They always say you never forget the first time. If I hadn't run out on you, Bertha, you might have been my wife. Everything you're seeing around you—and more—would have been yours."

"You think I ever gave you a second thought?" Bertha snarled at the screen. "You big-headed fool! You became a billionaire, not God." She sat back, arms folded over her bosom.

"Okay—Ray Darling," Cutthroat continued. "Ray, I know they call you Titan and from the pictures I've seen, it's with good reason. Of all the people in the room, I feel the worst about you."

"I don't understand this," Titan said, as everyone turned to look at him. Dymphna reached over the little table between them and squeezed his hand.

"By 1990 I had my hand in everything—real estate, oil fields, technology, politics. If there was money to be made, I was there. And one place to be making money in the eighties and nineties was entertainment. The days of a singer taking the stage with talent and a guitar were long over. I started backing those big tours with all the pyrotechnics. We needed acts that could keep people's attention. We were going for a *look*, talent be damned. Well, Titan, I don't need to tell you the rest, but I do need to let everyone else in the room know why you're on my 'make amends' list."

Cleo watched Titan as he put his hands over his face and plugged his ears with his thumbs. He obviously knew what was coming—even if no one else did. And he didn't want to hear it.

"Your mother could walk into a room and all eyes would turn to her. She was a pure spirit—just waiting for someone like me to make her a star. She knew how to dance and could go on forever. So what if she couldn't sing? Technology would take care of that! So we threw an act together. Your mom was tiny and cute as a bug, so we called her Sweet Darling. We put her on the stage and all the charts. She won a Grammy, for Christ's sake. There were rumors in the press that your mom wasn't actually singing, but we were cocky. We figured nobody cared as long as they were being entertained. Sweet kept begging us to come clean. She said she felt ashamed of winning that Grammy! Then, at one of the shows, something went wrong. I don't know what. But it was obvious your mom wasn't singing. She ran off the stage."

Cleo tried to keep her eyes on the video, but she kept looking toward Titan, who had not lifted his head.

"We didn't think it was going to be a big deal. Your mom was a sensitive soul . . . a real sensitive soul. We told her we'd be doing damage control. But she wouldn't listen."

Cleo could see her father fighting to control his breathing.

"She ran out of the building. She wasn't looking where she was going and got hit by a car." Once again, Cutthroat stopped talking. He cleared his throat and took a sip of water from a glass just out of sight of the camera. He continued, but in a husky whisper. "There was speculation that she ran into that car on purpose, but I know that isn't true. Ray, I swear, your mom would never have left you."

Titan continued to look at the floor. Cleo could see his shoulders softly shaking.

Cleo thought back to those days. Sweet Darling's death had been in all the papers, magazines, and TV news. She remembered her father being withdrawn and anxious. Every family get-together was interrupted by phone calls and messages. She never knew why. She never asked. Her remembrance was interrupted as her father continued his narrative.

"Sweet used to talk about you all the time. I kept meaning to do something for you. But my advisers said that I couldn't make any sort of reparation without admitting guilt. So I let the lawyers duke it out. But that is no excuse! No excuse not to do something for a little boy who must have been in pain over losing his mother."

Cleo bit her lip. Although by the nineties, she was an adult—married, then divorced and living her own life—she was always close to her father. Or so she thought until today. So many secrets.

Their family had had their own share of tragedy during those years. She could tell her father was struggling to keep his emotions under control.

"I lost my son and daughter-in-law just months after. My own grandson, Elwood, was left an orphan. But I just browbeat my newly divorced daughter into taking him in, rather than pay him any attention myself."

Cleo looked over at Elwood, who was taking in everything in his stoic fashion. She didn't want him to think she only took him in because his grandfather insisted. It was true, but she certainly didn't want her nephew to know it.

"It was as if . . . if I admitted my little grandson needed me, I was somehow admitting that Sweet Darling's son needed something from me, too."

Cutthroat paused and took another sip of water.

"I also lost my friend and partner, Sebastian Pennyfeather, that year." Cutthroat smiled grimly. "But enough about me. Elwood, let's move on to you. You've done all right for yourself. You might not care about money, but that's probably my fault. You most likely didn't see anything particularly rewarding on that path. I'm just guessing, of course, since I never asked you. I know I haven't said this—but I'm proud of you. But I still owe you. I owe you a grandfather. But, since I don't have time to give that to you, I'm adding you to my list. And one more thing, Elwood. You're just too damn serious. I'm hoping this little scheme of mine loosens you up a bit. I've never met a young person so dead set against a good time. OK, who's next?"

Cutthroat pulled his notes close to his face and put them down again.

"Now, I won't pretend to think I was powerful enough to stop the 9/11 tragedy. But I was working in politics—behind the scenes, of course—and I donated a lot of money to protect our interests in the Middle East. Did I ever think that something like 9/11 would happen? God, no. But did I do anything to protect America against it? No, again. So, Polly, if you're in the room, and I hope you are, I kind of picked you at random—to represent all the kids of the first responders who didn't make it out. The fact that your dad was just about to retire really nags at me. But I guess that doesn't really change anything."

Polly, who had her long legs tucked under her, and had been typing on her cell phone through most of the morning, stopped typing. While she didn't look at anyone, she blinked up at the ceiling, fingers pressed under her eyes to keep her makeup from running.

"You seem like a good kid who got an unlucky break, Polly. For whatever part I played in that, I'm sorry. And if any of this goes according to plan, I hope you can pay it forward to other kids in your situation."

"According to what plan, you damn fool?" Cleo heard Wally yell at the screen. "Like the old lady said, you weren't God."

Cleo raised her eyebrows. Her father *did* think he was God and nothing that ever happened in his life had made him think otherwise. Cutthroat Clarence, of course, couldn't see or hear any of this and just continued.

"That was the worst of it, but I still could be an asshole once in a while, just to keep in practice," he said. "Which brings me to Dymphna Pearl."

As Dymphna's name was spoken, Titan raised his massive head from his hands. It was now his turn to be the protector, it seemed.

"Sweet little Dymphna Pearl, who wanted nothing more than to raise a few sheep in the hills of Malibu and spin yarn," Cutthroat said.

Cleo was puzzled by her father's tone. Was he making fun of the young woman? Admiring her? Cleo had given up guessing.

"But that was not to be, was it, Dymphna?" He looked back at the camera, eerily posing the question. "I already knew I was dying when I got an offer to buy several prime acres in Malibu. The land you had your sheep on was among them. What can I say? I bought the acres. I don't even know what happened to you."

Cleo looked over at Dymphna, who sat, shoulders hunched and head bowed, Titan's huge hand on her shoulder.

"Well, that's just about everybody," Cutthroat continued. "Cleo, I've robbed you of your chance at the American Dream, too. Being handed everything is not all it's cracked up to be. I may be criticized for the way I built my empire—and rightly so. But I built it myself. There's nothing in the world like doing it yourself. I want you to have the chance to experience that."

Cleo bristled. Had she ever complained about her life? When her friends turned forty and wanted to make something of themselves by opening boutiques and spas, did she feel even a twinge to follow suit? No, she did not. If she wanted the American Dream, she would have just bought it.

Cleo looked over at the man in the winged-back chair. Had her father forgotten someone?

"OK, Cleo, one last thing. If you're not mad at me now, this will probably cement the deal," her father said to the camera. "I know I said you'd get your inheritance if you gathered all these people together, and I'm sorry to say, I lied to you. There is just one more step before that money is in your hands."

Cleo felt as if she'd been turned to stone. What did he mean? What did she have to do now? At that moment, the man in the winged-back chair leaned forward.

It was Marshall Primb, her ex-husband.

"I'm also including you and Marshall in this," Cutthroat said on-screen.

"Uncle Marshall?" Elwood's voice pierced through the stillness in the room.

Marshall Primb winked quickly at Cleo then turned his megawatt smile on Elwood. "How's it going, kid? Long time, no see."

# CHAPTER 5

Dymphna felt the color rising from her collarbone as her friends stared at her. Erinn, Suzanna, and their mother, Virginia, listened as Dymphna recounted what had happened at the mansion. Unlike the lavish buffet set up at the Beverly Hills house, Suzanna had laid out some simple scones and homemade lemon curd in her closed teashop. It was perfect. Dymphna was starving, but could only manage a small bite now and then.

"Go on." Suzanna, who was just starting her fourth month of pregnancy with her second child, stood up and was refilling tea mugs. "So the gazillionaire tells Chloe—"

"Cleo," Erinn corrected.

"Dear, it's Dymphna's story, let her tell it," Virginia said, patting Erinn's arm.

Dymphna smiled at Virginia's mild correction. Erinn might be forty-something, but once a mother, always a mother. Suzanna sat down heavily in her chair, propped her head on her fists, and turned her complete attention to Dymphna. All three women appeared to be galvanized.

Dymphna took another quick bite of scone and continued. "When Cutthroat Clarence told Cleo that he also needed to make amends to her ex-husband, Cleo totally lost it. She took turns screaming at the video, screaming at her ex-husband, and screaming at the lawyer. I got up to leave—I was terrified, but my friend Titan . . ."

"The bodybuilder who is a dresser in Las Vegas, who lost his mother," said Erinn.

Dymphna flinched. Titan's pain had been palpable. But Erinn was a TV producer and was a little more hardened than she.

"Good memory," Dymphna said.

"I'm taking notes," Erinn replied, indicating a legal pad in front of her. "This is a lot to take in."

"Titan said we had to stay," Dymphna said. "He pointed out that we still didn't know why we were all there."

"I assume you found out," Virginia said.

"Never assume, Mother," Erinn said.

"Well, in this case," Dymphna said, "it's all right to assume, because we did find out."

Suzanna's stomach started to growl. She rubbed her hands over her belly. "Sorry! The baby is demanding some jelly beans," she said, getting up and going to an antique hutch in the corner of the shop. She stretched to reach a high shelf and pulled down a jar of jelly beans in a glass jar with an ornate lid. She went back to her seat, where she grabbed a handful of candy and pushed the jar to the center of the table, indicating that the candy was up for grabs.

"Mr. Tensaw got everybody seated and started the video again."

"Didn't you say it was a DVD?" Erinn asked. "Although it could have been originally recorded on digital videotape, I suppose."

"Oh my God, Erinn," Suzanna said. "Nobody cares! Go on, Dymphna!"

"Cutthroat said that he knew he'd done each of us harm," Dymphna said. "But he didn't want to just give us money, he wanted to give us back the thing he stole from us."

"Which was?" Virginia said, digging through the jelly beans. Dymphna knew she was looking for a coconut-flavored one.

"The American Dream," Dymphna said.

Virginia stopped digging and the three women stared at her.

"Pardon me?" Erinn said, looking up from her notepad.

"He said he stole our chance at the American Dream," Dymphna said.

"What a cheapskate," Suzanna said. "Tell him you want the money."

"He's dead, dear," Virginia said to Suzanna, then turned to Dymphna. "Besides, it doesn't sound as if he actually took any money from any of you."

"Is he planning on giving you something as abstract as a shot at the American Dream?" Erinn asked. "Can you speak of a dead person's directive in the present tense? Shouldn't it be '*Was* he planning—'"

"Mom, just make her stop," Suzanna said. She looked pleadingly at Virginia and then back to Dymphna. "What happened next?"

"This is where it gets strange," Dymphna said.

"Oh no," Erinn said. "It's been strange for a quite a while now, but go on."

"He's leaving us a town," Dymphna said.

There was dead silence at the table. The intensity of her friends' expressions unnerved her. She looked down at the table, taking a sudden interest in her phone, which was upside down on the table. The case, a gift from Erinn, featured a picture of Snow D'Winter that Erinn had taken. Erinn considered Snow to be Dymphna's most photogenic rabbit, although Dymphna loved all six equally. At one time, her animals were her only family. Dymphna thought about the three women who had since become her surrogate family. Dymphna's introduction to the Wolf family had come about in the quintessential SoCal way. She'd been looking for a house in Santa Monica with a yard that would accommodate her furry brood and she'd answered Erinn's ad on craigslist. Erinn had a lovely Victorian with a perfect guesthouse and large yard. Now, when Erinn's mother, Virginia, introduced her daughters, she said, "This is my eldest, Erinn, this is my younger daughter, Suzanna, and this is Dymphna, my daughter from craigslist."

Dymphna realized her mind had wandered. "So sorry," she said, shaking her head. "Where was I? Does anyone remember?"

"We *all* remember," Erinn said. "You said, 'He left us a town.'"

"He said that he wanted us to have the opportunity to make something of ourselves, so he left us a ghost town in Texas."

"How are you supposed to make something of yourself in a ghost town?" Suzanna asked. "It's already a loser town, right? Everybody already left."

"I don't really have all the answers," Dymphna said. "He did say that he wanted us to realize our potential—and the potential of this town in Texas. It's apparently been abandoned for years, but it has running water and electricity. He said that if we all go—and we all *have* to go—and make a success of the town in six months, he would give us each three years' wages."

"Three years' wages?" Suzanna asked.

Dymphna said, "But Mr. Tensaw said that if our total earnings over three years didn't equal $100,000, then we'd be guaranteed that!"

"Did he specify what kind of success?" Virginia asked.

"Not exactly." Dymphna shook her head. "At the end of the day, we're getting the money whether we make anything of the place or not. I guess he figures if we're stuck there for six months, we might as well give it a shot."

"That's taking a lot for granted," Suzanna said.

"I can't believe he thinks he can dictate a crazy scheme like this and expect it to work!" Erinn said. "Although he doesn't have anything to lose at this point." At her mother's disapproving look, Erinn added, "What? Too soon?"

"Where in Texas is this place?" Suzanna asked, changing gears.

"It's someplace in the Texas Hill Country," Dymphna said. "I don't really know."

"Does this place have a name?" asked Virginia.

"Yes," Dymphna said. "It's called Fat Chance."

"Apt," Erinn said.

"Fat Chance is better than No Chance, I guess," Suzanna said, popping a lemon jelly bean.

"Although, frankly, Dymphna," Virginia went on, "you've already made something of yourself. You don't need to live up to some billionaire's idea of success."

"Thank you," Dymphna said, blushing. "But, you know, all those other people are counting on me. If I don't go, they don't get a chance to get their money."

"You just met these people," Suzanna said. "You need to decide what's right for you."

"I know," Dymphna said. "But we've been given a week to decide and I'm the only one on the fence."

"You're kidding," Erinn said. "I can't believe that Cleo is going to spend six months gentrifying a ghost town in Texas."

"I can believe it," Suzanna said. "If she isn't going to get her money unless she sees this through, you can bet she'll go."

"You don't even know her," Dymphna said, giggling.

"I know her type," Suzanna said.

"You do not know her type," Erinn protested. "How many billionaire heiresses do you know personally?"

Suzanna scowled at her sister.

"If you feel loyalty to the group, which I think is admirable of you," Virginia said, "what are your reservations?"

"I wouldn't be able to bring the rabbits right away," Dymphna said, her eyes tearing up. "I would have to make sure the place was safe for them. Texas is *hot*. I'd have to scout the place and make sure I can keep them comfortable. And I can't leave them here."

"Of course you can leave them here," Virginia said.

"That wouldn't be fair to Erinn," Dymphna said, reading the panic in Erinn's eyes. "They need tons of attention. I can't leave her to take care of six rabbits."

"Oh, I know how to take care of them," Virginia said. "You taught me how to feed them, shear them, and make the yarn! I know their schedule. They'll be fine! I promise."

"But, Mom," Erinn said, "you live here and the rabbits are at my place."

"Actually, that's even better," Virginia said. "I mean, Dymphna, it's certainly up to you, but it's going to get a little crowded upstairs at Suzanna and Eric's."

"Aren't you happy with us, Mom?" Suzanna asked.

"Of course, honey," Virginia said. "But Lizzy's almost four years old. And with the new baby coming, this would be a perfect time for me to leave." She turned to Dymphna. "I could actually move into the guesthouse. Then I'd be with the rabbits. It's a win-win. Unless, of course, Erinn doesn't want me to move in."

"Don't be silly, Mother," Erinn said.

Dymphna couldn't tell if Erinn was onboard with her mother living in her backyard or not. But there were other issues looming, so she laid them out. "But what about the podcast? What would we do about that?"

"Actually," Erinn said, "I was going to tell you tonight. We need to give the podcast a little break. I got a job on a new series—and I have to take it. Money is getting a little tight."

"If I get three years' salary, we'd have a nice nest egg," Dymphna said. "I could come back in six months with all that money and live in your backyard forever."

"If you have a nest egg, you probably won't want to live in my sister's backyard," Suzanna said.

"Yes, I would," Dymphna said. "I really would. I love you guys."

Suzanna and Virginia leapt up and smothered Dymphna in hugs, tears, kisses, and we-love-you-toos. Erinn, who was embarrassed by displays of emotion, started tapping at her phone.

"You need to do this," Virginia said, through tears. "You would have enough money to buy land for rabbits or llamas or goats or sheep and really have the life you deserve."

"We'll watch over the rabbits as if they were our own!" Suzanna added.

"Okay." Dymphna sniffled. "If you guys believe in me, I'll go."

"We do," Virginia said, kissing Dymphna on top of her head.

When the women finally finished their declarations of love and loyalty, Erinn looked up from her phone and said, "Did you know that 'Texas' comes from the Hasini Indian word *tejas*? It means friends."

"Perfect," Dymphna said. "'Cause I'm going to need all the *tejas* I can get."

# CHAPTER 6

Cleo's massive bed was barely visible under the dunes of clothes. Arms crossed, she surveyed her selection.

*What does one bring to a ghost town in Texas?*

She picked up her white mink coat and tossed it onto a Louis XVI bench. She'd always loved the elegant styling of the bench and now felt in solidarity with the misunderstood and beheaded king for whom it was named.

It was over a hundred degrees in the Texas Hill Country right now. Even at the end of her sentence in February, she was never going to need a mink. Following this logic, she also discarded a gray chinchilla jacket and a rich brown sable. She had never really needed furs in Los Angeles, but trips to cooler climates offered excuses to show them off. She thought perhaps she'd find a more appreciative audience in Texas, but Jeffries had looked on the Internet for what sort of weather she would encounter. The furs had to stay home.

She picked up her favorite coat—a vibrant full-length red fox fur. She wrapped her arms around it—she just couldn't leave it here. At the very least, she'd use it as a throw on her sofa.

*Will I even have a sofa?*

She put the fox coat back on the bed—it was coming with her. The clothes looked like the ingredients of one of the salads she ordered at the Cheesecake Factory. The more you ate, the more lettuce seemed to be left. She sighed and went to the mountain of shoes she'd selected. She picked up a pair of strappy sandals with Lucite heels. She was studying them when she heard a whisper of a knock on the bedroom door.

*That new maid needs to be more assertive!*

"Come in, Gilda," Cleo said, adding the Lucite heels to the Louis XVI bench.

"That's Hilda, ma'am," Hilda said, chewing on her thumbnail as she entered. "Mr. Tensaw is downstairs. He said he'd like to have a word with you before you leave tomorrow morning."

"I have a telephone," Cleo said.

"Yes, ma'am," Hilda said. "Would you like me to tell him that?"

"No, that's all right, Glinda. Tell him to come up."

"I'm already here," Wesley said, lounging in the doorway.

Cleo heard the new maid gasp—probably fearful she'd be reprimanded because Wesley hadn't stayed downstairs until summoned. Wesley looked annoyingly sure of himself perched in the doorway like that. He certainly seemed to be enjoying himself as this little family drama played out.

"Thank you, Heidi," Cleo said. "You may go."

"It's Hilda," Wesley and the maid said at the same time.

Cleo saw the maid shoot Wesley a grateful smile. She also saw Wesley cast an appreciative glance at Hilda's departing rear end as the maid scooted out of sight.

*He's old enough to be her father! But certainly hot enough to turn a girl's head.*

"Ten million dollars for your thoughts," Wesley said, with that crooked smile that made Cleo want to slap him.

He walked into the room, tossed aside the fur coats, and sat on the bench.

"I'm not speaking to you," Cleo said. "That was a dirty trick inviting my ex without telling me."

"I'm still following your father's orders, Cleo," Wesley said. "Believe me, I'm doing the best I can for you."

"I hadn't seen him for years," Cleo said. "I didn't even know where he lived!"

"Portland, Oregon," Wesley said.

"You know, Daddy said I should never have married him," Cleo said. "An older man, a Vietnam vet. Too many strikes against him."

"I wasn't aware serving our country would be held against a man," Wesley said.

"He just would never settle down," Cleo said. "At least he didn't settle down as long as I knew him. Do you know what he's doing now?"

"He's a carpenter."

"See? Daddy was right. He didn't amount to anything."

"Carpentry is a respectable profession," Wesley said. "Just ask Jesus."

"Very funny," Cleo said, picking up a pair of designer jeans. She held them out for his inspection. "Should I bring these? Texas means horses, right?"

Wesley nodded. "I'm only going to be a phone call away," he said. "You know that."

"If there's a phone!"

"I don't think your father is sending you back to the nineteenth century, Cleo," he said.

"Why is he sending me at all?" Cleo sank down on the bed, displacing four pairs of evening pumps, which clattered to the floor.

"People get funny ideas when they're dying," Wesley said. "I think your father had deep, deep regrets about a lot of things—and throwing money at those regrets wasn't going to work."

"Right," Cleo said. "So withholding all the money is going to make everything all right, is that it?"

"I couldn't say," Wesley said. "But you've got to see this through, whether you like it or not."

"But it's a ghost town! Jeffries says it's not even on Google Maps!"

"I know," Wesley said. "I've printed directions on how to get there."

"But there are eight of us! Where are we going to live? How are we going to shop? Can I get my nails done? There are a lot of questions."

"I'm pretty sure your father anticipated all of them," Wesley said. "And while I can't speak for him, I'm going to guess that, no, you aren't going to be able to get your nails done."

Cleo blinked back tears.

"You've just got to make the best of it," Wesley continued. "Be a good sport."

"A good sport? Have you met me?"

Wesley surveyed the pile of clothes. "You're not going to be able to fit all that in the RV, you know."

"Oh, you think I'm going to get in an RV?"

"It's one of the terms," Wesley said. "Your father chartered a private RV and it will take you all, in absolute comfort, to Fat Chance."

"There is nothing private about traveling in a bus with seven other people," Cleo said. "I'm taking our plane."

"One, it's not your plane—yet," he said. "Two, you seem to forget you have no money. How are you going to pay the pilot or buy the fuel?"

Cleo collapsed backward onto the bed, stabbing herself in the head with a stiletto heel. She hurled the shoe across the room. Sitting back up, she glared at Wesley.

"I could sue you," she said.

"No, you couldn't," Wesley said, chuckling. "You don't think that's the first thing your father locked down? And even if you tried, your money would still be tied up until this is over. Why not take the Martha Stewart approach? Just do the time and get on with it."

"That would make *your* life easier, wouldn't it?" she said.

"Oh, I almost forgot," Wesley said. "Here's a debit card. It has five thousand dollars on it."

"Five thousand dollars?" she asked, staring at the plastic card Wesley put in her hand.

"For incidentals," Wesley said. "And you should be very pleased. Your father is only giving the others a thousand dollars each."

Cleo started packing, furiously. "Thank God for credit cards," she said.

"Your credit cards are canceled," Wesley said.

Cleo froze. Maybe Wesley was right. She should just do her time and get it behind her. There was no way she could outsmart or out-think Cutthroat Clarence.

"You're really enjoying this, aren't you?" she asked Wesley.

"In my weaker moments."

"What about my staff?" Cleo asked, changing gears. "What are my secretary, driver, butler, pool boy, and all the other people who run this house supposed to do?"

"Your father has made provisions," Wesley said. "You worry about you."

By morning, Jeffries had loaded the town car with seven suitcases and a garment bag. Cleo was exhausted, and the strain of the recent week was showing in the bags under her eyes. She did the best she could to reduce the swelling with cool teabags—there was no time or money for a facial. Jeffries came out of the house carrying a small, inexpensive bag.

"Are you ready to go, Jeffries?"

"Yes, ma'am, I am all packed." Jeffries held the small suitcase aloft. "The GPS should get us as far as Austin and I have directions from there. Mr. Tensaw gave me all the confirmation numbers and addresses for our accommodations. We are all squared away."

He slid his suitcase into the front passenger seat—there was not an inch of space in the trunk—and climbed into the driver's seat. Cleo climbed into the back. She told Jeffries that she needed him to drive her to Texas. If her father wanted her to economize, fine. She wouldn't fly. Besides, she'd need a car and a driver in a godforsaken ghost town. She hoped it hadn't occurred to Jeffries that she was kidnapping him. She'd make it up to him when she got her money. Besides, he was a loyal family servant. He would *want* to help. As they pulled out of the driveway, she looked at him in the rearview mirror, where she could see only his eyes—focused on the road ahead. She wondered if perhaps she should have just asked him.

# CHAPTER 7

Dymphna waited outside Erinn's wooden front gate, having said good-bye to her rabbits and surrogate family. She insisted on meeting the RV by herself—she didn't say so, but she wasn't sure she'd have the resolve to board if any of her loved ones were around. She knew this was an opportunity to get enough capital to finance the life she wanted for her rabbits, but she was not entirely convinced that Cutthroat Clarence actually owed her anything. While she didn't actually believe that all was fair in love and war, Dymphna suspected that Clarence Johnson hadn't been the total black-hearted opportunist he painted himself to be. Erinn's exhaustive research—and a touch of her own—revealed a more complex man. He gave billions to charity. He'd made some terrible mistakes, but he'd attempted to rectify them—albeit at the last minute. Erinn thought it was a bid for redemption, a deal with God. Dymphna thought it revealed a good soul . . . even if it was one that had been buried deep within the businessman. She liked the idea that she would have to earn this prize. If Cutthroat had just written her a check, she wasn't sure she could have accepted it.

The black-and-tan RV stopped inches from the curb. It loomed over her; she had never seen an RV this size. The door swung open. Dymphna lifted her battered carpetbag onto the step. The driver reached for it.

"I'll keep it with me," she said. "It has my knitting."

She was a little too nervous about the future to actually feel anything like a genuine smile, but she attempted one anyway. After all, it wasn't the driver's fault she was on her way to a ghost town in Texas for six months.

Dymphna climbed aboard and the door made a soft hissing sound behind her as it closed. She was the first one aboard. She looked around, stunned at the opulence of the interior. The door to the RV was behind the front passenger's captain's chair. The front of the RV looked like a futuristic spacecraft, with more buttons and levers than she could imagine operating while still keeping a vehicle on the road. To her left, there was a kitchen, a desk, a flat-screen TV, a dining area with a built-in wet bar and china cabinet, several built-in couches, and two more captain's chairs behind the driver's and front passenger's seats. There was also a hallway, but Dymphna didn't think she should go exploring just yet.

She looked back at the driver, who had stowed her bag . . . somewhere . . . and was climbing back into his seat. She didn't want to appear haughty or rude, so she scrambled into the seat next to him.

As she reached for the seat belt, the driver said, "Can't sit up here, miss. Against policy. Please make yourself comfortable in the back."

Dymphna flushed. She was sure Cleo would know that sitting next to the driver was verboten. She said a little prayer of thanksgiving that Cleo wasn't around to witness her faux pas.

*Why am I worrying about her?*

She decided to sit at the dining room table—there was a hollowed out center with lovely apples and pears nestled in it. She assumed that a bowl sitting *on* the table instead of *in* it would slide right off at the first turn. She realized that, as comfortable and inviting as the RV seemed, it was battened down as tight as a ship. She took an apple out of the bowl and pressed on it to make sure it was real—every piece of fruit in the bowl looked too perfect. But they were real, all right! She rubbed the apple on her sleeve to make it shine. Before she took a bite, it occurred to her that perhaps the fruit was just for display and she shouldn't eat it.

"Would you like an apple or a pear?" Dymphna swiveled in her chair to ask the driver.

"No, thank you, ma'am," he said. "But you go right ahead."

Dymphna took a big bite of the fruit, pleased with how she'd handled the situation. The RV took off—she was on her way. The vehicle was incredibly agile for its size. She could see people straining to see inside. She blushed, sure that everyone thought there must be a famous person lurking within.

"Where are we going?" she called up to the driver, to distract herself from worrying about the gaping onlookers.

"Los Feliz," the driver said.

She was surprised how casual he sounded. She would have been extremely jumpy driving this whale of an RV.

"Next passenger is Professor Elwood Johnson. That's the last of the locals."

"Oh?" Dymphna said. "What about Ms. Johnson-Primb?"

The driver shrugged. "I don't have her on my list."

Dymphna felt suddenly more at ease. She couldn't imagine traveling for two days with that woman. The trip suddenly seemed much more interesting.

Mr. Tensaw had sent each of them a follow-up letter, with a debit card loaded with a thousand dollars and the directive that they would all be taking an RV to Fat Chance. Now that she thought about it, the geography didn't quite work. She knew everyone else lived out of state, but, except for Titan in Las Vegas, none were between California and Texas. And even Las Vegas would be out of the way.

"I'm a little confused," Dymphna admitted. "How are we going to pick up Bertha, Polly, Titan, Marshall, and Wally?"

She was pleased with herself for remembering everybody's names. Dymphna and Erinn had Facebook-stalked everyone but Bertha (who wasn't on it), so she had at least a little information on all of them.

"Picking everybody else up at the airport," the driver said. "All their flights got in about the same time."

It was inconceivable how much money Cutthroat Clarence was spending on this crazy idea of his. He'd paid to fly each of the out-of-towners in and out twice in the same week—once to have the initial meeting at Cleo's and now for the trip to Fat Chance. For a man who was dying of cancer, he seemed to have considered every detail. She thought how much easier it would have been for him to just tell his advisers to send everyone some money. She didn't know about the rest of the group, but she sort of admired him for working so hard on this escapade. Especially since she suspected that Ms. Johnson-Primb was looking for loopholes!

Dymphna looked out the window as they passed the Silver Lake Reservoir. They climbed up a steep street not much wider than the RV. The driver pulled smoothly to the curb as Professor Johnson and an enormous wrinkled dog came out of a duplex. His half of the yard was a vegetable garden. She wondered if the occupant of the other unit in the duplex would water the vegetables while Professor Johnson was out of town. She also felt a pang of remorse that the professor's dog was making the journey with them, but not her rabbits. On the other hand, if Professor Johnson's dog was coming along, perhaps it was a good thing that her rabbits were safe in Santa Monica.

The door swung open and the driver repeated his routine. He grabbed the professor's bag and ushered him inside. The professor also had a messenger bag slung across his body, but he didn't relinquish that to the driver. The dog looked up into the cab and sat down on the street. Professor Johnson went back out, got behind his dog, and pushed him bodily into the RV. Dymphna looked at the dog. It was tan with a black saddle and muzzle. It had sad, sleepy eyes and a forlorn expression. The droopy ears added to the animal's depressed appearance.

"Hi, boy," Dymphna said, guessing by the black, masculine collar that she was speaking to a male.

That was enough for the dog. He shook himself happily, sending spittle flying over the inside of the RV. The driver probably didn't know there was a long line of dog slobber on the back of his shirt. Dymphna decided it was probably best not to mention it.

The dog loped over to her, settling down with his head in her lap. They let out a collective sigh.

Professor Johnson sat in one of the captain's chairs in the rear section. He obviously knew not to sit next to the driver.

"Hello," Dymphna said.

"Hello," Professor Johnson said.

"So," Dymphna said. "You're a professor."

"Yes," he said.

"And this is your dog?"

"Yes."

Dymphna was terrible at small talk, but she felt she'd met her match. She patted the dog's furrowed brow.

"Is this a bloodhound?" she asked, briskly rubbing the dog, whose skin oozed like a mudslide under her ministrations.

"Well, technically, he's a Chien de Saint-Hubert," he said. "But bloodhound will do."

*Thank God.* "Are you excited about the trip?" she asked.

"I find it interesting that my grandfather formulated this little production and died just as I started my sabbatical year," he said. "It's the only way I could have gone."

"You think your grandfather *planned* to die during your sabbatical?"

"Stranger things have happened." He shrugged.

*No, they haven't.*

The bus lurched forward. The dog's toenails skidded on the laminate flooring.

"What's his name?" Dymphna asked, patting the wobbling dog again.

The dog lost his fight with gravity and thudded to the floor, legs splayed.

"Thud," Professor Johnson said.

"Pardon me?"

"Thud. His name is Thud—for obvious reasons."

Dymphna and Professor Johnson stared at the melancholy heap on the floor.

"Good name," she said.

"Thank you."

Professor Johnson signaled the end of the conversation by opening a large newspaper—it appeared to be called *Old News*, and had a banner headline about ancient China. Dymphna felt awkward just sitting there, but reading in a moving vehicle made her nauseous, so she pulled out her latest knitting project—a sweater in a pale yellow. The touch of the yarn moving softly through her fingers made her miss her rabbits. She tried not to cry—was she really up for this trip? Thud seemed to sense her anxiety and scooted across the floor to put his head on her feet. He drooled on her shoes.

In no time at all, Dymphna had finished a sleeve and they were pulling in to LAX. The sign overhead read Arriving Passengers.

With Titan looming above the crowd, it wasn't hard to spot them. The sight of the RV apparently intimidated the drivers of several smaller vehicles. One by one, they pulled away from the curb without a fight. The driver swung the door open and dismounted to deal with the luggage. Thud lifted his head from Dymphna's shoes. She watched as Professor Johnson continued to read, but without missing a beat reached up and grabbed Thud's collar as the dog made for the stairs.

Thud's tail wagged violently as the passengers started to board. Dymphna could see Titan helping Old Bertha (she tried not to think of her as "Old" Bertha, but it was difficult) into the RV. Bertha grabbed the railings with both hands and heaved as Titan pushed.

Once inside, Bertha glared directly at Dymphna—who was looking at her—and Professor Johnson—who was not. Bertha gave Dymphna a curt nod and lumbered to the front of the RV. Dymphna was about to tell her not to sit by the driver, but couldn't work up the courage to speak. Bertha didn't seem to invite conversation any more than the professor did.

Next aboard was Titan. Dymphna felt herself relax as soon as she saw his colossal frame filling the doorway. He beamed at her, but was soon distracted. He saw Thud.

"Hello, beautiful boy," Titan said, kneeling in the middle of the narrow room. "Aren't you a good dog!"

Thud broke free of Professor Johnson's grip and put both paws on Titan's shoulders. The two of them happily wrestled each other to the floor. Dymphna was afraid the shifting of all that weight might tip the RV, but the vehicle seemed stable.

"Okay, move it," came the sudden voice of Wally Wasabi. "I gotta—get by."

"Oh, I'm so sorry," Titan said, getting off the floor and returning his attention to Dymphna. "Hi, honey!"

Titan gave her a big hug as Wally Wasabi slunk by, disappearing into the back section without another word. Polly Orchid, in black leggings, a black ruffled skirt, black tunic, and her signature kohl-rimmed eyes, climbed up the steps two at a time. She still had her bright red hair with the shaved sides, but had replaced the white lipstick with black. Thud was on his way to greet the newcomer, but Professor Johnson grabbed the dog's collar again.

"He can be a bit enthusiastic," Professor Johnson said to Polly.

"No worries," Polly said, a giant smile emerging from her black lipstick. "I love dogs."

Professor Johnson kept his grip on Thud and went back to his reading. He glanced up one more time at Polly and said, "By the way, thank you for your father's service."

Polly nodded, once again trying to keep her tear ducts from overflowing by pressing on her lower eyelids. Dymphna and Titan exchanged a conspiratorial look. Clearly, the Johnsons were a cold bunch, but maybe the professor wasn't a complete icicle. By the time they turned to smile fondly at the girl, she was absorbed in her cell phone.

The whole RV shook as Marshall Primb climbed on board. He

was only about half the size of Titan, but he seemed to be in perpetual motion.

"OK, OK," he said, clapping his hands together, then waving them in the air. "Let's do this!"

Dymphna thought his frenetic energy was impressive, but she noticed that Bertha swung her seat around to look out the front window. The older woman was obviously not a fan of noisy men. Thud strained to get free. It was clear another wrestling partner had joined the party. The driver, having divested the curb of all luggage, climbed back on board. Marshall took a seat at the dining room table with Titan and Dymphna, offering his hand to each before he sat.

Dymphna couldn't help herself. She turned to the front of the RV to watch the drama unfold between Bertha and the driver.

The driver said his well-rehearsed line. "I'm sorry, ma'am. Against policy. Please make yourself comfortable in the back."

"Bite me," Old Bertha said, staring determinedly out the front as she fastened her seat belt. It clicked with a resounding finality.

They were on their way. Dymphna tried to make conversation with Polly. Although Dymphna was Polly's senior by about five years, Polly was certainly the closest of the travelers, with the possible exception of the antisocial Wally Wasabi, to her own age. As if Polly could sense Dymphna's interest, she looked up from her phone.

"I've never been to Texas," Polly said.

"Neither have I," Dymphna said, hoping to get a grip on a potential bonding moment.

"It's crazy big," Polly said, showing Dymphna a colorized map of the state on her phone. "Did you know that the most popular snack food in Texas is peanuts floating in Dr Pepper?"

"No, I didn't know that," Dymphna said. She could feel the potential bonding moment slipping through her grasp.

"I don't drink soda," Polly said, looking up with a stricken face.

"I . . ." Dymphna could think of nothing comforting to say.

Polly sighed and swiped at her phone. Dymphna could see the screen fill with words.

"I never got the hang of reading a book on my phone," Dymphna said.

"Oh, I love it!" Polly said. "I use my phone for everything. Right now, I'm reading a series of short romances by a woman named Mimi

Millicent. She actually writes her stories *on* her phone. They're awesome."

She left Polly to stare at her phone and turned to Titan. "Are you excited about the trip?"

"Sort of," Titan said. "I've been working on a show in Vegas with my friend Maurice. He's a top dresser in Vegas and he got me the job. It's the longest I've ever been in one place. I'm just afraid this is just a crazy rich man's joke and I'm leaving a good thing for some stupid wild-goose chase."

*I know what you mean.*

Marshall turned out to be the chattiest among them.

"This is just insane, isn't it?" he asked the group. "Old Cutthroat pulling a stunt like this?"

No one answered him. Dymphna wondered if this was out of shyness, like with Titan and Professor Johnson, or rudeness, like Bertha or Wally Wasabi, or cell-phone absorption like Polly. She felt she didn't fit into any of those categories, so she spoke up.

"It's a little unusual," Dymphna agreed.

"I noticed that these gentlemen have spectacular nicknames—Titan, Wally Wasabi." Marshall turned to Professor Johnson. "Except for you and me, Elwood."

"Apparently, yes," Professor Johnson said flatly.

"I mean, 'Elwood'—that's some handle," Marshall said. "I remember telling your mom and dad, God rest their souls, that Elwood was way too much name for a little boy."

Dymphna had forgotten that Marshall had been part of the Johnson clan for several years.

"Did you get a nickname in school? Woody? Woodstock? Anything like that?"

"No," Professor Johnson said.

"So, what do your friends call you?"

"Professor Johnson," the professor said, pointedly returning to his paper.

"Catchy," Marshall said, winking at Dymphna.

Dymphna blushed. Marshall was pretty old, probably around sixty, but he was masculine in a way that men of her generation rarely were. She couldn't picture Marshall refusing to leave the house because he had no hair gel.

"Well, I've been thinking." Marshall turned his attention to Dymphna and Titan, apparently not at all put off by Professor Johnson's snub. "I want to be called Powderkeg from now on."

Dymphna and Titan nodded.

"All right," Titan said. "We'll call you Powderkeg."

"Oh no!" Marshall slapped the table. "Not like that! You've got to say it like a pirate! Powwwwwderkeg! Maybe squint one eye when you say it."

Titan jumped at the loud noise, but Dymphna started laughing. Polly laughed, too. At that moment, a life preserver couldn't have been more welcome than Polly's black-rimmed smile. It felt wonderful to release all the tension that had been building up as one after another of the new residents of Fat Chance, Texas, boarded the RV. Marshall tossed an appealingly crooked smile Dymphna's way.

"Okay, Dymphna Pearl," he said, Dymphna's blush deepening. "Let's hear it."

"I can call you Powderkeg," she said. "But I can't close one eye at a time."

"Like this," Powderkeg said. He winked at her.

For the first time in her life, Dymphna really regretted her inability to wink back.

Powderkeg turned to Elwood. "You can call me Uncle Powderkeg, if you want."

# CHAPTER 8

Dymphna Pearl was dreaming.

In her dream, she was surfing a huge wave, barreling toward the California coastline. The wave kept getting bigger and bigger, until she was a speck riding a living, breathing, wild animal of blue-black water. When the wave crashed over the bluff of Santa Monica, she had to lie flat, gripping the board, to keep from falling into the sea. She held tightly to the surfboard as it arched up—past Los Angeles, over Las Vegas—then landed like a jetliner in a gentle green valley by a lake. She was still facedown on the surfboard, afraid to look up. The far-off mechanical voice of a GPS whispered in her ear.

"Oh, Dymphna! Wake up! You have reached your destination."

"I don't know my destination," Dymphna said, fighting to stay asleep.

"Be that as it may," the mechanical voice intoned as the surfboard morphed into the RV, "your destination is on your left."

Dymphna's eyes opened. She looked around. She *was* in the RV. She realized this was not a dream. Well, the surfboard and flying over Vegas clearly was, and while global positioning units had gotten very advanced, they still didn't call you by name or use expressions like "be that as it may." But the rest was real. The RV was parked on a turnout on a desolate highway. There was nothing but silence. She looked around the cavernous interior of the RV. She counted—one, two, three, four, five sleeping figures—not to mention the driver, who was asleep with his feet propped up on the massive steering wheel. Someone was missing. She saw that the door at the front of the cab was open. Tossing a light knitted shawl around her shoulders, she got out of the gigantic RV. The area was socked in, in a thick fog. She walked toward the outline of a man.

Once they'd seen highway signs for Austin late last night, they'd all voted to keep going. Dymphna had no idea how far outside the city limits they were—an hour? Two hours? Three? She'd fallen asleep while the neon lights of the college town still lit up the sky and country music rode on the wind.

"Professor Johnson?" Dymphna called out as she made her way over to him.

The fog was so dense, she couldn't tell if the professor shrugged a greeting or, more likely, just ignored her. He had a real paper map in his hands and was scanning the horizon—what there was of one in the fog.

"I wasn't expecting fog this dense in Texas," Professor Johnson said. "It feels like a London particular from Victorian England. Without the soot, of course."

Dymphna assumed a London particular must be the professor's learned term for a pea soup fog.

"Oh," Dymphna said, racking her brain for any interesting tidbit she might know about fog or Victorian London. She came up blank. She missed Erinn. Erinn would know everything there was to know about fog, London, Queen Victoria, *and* soot. She knew everything about everything. Granted, Erinn could be downright boring in telling you more than you wanted to know about any given subject, but she was never at a loss for words.

But Erinn wasn't here. As usual, Dymphna was desperate for a way to make conversation with this man.

"I had a dream just now," she said. "The GPS said we'd arrived."

"That was a dream, all right. Our GPS gave up about two hours ago," he said. "But the driver and I came to the conclusion that this is the place."

"That's good!" Dymphna smiled encouragingly.

"Oh?" he said. "Do you see a town here?"

Every way she looked, she saw nothing but shadowy hills spread lavishly with mist.

"I mean, obviously not right *here*," she said quickly. "Maybe when the fog clears, we'll see it."

"Like Shangri-la," Professor Johnson said.

"Or Brigadoon," Dymphna said as the two of them stared into the space where the town should be.

Unlike the fog, but like every other conversation they'd had, this one vaporized.

The seven of them had traveled together from Southern California to Central Texas in the behemoth chauffeured RV provided by their eccentric and deceased benefactor. Dymphna had thought an adventure of this nature—or the stress of it at least—would have resulted in some sort of bonding. Even the small inroads she'd made with the others paled in comparison to her total failure at thawing Professor Elwood Johnson.

"Where is Thud?" she asked.

"He's a bloodhound," Professor Johnson said. "He's off . . . sniffing."

"Maybe *he* can find the town," Dymphna said.

"I have a PhD from Harvard in natural science," Professor Johnson said.

"I know. You've mentioned that several times."

"My point is," he said defensively, "if I can't find the town, what makes you think he can?"

"I just thought . . . ," she said. "Well . . . he has other skills."

Professor Johnson whistled for the dog. Thud bounded out of the brush, wrinkles and spittle flying. He had a large, rectangular piece of wood clamped in his mouth.

"What have you got there, boy?"

Professor Johnson always seemed a little less intimidating when he was interacting with his dog.

"Thud, let go!" he said, finally pulling the wood from the dog's mouth.

Thud relinquished his prize and sat down, tail wagging furiously.

Dymphna stood over the professor, who had laid the plank on the ground. As he knelt, he started wiping away some caked mud. She realized the sun was up, but the fog was still so thick she could barely make out the weather-beaten letters that were appearing by inches.

Dymphna stood over the professor. Wrapping the shawl around her, she squinted down at the sign.

"What does it say?"

"It says—"

"Welcome to Fat Chance, Texas!" called out a new voice from somewhere in the fog. If a wheelbarrow rolling through gravel could be given a voice, this would be it.

Dymphna peered into the fog. She shot a glance at Professor Johnson, who was wiping his glasses as he peered nearsightedly in the same direction. Dymphna found herself standing closer to Thud, who did not seem at all alarmed as the crunching footsteps approached. Dymphna could make out the approaching figure of a man. He wore a pair of long Hawaiian board shorts that almost crested the tops of thick-soled hiking boots. Completing this rather unusual ensemble was a stained T-shirt, which may have been white once in its dreams. The man's large, battered cowboy hat rested on the back of his head, a shock of white hair poking out from underneath. His piercing, silver-tinged green eyes peered out from a pair of oval glasses. He also sported an enormous white beard. Between the hair and the beard, there was no more than a strip of tanned face showing. He reminded Dymphna of a large angora rabbit. The man continued advancing on them. Professor Johnson grabbed Thud's collar, although Dymphna thought it was probably more for show than any worry that the bloodhound was going to attack. She could feel the dog's tail whapping against her leg.

The man stopped about three feet in front of them. He didn't smile. He thrust out his chin at Thud. "That your dog?"

"Yes," Professor Johnson said.

The man now thrust his chin at the Welcome To Fat Chance, Texas sign in Professor Johnson's hands. "That's my sign," he said.

Dymphna noticed the man had his right shoulder angled back at an unnatural angle. She wondered if there was something wrong with his arm, but as the fog started to clear, she saw that he was resting his fingertips on the butt of a gun. The gun was in a holster buckled across the man's hips. At a distance, the holster had blended in with the loud board shorts, but as he got closer, there was no mistaking it.

The man suddenly whirled on the RV. He yelled out, "Throw your weapons down and come out with your hands up."

"Sir, this RV is coming in from Los Angeles," Professor Johnson said. "We don't have weapons."

One of the windows opened slowly and a man's hand appeared, palm up. In the palm was resting a pistol. The hand dropped the gun to the ground as the door hissed open. Powderkeg came down the steps into the open with his hands locked over his head.

"Good morning, Vietnam!" the old man said. "I know that gun."

As Powderkeg moved toward the side of the RV with his hands still clasped over his head, another gun hit the dirt—this one a semiauto-matic handgun in dark gray and alarming pink. Old Bertha heaved herself down the stairs, glaring at the old man.

"A lady can't be too careful," she said, putting her hands in the air and moving toward Powderkeg.

A switchblade was next out the door, followed by a glowering Wally Wasabi.

"Dude," Wally said. "You suck."

"Move along, sonny," the old man said. "And get those hands in the air."

"Whatever," Wally Wasabi said, but he moved down the steps of the RV with his hands up.

"How did they get all those weapons on their planes?" Dymphna whispered to Professor Johnson.

"You can put a switchblade in checked luggage," Professor John-son whispered back. "And if you let TSA know you're bringing a firearm—ahead of time in writing and you have a permit—you can bring it in checked baggage, as well."

"Wow." Dymphna's voice was so soft, she could barely hear it her-self. "Who knew?"

"I did," the professor said. "And every TSA agent in America."

Dymphna looked at him. He clearly wasn't showing off, just stat-ing facts.

"Any more weapons in there?" the man with the gun said.

A hairbrush came flying out the door, knocking the hat off the old man.

"I'm so sorry," Titan said as he stumbled out the door. "I didn't mean to hit you."

The old man picked up his hat and placed it back on his head. "Take more than a hairbrush to do me in. Is that everybody?"

"Everybody but the driver," Old Bertha said. "And a sweet young girl who is perfectly harmless."

"OK, driver," the old man called in. "I want you to check the en-tire interior for any other weapons and then come on out. Slow-ly."

The old man drew out the word "slowly." Dymphna wondered if he'd watched too many westerns. He didn't really look like a real cowboy. He *was* wearing a cowboy hat, but those Hawaiian shorts and hiking boots told a different story. Cowboy or not, that gun looked real—and she was going to pay attention. She could hear the driver rummaging around. When he came out of the RV, Dymphna instinctively moved toward him. He was carrying her knitting needles, one of them looped with her precious yellow yarn. She let out a whimper as the driver held them in the air.

"Do I really have to throw this on the ground?" the driver asked. "This lady has been working awfully hard—knitting away the entire trip."

Dymphna was touched. The driver had kept to himself. She hadn't exchanged more than a few perfunctory words with him since the trip began. She didn't even know his name. She couldn't believe he had noticed she'd been knitting, let alone taken on a man with a gun on her behalf.

"Hand the one needle over to me," the old man said. "Slow-ly."

The driver handed the old man the free knitting needle and passed the remaining needle and yarn to Dymphna, who cradled them in her arms. The old man studied the needle, tucked it into his holster belt like a sword, and then turned toward Professor Johnson.

"What about you?" the old man asked. "You got any weapons?"

"I don't believe in weapons," Professor Johnson said, hands in the air, the Fat Chance sign leaning against his shin. "Besides, I have my dog."

The old man started laughing. "Come 'ere, pooch," He pulled a piece of dried meat from his pocket.

Thud pulled free of the professor's grip and bounded over to the man, who held the jerky aloft.

"Sit," the old man commanded.

Thud's haunches landed in the dust, his eyes never moving from the piece of meat. The old man tossed the meat into the air and Thud rose up and caught it in his gigantic jaws.

"I've already met your dog," the old man said to Professor Johnson. "He came into town and I gave him some of this." He pulled out another piece of jerky and threw it to the dog, who once again caught it in midair.

"Town?" Professor Johnson asked, starting to lower his hands until the old man started fingering his gun again.

"Yeah," the old man said. "I'm the mayor."

"The mayor." Dymphna tried not to make the word into a question.

She exchanged a look with Titan. She noticed Powderkeg never took his eyes off their host.

"Yes," the old man said. "My name is Pappy and I'm the mayor of this place."

"We're not even sure where this place is," Old Bertha said.

The old man pointed to the sign leaning on Professor Johnson's legs. "Like the sign says. Fat Chance, Texas."

"This is bogus," Wally Wasabi said. "You're not going to shoot anybody."

"Oh yeah?" Pappy stalked toward Wally Wasabi, who didn't flinch but stared back calmly into the old man's face. They were nose to nose for several seconds. Dymphna was starting to feel light-headed, when Pappy broke the stalemate.

"Wait a minute," he said, as if he'd forgotten all about his show-down with Wally Wasabi. "Didn't you say there was somebody else on that bus?"

"Yeah," Polly said, appearing in the door of the RV, Goth makeup freshly applied.

Pappy was clearly taken aback by Polly's ghoulish appearance. "That's a look," he said, walking over to her.

Dymphna had gotten used to Polly being friendly and personable on the bus, and had forgotten what an interesting first impression the girl made.

Pappy reached up to take Polly's hand. "Come on out," he said. "Don't be scared."

As soon as Polly was on solid ground, she let out a tae kwon do *kiai* yell and flipped Pappy into the dirt, her foot on his throat.

"I'm not as harmless as I look," Polly said, releasing Pappy's throat and staring down at him.

"I'm sorry to have underestimated you, little girl." Pappy sat up and rubbed his throat.

In an imperceptible flash, Pappy's hand shot across Polly's ankles. She landed on her butt, sending a cloud of dust into the air. Dymphna saw Powderkeg take a step toward the scene, but Titan stopped him.

"I think she's got this," Titan whispered under his breath.

Pappy and Polly scowled at each other from their sitting positions. Polly's muscles tightened, ready for more action.

"Hold it right there," Pappy said to her. "I'm an old man and that's my only move."

The group relaxed. Polly sprang to her feet and offered Pappy a hand, before rethinking and pulling her hand away.

"No funny stuff," Polly insisted.

"Yeah, yeah," Pappy said. "Get me up."

Polly hauled him to his feet. "This isn't a very nice way to greet us, you know."

"Well, you got me there, little lady," Pappy said, smacking dust from his Hawaiian shorts and breaking into a deranged grin. "OK, everybody, you can pick up your weapons."

"I don't understand," Dymphna said. "We're free to go?"

"You've always been free to go," Pappy said. "But now you're also free to pick up your weapons."

"I could have had a heart attack," Old Bertha said.

"Well, I'm sorry, ma'am," Pappy said. "But I just wanted to make sure you were the right crowd."

"Right crowd?" Polly asked. "How many recreational vehicles on steroids roll through here?"

"None," Pappy admitted. "Cutthroat said you all were coming, so I've been expecting you. But I had to make sure it was you! I mean, if the media got wind of this crazy idea of Cutthroat's—who knows how many lunatics would be showing up? Nothing personal, of course."

He looked around at the group. "Y'all fit the description," he continued, counting heads. "But aren't we missing somebody?"

"Hold on," Professor Johnson said. "Let's not get ahead of ourselves here! What do you mean, you were expecting us?"

"Y'all think Cutthroat would send a bunch of babies like you to the middle of nowhere without assistance? I'm here to oversee this whole experiment. Who do you think got the electricity and water going around here?"

"You?" asked Titan.

"Hell, no," Pappy said. "I just said I *oversee* the place."

"Can I drive this RV down that road?" the driver interrupted. "Looks pretty steep . . . and narrow."

The group turned and looked at the trail behind Pappy. The fog had evaporated and they could see the trail suddenly dipping into a valley, most of the road disappearing around a sharp bend. The pitch of the road wasn't the only problem. There was also an enormous rut carved out in the middle—a huge seam yawning in the center of the trail. Everyone stared at Pappy, who was shaking his head.

"Afraid not," he said. "The road washed out about five years ago."

"Some overseer," Wally Wasabi said under his breath. Titan nudged Wally's sneaker with his own foot, trying to keep the newly won peace.

"Yep," Pappy said. "I can't even get my own car up and down anymore."

Everyone followed Pappy's gaze, which settled on an ancient VW bus. The bus was missing its top. In its place was a large beige tarp fastened on either side with thick twine. The tarp followed the curved lines of the roof, and looked like a futuristic Conestoga wagon.

"I call her the Covered Volkswagen," Pappy said.

"How do we get our things down to Fat Chance?" Dymphna asked.

"Carry 'em," Pappy said.

The driver had quietly unpacked the suitcases and boxes from the RV. The luggage sat on the ground, metal buckles and locks winking in the sun.

"I can't walk down that," Old Bertha said, arms folded across her chest in determination.

"You gotta," Pappy said. "Might as well get used to it. Like I always say, up and down is the only way in and out. Of course, I say that to myself, 'cause nobody else has been here in years."

Dymphna tried to steady her heartbeat as she watched the driver. He appeared to be getting ready to desert them—leaving them with this madman.

"We're supposed to carry all this down there?" Wally Wasabi asked.

"Keep your pants on," Pappy said, eyeing Wally Wasabi's sagged jeans. "Or in your case, pull your pants up. Jerry Lee is gonna give you a hand."

He let out a shrill whistle that pierced the morning. "Jerry Lee," the old man barked. "Get up here."

The group stared down the road. Nothing moved in the still morning air. Dymphna wondered if Pappy was insane. Then she heard it. The tiniest hint of sound. Possibly a branch moving. She looked at Thud, who had gotten to his feet, the hair on his back bristling. She couldn't see it, but something was headed their way. Professor Johnson grabbed the dog's collar as an old mule came morosely up the hill and stood next to Pappy.

"This is Jerry Lee," Pappy said, scratching the animal between its enormous ears. "Named him that 'cause he's entertaining, but sometimes he can be a real jackass."

Pappy slapped his thigh. Clearly being alone did not stop him from enjoying his own jokes.

"That's a mule," Professor Johnson said, looking at Jerry Lee. "A jackass is a donkey."

"A jackass can be a person, too," Pappy said.

"I hate to interrupt, but I have to head back to Los Angeles," the driver said, looking at the anxious faces of his former passengers. "Happy to take anybody with me—looks like this will be your last chance to change your minds."

Dymphna's body shook like an earthquake had gone off inside her. She thought the driver looked extremely worried. Well, he didn't sign up for this. She did. She shook his hand.

"Thank you for everything," she said. "We'll be fine. Really."

The driver started to speak, but Dymphna held up her hand.

"We all agreed to this," she said. "You have a safe trip back."

"If you're sure," the driver said.

She smiled. "I'm sure."

*I'm not sure!*

By the time she'd turned back, everyone was carrying armloads of luggage. Dymphna watched Powderkeg and Pappy as they compared pistols.

"I knew you were the veteran as soon as I saw your Colt," Pappy said. "I'm carrying the same kind—western style, of course. It'll be good to have some backup around here."

*Backup?*

Everyone stood in silence for a moment as the RV disappeared down the road that had brought them all here.

Old Bertha was the first to speak. "Well, Jerry Lee is loaded up with suitcases," she said to Pappy. "You go down there and unload. Then send the mule back for me."

Pappy slapped her on her ample bottom. "Come on, old girl. The walk will do you good."

Dymphna's jaw dropped in disbelief. This man had obviously been long out of touch with most of civilization if he thought it was acceptable to smack a woman's rear. Polly's eyes blinked rapidly in their kohl-rimmed sockets. Old Bertha looked furious, but held her tongue.

Titan was making sure the luggage was secure on Jerry Lee. Pappy came over and patted Titan on the shoulder.

"Good job, son," Pappy said. "Jerry Lee needs new shoes. Cutthroat left you the forge, so you and I are going to be good friends."

Titan's eyes widened as Pappy led Jerry Lee onto the trail.

"What's a forge?" Titan whispered to Dymphna as the band of travelers made their way down the hill, dodging the worst of the ruts.

"I don't know," she said. "I guess we'll find out."

Dymphna felt bad about lying. She knew what a forge was, but thought it might scare Titan off. And she really wanted him to stay.

# PART TWO

# CHAPTER 9

Powderkeg and Wally were in the lead as the group headed carefully down the trail. Dymphna found that strange, as they didn't know the territory. Shouldn't they wait for Pappy to show them around? Weren't all of them still guests? She didn't have much experience with men, but she had a sense that there were some subtle testosterone challenges going on. Dymphna noticed that Pappy, for all his wisecracking at Old Bertha's expense, was being very gentlemanly, putting out his hand to guide her over the particularly wide ruts. Professor Johnson, Dymphna, Polly, and Titan followed cautiously behind Jerry Lee's hindquarters as the mule lurched into town carrying his share of the luggage. Thud threaded his way in and out of the bushes and sniffed at Jerry Lee's heels.

Polly tapped away wildly on her phone. She looked up at Dymphna in a panic. "There's no reception," she said. "Our phones are useless out here!"

"We'll be okay," Dymphna said.

"I'm right in the middle of a Mimi Millicent story!"

Dymphna tried to think of something comforting to say, but Polly didn't seem like someone who was going to function very well without a cell phone signal. Both women looked up and saw Fat Chance at the same time. They gasped at their first glimpse of their new home.

A sun-baked wooden walkway ran the length of eight brown and gray buildings clustered together at the bottom of the trail. They looked like something out of a history book or movie set. There was one building on what would have been "the other side of street," had there been a street. Another building, the largest of them all, sporting a lopsided sign that said Creekside Inn, sat slightly off by itself at a disturbing angle to the street. A final set of buildings, set off from the town, up a slope, looked somewhat like a tiny farm, with a ramshackle house, a barn, and another outbuilding. Although it was a short distance away, there appeared to be a few animals grazing in a penned yard. A creek ran along the back of the town but circled around to the side of the aptly named inn, then continued onto the lower portion of the property line of the little farm, before finally spilling into a small pond.

"If Norman Bates comes out of that inn, I'm going to scream like a girl," Titan said.

"Who is he?" Professor Johnson asked, stepping carefully over a large rock protruding from the road.

"*Psycho*?" Titan said.

"Oh! He's psycho," Professor Johnson said. "I guess that could happen to anybody out here." He walked ahead of them to get his dog away from the mule.

"What planet is *he* from?" Polly asked.

Powderkeg and Wally waited at the bottom of the hill for everyone to regroup.

Pappy returned to host-captor mode. "OK, see that brown building that's sort of leaning to the left?" He pointed vaguely toward the buildings on the walkway. "That's City Hall."

"You mean shitty hall," Wally said, poking Polly in the ribs.

Polly snickered, but Pappy's smile disappeared. He walked over to Wally Wasabi and put a hand on his shoulder.

"Listen, son," Pappy said. "There are ladies present. I don't think we need to be using that sort of language."

Dymphna was worried that every day here was going to be spent waiting for a fight to erupt, but Wally Wasabi backed down. Surprisingly, he looked straight at Old Bertha and said, "Sorry, ma'am."

"As I was saying," Pappy said, tying Jerry Lee to a hitching post. "That building in the middle is City Hall. Let's all head in there and I'll start distributing the property."

"Property?" Powderkeg asked. "We get property?"

"Don't you people know anything?" Pappy asked, as he looked around at the bewildered faces. He shook his head. "I don't know if Cutthroat died before giving out the details or if he just decided to leave everything to me. 'Cause . . . you know . . . I'm the mayor and all."

"This is not Chicago in the nineteen thirties," Professor Johnson said. "It is not the job of the mayor to distribute property."

"That's debatable," Pappy said, ushering everyone up the stairs into the swaybacked City Hall. "Of course, it's not debatable *here*, since I pretty much have all the cards and all the property, but go on."

"You are not the mayor," Professor Johnson continued. "The mayor is an elected office. No one elected you."

Dymphna looked around the hall. It was one story, and contained several stools and mismatched chairs. A table was at one end, with a gavel resting on the scarred top. Pappy sat down at the table. He picked up the gavel and whacked it. The cracking sound reverberated through the room.

Dymphna peeked at Titan, who looked like he was ready to bolt, then at Powderkeg, who looked like he was going to explode with laughter.

Pappy looked solemn. "I admire"—he pointed the gavel at Professor Johnson—"Professor Johnson, right? I admire Professor Johnson's enthusiasm for civics, so I'm going to do this right. Now, Cutthroat left me in charge of this town to help y'all, but if you don't want any help, that's fine. I can just take Jerry Lee and be on my way. Otherwise . . . well, all in favor of me retaining my position of mayor, raise your hand."

Bertha was first with her hand in the air, followed by Titan, Dymphna, Powderkeg, and Polly.

"That's enough," Pappy said. "I'm still the mayor."

"Says who?" Titan asked.

"Says me," Pappy said.

"If I may interrupt this witty repartee," Professor Johnson said, "that is not the way an election works."

"I got five votes," Pappy countered. "That's the majority."

"Voting is done in secret," Professor Johnson insisted.

"Not here." Pappy looked around as if he were playing to an invisible crowd.

Professor Johnson continued to scowl over this travesty of the American electoral system as Pappy continued. "You better back down, there, Professor, or I'll throw you in jail."

"Oh, so you're the jailer, too?" Professor Johnson asked.

"Well, technically, the sheriff. But yeah."

"Oh, the mayor *and* the sheriff." Professor Johnson looked around at the group, seeking support.

"And the banker," Pappy added.

"This is insane."

"Are you just noticing that?" Wally asked, but his natural hostility seemed to have dissipated a bit. He actually seemed to be enjoying himself.

"Come on, come on," Powderkeg said. "I'm sure we can settle this like reasonable people."

"I don't think reasonable is much of a buzzword around here," Titan whispered to Dymphna.

Dymphna turned to see how Polly was processing everything—she was starting to feel protective of her. But Polly was staring at her phone as if she'd never seen it before. She must have felt Dymphna's eyes on her, because she suddenly looked up.

"I rebooted and everything," Polly said, eyes glistening. "There's no cell phone reception."

Thud, who had been wandering in and out of the building, started barking wildly. All discussion ended as everyone filed out to see what had the dog in such an uproar. Professor Johnson ordered Thud to be quiet. The entire group, so at odds with one another a few seconds ago, stood together in silence. Then they heard it, the faint *beep beep* of a car's horn.

For one brief moment, Dymphna's heart leapt. A car! A car that went places! A car that could take them out of Fat Chance!

Thud raced back up the trail. Without so much as a nod to one another, Dymphna, Titan, Polly, Powderkeg, and Professor Johnson chased after the dog. Dymphna was halfway up the hill when she turned around to see Pappy and Old Bertha sitting on the steps to the wooden walkway. She smiled as she watched them. From a distance, they looked like any normal, sane couple you might meet at the tea shop back in Southern California. Pappy seemed to be inching closer to Old Bertha. Maybe a romance would blossom in the hills of Texas? She saw Old Bertha slap Pappy's hat into the dust.

*Maybe not.*

Wally was sitting off by himself—just like he had for the entire RV trip. She wondered if he was ever going to make an effort to be part of the group.

The horn was still blaring and getting louder as Dymphna got closer. She hopscotched over the worst of the ruts.

"Come on, Dymphna," Titan said, holding out his massive hand to haul her to the top of the trail.

As they cleared the top, Dymphna saw Cleo furiously beeping the horn of the town car. Jeffries, whom Dymphna remembered from Cleo's house, was leaning against the trunk of the car, arms crossed, ignoring the racket and watching Thud pee on a back tire.

Cleo spotted the little band of newly minted townspeople coming toward her and stopped blasting the horn. "Thank God," she said. "We were lost!"

"I was wondering if you were going to figure out where to stop," Powderkeg said.

"As if you care."

"I do care."

Dymphna, who seemed to have turned into a romantic overnight—possibly because she had no rabbits to worry about—thought this was incredibly sweet of the rough-hewn veteran.

"Don't give me that," Cleo said.

"I *do* care," Powderkeg insisted. "I mean, there's no money for me in six months unless you're here, so I'm ready to deal with whatever you have to dish out."

While Cleo and her ex argued, Dymphna went over to Jeffries, who had opened the trunk.

"Do you need some help with that?" Dymphna asked, glancing over at Powderkeg and Cleo. "Looks like they might be awhile."

Jeffries smiled at Dymphna and handed her a suitcase embroidered with roses and the monogram *cPj*.

"We passed the RV. The driver told us where to stop," Jeffries told Professor Johnson, who was pulling his dog away from the car.

Polly came over and looked into the overstuffed trunk. Cleo abruptly grabbed the suitcase out of Dymphna's hands and gave it back to Jeffries.

"That's all right, dear," Cleo said, frantically trying to push her hair back into place but instead making it stand on end. "Jeffries will get everything. Won't you, Jeffries?"

Jeffries looked down the pockmarked road and shook his head."The town car won't make it down there," he said. "This is the end of the line, Ms. Johnson-Primb."

"Jeffries, I thought you'd consider staying!"

"Why would you think that?" Jeffries asked, genuinely startled.

"Well..." Cleo stalled. "I thought you might... feel it was your duty."

"My duty?"

"Or something like that," Cleo added weakly.

Jeffries started again to distribute Cleo's luggage—returning the embroidered suitcase to Dymphna's hands. Cleo was clutching a makeup bag as if her life—and profile—depended on it. Titan could barely see over the top of his own stack of matching suitcases. Polly had the unwieldy garment bag. Professor Johnson had a second set of luggage. Even loaded down with luggage, no one in the group moved.

Only Powderkeg had his hands free. He was clearly enjoying every minute of Cleo's power struggle with the help.

"Please, Jeffries," Cleo said, as she watched her precious luggage being passed around. "I don't know what I'd do without you."

Jeffries had one more embroidered suitcase in his hands. He put it on the ground.

"All right, Ms. Johnson-Primb, I'll stay," Jeffries said.

"You will?" Cleo relaxed her grip on the makeup bag.

Dymphna's eyes widened. She had not expected this! She shot a glance at Powderkeg, whose mouth dropped open in surprise.

"Yes, ma'am," he said. "On one condition..."

"Anything, Jeffries," Cleo said, sounding a little more in control of herself.

"I've worked for your family for twenty-five years," he said.

"And we have valued every minute of your dedication."

"I'll stay," Jeffries said, "if you can tell me my first name."

"I guess Rumpelstiltskin is too much to hope for," Cleo said faintly.

The residents of Fat Chance, who were making an effort to look like they weren't listening, gave up the pretext and stared at Cleo.

"Well," Cleo said. "Well, it's... it's..."

Cleo grabbed her hair and looked at the ground, clearly racking her brain. Jeffries clicked the trunk closed. As he opened the driver's-side door, he tilted his head as if studying Cleo.

"You have a safe stay here, ma'am," he said. "And if you don't mind my saying so, I think this is going to do you a world of good."

Before Cleo could say another word, Jeffries disappeared into the town car and drove away. Cleo stared after the car as if she were forcibly rooted to the earth. Powderkeg came forward and put an arm around her.

"It's Donald," Powderkeg said.

"What?" Cleo said, as if emerging from a dream.

"Donald. That's Jeffries's first name."

"How can you possibly know that?" Cleo demanded.

"I lived with you for five years," Powderkeg said, shaking his head. "I saw the man every day. How could you possibly *not* know that?"

Cleo thrust her makeup bag at him. He took it, but was clearly enjoying himself.

"I bet you tried just about everything to get him to stay," Powderkeg said. "Did you offer to marry him?"

"Oh, for God's sake, Marshall." Cleo picked up a sack of jewelry that had fallen out of one of the bags. "Grow up. This isn't *Downton Abbey*."

"Awww, come on, Cleo," Powderkeg said. "It wouldn't be the first time you married below your station."

Cleo stomped ahead of the group to walk down the hill with Professor Johnson and Thud. Thud attempted to jump on Cleo, but the professor managed to rein him in. Clearly, Cleo was not in the mood for a frisky bloodhound.

"Wow," Polly said. "They run with scissors."

"I know, right?" Titan said.

Titan and Polly waddled down the hill. Dymphna looked after them. They made a cute couple.

*Maybe Titan and Polly . . . oh, wait, Polly isn't exactly Titan's type!*

Powderkeg picked up the small suitcase that sat orphaned on the side of the road and fell into step with Dymphna as she headed down the trail.

"I figured it might be a bad idea to tell her to start calling me Powderkeg," he said, barely suppressing his delight.

"Yeah," Dymphna said as she looked down the road to Fat Chance. "Too soon."

# CHAPTER 10

Cleo grabbed her nephew's arm as she took in the wreckage that was Fat Chance, Texas. She stared at the ramshackle buildings and the makeshift boardwalk. She choked back outraged tears.

"I can't believe your grandfather has done this to me," she said, looking helplessly at the professor. "Did you know Jeffries's first name?"

"Well . . ." Professor Johnson stalled. "Well . . . actually . . . yes."

"Why didn't you say something?" Cleo asked.

"Jeffries didn't ask *me*."

"This is a nightmare." Cleo forced her feet to move toward town.

"It gets worse." Professor Johnson nodded toward Pappy, who was headed toward them with his strange hiking-booted gait.

"Hello, Cleo," Pappy said, offering a cracked and calloused hand for shaking. "Good to see you! I thought maybe you'd backed down."

"Do I know you?" Cleo hesitantly offered up just four fingertips for a handshake.

"Oh no, no, of course not," Pappy said. "I just . . . well, you're the only one on Cutthroat's list I haven't met yet."

"This is Pappy," Professor Johnson said. "Grandfather left him here."

"He left you here?" Cleo asked. "I'm so sorry, Mr. Pappy. I think my father was losing his mind toward the end . . ."

Thud looked up in surprise as Pappy let out a laugh that echoed through the hills.

"Don't you worry," Pappy said. "I'm here of my own free will. Been here for almost thirty years. Happy to help you all get settled."

"That's very kind of you," Cleo said, taking heart that someone could survive thirty years in Fat Chance.

Pappy reached for one of Cleo's bags. "Let's get a move on. I want to get back to that town meeting."

"We're having a town meeting already?" Cleo asked.

"Yes," Professor Johnson said. "We were electing a mayor."

Pappy bristled. "We were *not* electing a mayor. I'm the gob-derned mayor, son, and you better get used to it."

Professor Johnson was about to argue when he felt a light pressure on his arm. His aunt had regained some of her Beverly-Hills-matron composure. Her touch meant "Just keep smiling, we will deal with this later."

"Fine," Professor Johnson said to Pappy. "Lead the way. We'll follow you into City Hall."

"You'll follow me into City Hall, what?"

"Pardon me?" Professor Johnson asked. He glanced at his aunt, who was still wearing her shell-shocked beauty-queen smile.

"You'll follow me into City Hall, Your Highness!" Pappy said, grabbing another of Cleo's bags from the professor and heading toward the tilted buildings. He must have been carrying sixty pounds, but walked as if he were carrying a briefcase with nothing more than a newspaper inside.

"It's not Your Highness," Professor Johnson said to Pappy's back. "It's Your Honor!"

"What was that?" Pappy asked.

"Your. Hon-or." Professor Johnson pronounced every syllable carefully.

"Just so we understand each other"—Pappy turned to Cleo— "that's one serious boy you got there."

"I'm glad we're providing you with some entertainment," Professor Johnson said. "But this is not what the Founding Fathers had in mind, you know."

"Look around, Professor," Pappy said, turning around. The ram-shackle buildings of Fat Chance, Texas, were starting to absorb another day of sun. "I think this is about as far from what the Founding Fathers had in mind as you can get. We're on our own!"

Pappy pivoted and continued walking. It could have been the heat or the luggage, but as hard as they tried, Professor Johnson and Cleo could not keep up with Pappy.

Cleo looked down at Thud, whose wrinkled, drooling face seemed even sadder in Fat Chance than it had in Los Angeles. She wondered how long it would take until all of them looked like that.

Pappy might have been joking when he referred to himself as Your Highness, but there was no denying the man was the very definition of large and in charge.

"So, like I said," Pappy reiterated to the assembled group that now included a dehydrated Cleo, "I run the bank and the jail. I'm going to declare City Hall a neutral space. We can air our differences here any time."

"Seems like we'd need a space about the size of the Empire State Building for that," Professor Johnson said, as Pappy ushered them into one of the buildings.

Instead of sitting in the assembled seats with the others, Professor Johnson leaned against a back wall to protest the handling of this local government. Thud stared back evenly at the group, but neither he nor the professor stirred.

"Thought that might smooth some feathers around here," Pappy said under his breath. "Now, I'm going to distribute these buildings and they're yours to do with what you will."

Dymphna couldn't begin to imagine what anyone could do with the buildings.

"I'm going start with the buildings in town," Pappy said, waving vaguely around. "You know, the ones that are all connected. Cutthroat made sure each building was stocked with enough supplies to get you going."

"This is bullshit," Wally Wasabi said. "What? Are we on *Survivor*? Is this some lame reality show where challenges are made up?"

Dymphna hadn't thought of that. She found herself feeling hopeful that somehow this was just an elaborate joke, and within moments they would all be in the hands of a TV crew pointing out the hidden cameras. As she looked around, she could see that the idea appealed to almost everyone in the room.

"No," Pappy said. "These challenges will all be real. But Cutthroat was a good businessman. He always bought in to a good idea—he never started from scratch. He's just offering you all the same as he took, that's all."

The moment of hopefulness deflated like an air mattress after the guests had gone.

Pappy went on. "OK," he said, looking down at the sheet of paper in front of him. "Powderkeg—" He looked up and scanned the room. Powderkeg raised his hand in a salute.

"*Powder*keg?" Cleo asked, jumping to her feet. She sounded absolutely outraged. "What is wrong with you, Marshall?!"

"Powderkeg," Powderkeg said gravely.

"This is not a joke," Cleo said.

"Oh, I think we might as well have some fun. Don't you? Try it out! Powwwwwwwderkeg!"

Dymphna, who was sitting between Polly and Titan, tried her best to look straight ahead. But Titan reached over and took her hand, giving it a squeeze. A tiny snort escaped her lips, which sent Polly into a fit of silent laughter as well. They tried to compose themselves as Cleo glared at them.

"I'm glad I can be of some amusement for the three musketeers," Cleo said, sitting down.

It was not in Dymphna's nature to be rude, and she did feel sorry for Cleo, who obviously wasn't one to roll with the punches. But as sorry as Dymphna felt for Cleo, she enjoyed becoming part of a group of friends. Polly, Titan, and she had sort of gravitated toward one another. It was like being back in grade school, alone and adrift until you finally settled in with a few people who might just have your back when the chips were down. Dymphna wiped her eyes and caught a wink from Powderkeg. It was clear he felt the three musketeers were on his team!

"Can we move on?" Pappy asked, looking around the room. Once everyone had settled, he continued. "OK, Powderkeg, the building on the northwest corner is the woodshop. That's yours. There's electricity and some tools that I hope make sense to you, 'cause they sure didn't to me—and some lumber."

Dymphna saw a slight shift in Powderkeg's cocky attitude. He looked genuinely emotional.

"That—" Powderkeg said. "That's very generous. Thank you. I never had my own shop."

"Don't thank me and don't blame me later," Pappy said. "Moving on. Next in line is the Chinese laundry. That goes to Wally Wasabi for obvious reasons."

Now it was Wally's turn to leap into the air.

"I'm Japanese," he said, pounding his chair up and down. "I knew that capitalist pig was a racist!"

"Oh, calm down, Rocket! I was just having some fun with you," Pappy said, then added, sotto voce, to the room, "I won't try that again."

Everyone in the room was so rattled by Wally Wasabi's outburst that Pappy's calming tone did little to soothe the electricity in the air.

"Anyway, there's probably not even a way to make a go of a laundry out here," Pappy continued. "Cutthroat left you a store. Just like the one he sold from under your great-grandpa."

"Whatever," Wally said, slumping back in his seat.

"Polly," Pappy said. "You're next."

Dymphna could feel Polly stiffen next to her.

"I seriously don't have any idea what Cutthroat had in mind when he decided this," Pappy said, shaking his head. "He left you a millinery."

"I don't even know what that is," Polly said to Dymphna in a panic.

"It's a hat store," Dymphna said, not sure if that was any comfort or not—what was anybody supposed to do with a hat store in the middle of nowhere?

"What am I supposed to do with a hat store in the middle of nowhere?" Polly asked Pappy.

"You got me, girl," Pappy said.

"I mean, I know how to sew, but that doesn't have anything to do with hats!"

"The place has more than hats. There's lace and feathers and all kinds of crazy things. You'll have to make some sense of the place yourself."

"May I ask where you bought all these supplies?" Cleo asked.

"I didn't buy anything," Pappy said. "Cutthroat did. Supplies have been arriving for over a year. Got to the point that the UPS guys wouldn't even carry the boxes down the hill anymore. Jerry Lee and I had to haul it all down ourselves. That's one reason I'm glad you all are finally here. I was getting tired."

Dymphna felt the anticipation mount, waiting for her name to be called.

Pappy flicked through some notes. "Carpenter shop . . . grocery store . . . millinery . . . OK, here we are. Next are the bank and the jail. Thought that was kind of poetic. And as you know, they both belong to me, seeing as I'm the banker and the sheriff."

Dymphna turned to look at Professor Johnson, who noisily cleared his throat in the back of the room.

"Oh, what now?" Old Bertha asked, clearly as anxious as Dymphna to find out what this old codger had in store for her.

"Well, I'm sure this is of no interest to anybody," Professor Johnson said, "but sheriff is an elected office as well."

"You're right," Powderkeg said. "That's of no interest to anybody. Come on, man, this is the Old West—get with the program."

"Am I done here?" Wally said. "Can I head out to the store?"

"You're free to go," Pappy said. "The place isn't locked. Be careful, though."

Wally almost sprinted to the back of the room to pick up his backpack and duffel bag, but turned around and looked at Pappy. "Careful of what?"

"Fancy."

Dymphna thought it was impossible for Wally to look any more annoyed, but she was wrong. She could see his jawline pulsing.

"Fine," Wally said. "I'll bite. Who is Fancy?"

"You'll bite?" Pappy slapped a Hawaiian-print knee. "Well, son, you may have met your match. 'Cause she might just bite you right back!"

"There's somebody else here?" Wally asked.

"No . . . well, sorta." Pappy let out one of his braying laughs. "She's a buzzard. She's got a bad wing. So she just hops around here making trouble. I'd give her a wide berth if I were you. You get too close, you could lose a finger."

Wally looked out the door. "Crap," he said, putting down his duffel bag and taking his seat.

Dymphna was curious if Fancy was on the sidewalk, but wasn't sure if she really wanted to find out.

"I hate buzzards," Titan whispered to Dymphna.

She felt him shudder beside her. "I don't really know much about them," she said.

"Me either," Titan said. "But I hate them in theory."

Dymphna wasn't really looking forward to meeting Fancy, but she was a firm believer in the natural order of things. If there was any place a buzzard had a right to be, it was in the middle of Fat Chance, Texas.

"Marshall . . . ," Cleo said.

"Powderkeg," Powderkeg reminded, wagging a finger at her.

"All right, fine! Powderkeg! Do you have your gun with you? What a stupid question. Of course you do. Go out there and kill that bird."

Powderkeg didn't move a muscle. "I'm not killing anything that hasn't caused me or anyone else any harm—and is named *Fancy*. Pappy, let's get back to business."

"OK," Pappy said. "Well, the next building in line is this one— City Hall. And then . . . Cleo, you're up next."

Dymphna studied Cleo, who stared straight at Pappy. Cleo betrayed no emotion. She looked no more concerned than if she were waiting to see if she won the cruise at a charity auction. Only when she looked a little closer could Dymphna see Cleo was biting her lower lip.

"Well?" Cleo asked. "What did Daddy leave for me?"

"The café," Pappy said.

Cleo looked down at her shoes and shook her head. Everyone waited for more of a reaction, but none was forthcoming.

"What are the chances that woman can cook?" Polly asked Dymphna in a low voice.

Dymphna shrugged. She didn't want to be unkind, but she was wondering the same thing. She hoped Wally Wasabi's store had something she could prepare herself—if she had a kitchen. Leaving herself in the hands of Cleo's cooking seemed like even more of a gamble than moving to Fat Chance.

"Professor, you've got the saloon next to your aunt's café."

"A saloon?" Professor Johnson said, standing straighter. "You mean, a bar? That's crazy. I don't drink!"

"It gets crazier," Pappy said. "There's no alcohol."

"How am I supposed to run a bar with no alcohol?"

"You seem to think I'm the answer man," Pappy said. "*You*'re supposed to figure it out, remember?"

Professor Johnson slumped back against the wall again as Pappy continued.

"OK, Bertha, now we come to you," he said. "I don't know if you noticed the large building off to the west."

"I did," Bertha said, narrowing her thick eyebrows. "It's crooked."

"It is crooked, but it's sound," Pappy said. "Tested it myself. That's the hotel. And it's yours."

"What am I supposed to do with a run-down hotel?" she asked.

"What are any of us supposed to do with anything?" Wally asked.

"You folks really are not in the spirit of this thing at all," Pappy said. "Give it a chance! Anything can happen out here."

"Whatever," Wally said.

"OK, Titan," Pappy said. "We've already discussed that you're going to take over the forge that's right across the street."

Titan smiled and nodded, but as soon as Pappy looked down at his paperwork, Titan whispered to Dymphna, "I still don't know what that means!"

"You make horseshoes," Pappy said. "And other things out of metal."

"Like titanium?" Dymphna asked. "Titanium for Titan?"

"Oh, how cute would that be?" Pappy smiled, then quickly returned to his scowl. "No, not titanium. That's a little rich for our blood. We've got some iron and some steel back there."

Titan looked panicked. "I don't know how to do anything like that."

"Don't worry about it," Dymphna said. "I think there's a steep learning curve ahead for everybody."

"Maybe I could trade with Polly," Titan said. "I'm good with hats."

Dymphna realized Pappy was speaking to her. She squeezed Titan's hand as she realized she was the last one to be getting a new . . . what? Home? Profession?

"So, Dym . . . Dymph . . . how do you say your name?"

"It's Dymphna. Like a woodland nymph with a D in front of it. I'm named after the patron saint of the insane."

"Are you now?" Pappy said. "Well, that sounds just about perfect for Fat Chance, doesn't it?"

Dymphna smiled. Being named after Saint Dymphna clearly didn't give her any special powers to determine whether Pappy was out of his mind or not.

"Well, Dym . . . do you mind if I call you Dee?" Pappy asked. "Cutthroat really felt bad about the wrong turns he took with all of you, but you being the last, well, that kind of stuck with him. So he's set you up on that little farm on the rise just outside of town."

"I saw it when we came in," Dymphna said. "It looked like it had a few animals in a pen."

"That's right," Pappy said. "You got yourself a few Angora goats and chickens. You know what you're doing with animals? The goats have been sheared for the season, but they'll be needing shearing again in five months. You'll still be here and I have to be able to count on you. I mean, the rest of these folks can screw up and nobody gets hurt. But you're going to be in charge of living, breathing creatures. I've been watching over those animals myself for a good long while, so I got a vested interest in their well-being. Can I trust you?"

"Yes, sir," Dymphna said, not believing her luck. She would have animals to care for! "You can trust me."

Thud suddenly started barking furiously. Cleo screamed and jumped up on her chair.

"What's going on?" Polly yelled over the noise.

"Git!" bellowed Pappy.

Dymphna looked at Pappy just in time to see him throw the gavel at the front door. Standing in the doorway was an enormous red-beaked buzzard. As much of an animal lover as Dymphna was, she would be hard-pressed to come up with anything positive to say about Fancy. Her feathers were mottled, her head bald and scorched looking. Her gaze was fierce and bold, one eye darting around the room and the other scrunched shut.

The gavel clattered at the bird's feet.

Fancy stood there, glaring at her new neighbors.

# CHAPTER 11

Cleo stood in the doorway of the café. She was no novice to restoration. She sat on the board of several Los Angeles conservation groups and had passionately fought to save more buildings than she could name. She recognized arrested decay when she saw it, that befuddling business of shoring up dangerous old buildings but not restoring them to their original condition.

Fat Chance had arrested decay written all over it.

The café had a solid wooden floor, tables and chairs in various degrees of disrepair, a podium, a long counter, and two ceiling fans. She located the light switch and turned the fans on. Miraculously, they worked.

*Why ceiling fans but no air conditioner?*

How had her father made these arbitrary decisions? Would she ever know? She walked through the doorway into the galley. Had he decked out the place in Viking and Wolf appliances to look like an old-timey kitchen, or did he just get some old relics to wheeze through this madness with her?

Relics it was. There was an old gas stove (at least it wasn't wood burning), a dented refrigerator, deep steel sinks, scarred wooden countertops, and a redbrick floor. She pulled open several of the drawers and discovered all the essential utensils: a whisk, measuring cups and spoons, a ladle, a carrot peeler, several sharp knives, and a honing steel. Cleo moved to the sink and turned on the water. The spigots ran hot and cold—good news. Opening the refrigerator, she saw that it was stocked with essentials. Eggs, butter, cheese, milk, some vegetables. Where did they come from? How had they gotten there and how long had they been there?

Cleo banged around the cupboards until she located a saucepan. New cookware. Thank God. She filled a pan with cold water and gently floated an egg in it. The egg hovered indecisively for a few seconds, but ended up balanced on its smallest tip, with the large tip reaching for the top. Translation? It was probably close to three weeks old. Still good, but not perfect. Cleo wondered if her father had this sort of experimentation in mind when he'd sent her to Le Cordon Bleu in Paris all those years ago.

Thud came bounding through the kitchen doors, followed by Professor Johnson, who was carrying some of his aunt's luggage. Thud put his paws on the kitchen counter and started sniffing.

"Get down, Thud," Cleo said. "Elwood, control your dog."

"That's a futile request, Aunt Cleo," Professor Johnson said. "He's in the lawless Old West, where men and dogs make their own rules."

"Well, it may be the Old West out there, but in here, I make the rules." Cleo lifted Thud's paws off the countertop. She pointed her finger sternly at Thud. "No dogs on the counters."

Thud licked her outstretched finger, then put his paws back up on the counter. Cleo could just imagine what her cooking instructor would say if he even saw a dog in the kitchen, let alone sniffing along the countertop.

"Where do you want these?" Professor Johnson said. "The rest of your things are right outside."

"Well, I . . ." Cleo looked around. The building consisted of a café in front, a small kitchen in the back, and a tiny bathroom outfitted with a toilet, a sink, and an old cabinet. "I don't have any idea. Daddy seems to have forgotten to give me a place to live."

Thud suddenly started barking furiously. He chased a mouse across the floor. When the mouse dove into a hole in the wall, Thud stood snapping desperately where the mouse had been.

"Elwood," Cleo said, "would you please do something? Or does the mouse get to make its own rules, too?"

"So far, it would seem fair to say yes," Professor Johnson said. "But it appears Thud might be a game changer. You may borrow him if you like. Although I would suggest getting a cat."

"Where am I supposed to get a cat?" Cleo asked, close to tears.

"You want a cat?" Pappy's voice boomed through the kitchen. "I can get you a cat."

Cleo tried to pull herself together. It was one thing to fall apart in front of her nephew, but coming apart in front of Pappy was something else altogether. Pappy walked through the kitchen and hoisted himself onto the counter. He had obviously gotten the "lawless Old West/making your own rules" memo.

"I just wanted to see if you needed anything," Pappy said. "Besides a cat."

"A bedroom might be nice," Cleo said.

"Oh yeah, some of the buildings don't have bedrooms," Pappy said.

"What am I supposed to do, pitch a tent?"

"OK, one cat and one tent," Pappy said. "Anything else? Jerry Lee and I will be running into town in a few days, so I thought I'd start a list."

"Going into *town*? A *real* town?" Cleo tried to modulate her voice. "Where I can buy things?"

"Of course there's a town! How do you think I've survived out here? Magic?"

"Magic is as good a guess as any," Professor Johnson said, trying to pry Thud away from the mouse hole.

"There's a town called Spoonerville about four miles from here," Pappy said. "Use to take the Covered Volkswagen up there every month or so. But the dang thing overheats now, so now it's just me and Jerry Lee. I can only get what we can carry between us."

"I Googled this whole area while we were in Los Angeles," Professor Johnson said. "I didn't see any towns nearby. Only a big ranch."

"That's 'cause it's not officially called a town," Pappy said. "It's just a little bitty place in the middle of the Rolling Fork Ranch."

"But they're happy for you to come buy supplies?"

"Haven't run me off yet," Pappy said.

As happy as Cleo was to hear that there was some semblance of civilization nearby, riding a mule four miles into town every night couldn't possibly be anybody's idea of a *plan*.

"What about my sleeping arrangements?" Cleo asked.

"Cutthroat told me that I was supposed to let you all figure things out for yourselves," Pappy said. "But you're new and you're tired, so I'm going to take mercy on you this once."

Cleo and Professor Johnson stared at Pappy. Pappy stared back at them. Cleo blinked first.

"Thank you, Pappy," she said in her best Beverly Hills voice. "What do you recommend?"

"Well," Pappy said, "we do have a hotel."

# CHAPTER 12

Although it made sense that his saloon was connected to his aunt's café by an archway, Professor Johnson couldn't imagine having to deal with her every day for six months. Family gatherings two or three times a year were about all he could handle. Not that family gatherings were *always* terrible. He patted Thud's head as he remembered the Christmas four years ago when his aunt presented him with the puppy that would grow into Thud.

"My Better Beverly Hills committee is focusing on rescuing dogs this year," Cleo had said, handing Professor Johnson the little brown-and-black dog with the forlorn expression. "You know, 'shop at a shelter, not at a breeder,' that sort of thing."

"You rescued this guy?" Professor Johnson had said, holding the puppy up and examining him. "I don't know much about dogs, but he looks like a purebred bloodhound to me."

"Well, of course he's a purebred," Cleo had said. "I needed him for a photo-op."

"I don't think that's quite the spirit, Auntie."

"Fine, Elwood. If you don't want the dog, I suppose he can stay with me. I certainly can't let it get around that I returned him."

"That's all right, Auntie," Professor Johnson had said, knowing a duplex apartment in Los Feliz wasn't exactly the perfect place to raise a bloodhound. "I'll take him."

From that moment, Thud *was* a rescued dog.

Professor Johnson watched Thud sniffing out every corner of the saloon and made a mental note to investigate whether dogs were allowed on patios and in restaurants in Texas. He knew Pappy would say not to worry about it, but he was a stickler for rules. Although his grandfather, according to his own testimonial, seemed to have broken every *moral* code, Cutthroat always worked within the law.

The floors in the saloon had seen better days. But the bar itself was a work of art. It had a marble top, with a copper gutter running along the lip and a heavily carved dark wood base. He figured that the marble top probably kept drunken cowboys from carving graffiti into it. Behind the bar was a darkened, wavy mirror. He wondered if glass cleaner would save it or if he should start over with a new one.

*How am I supposed to start, let alone start over?*

The professor looked through his inventory. He found a limited assortment of small ware, bowls, trays, and—testing the taps—running water.

Cleo walked through their connecting archway dragging one of her heavy suitcases. Professor Johnson picked it up and put it on the bar.

"Thank you, Elwood." Cleo breathed heavily from the exertion. "I brought a full bar from home for emergencies, but it looks like you're going to need these more than I . . . well . . . that might not be true. But at least I know where to find the vodka if I need it."

Professor Johnson looked over the assortment of first-class liquor his aunt was providing. Cleo took a seat at the bar. He glanced at his shelves. He'd have to do some heavy cleaning before these bottles could be displayed.

"Thank you, Auntie."

"Don't mention it. Make me a martini, no salad."

"No salad?"

"Yes, it means no onions or olives. Not that it matters—I didn't bring any olives or onions."

"And I don't know how to make a martini."

"Then we'll keep it simple. Just make me a scotch and soda."

"I don't know how to make a scotch and soda either."

"Scotch on the rocks?"

The professor looked behind the bar and spotted a tiny refrigerator. He opened the door.

"No ice," he said, pouring some scotch into a tall highball glass.

"Wrong glass, dear," Cleo said, but she took the drink. "You'll figure it out. Although I don't know how. You can't exactly take an online course out here, can you?"

The professor shook his head.

"I'll make a deal with you," Cleo said. "I'll teach you how to be a bartender—I know just about every important drink—if you'll do some prep work in the café. It could be our first successful barter."

"Let me think about it."

"This is an offer you can't refuse," Cleo said, leaning across the bar. The two of them stared at each other. Cleo offered her hand.

"You're going to be very good at this, Aunt Cleo," Professor Johnson said, shaking her hand.

"You know something? I think I just might be. Will you be going over to Old Bertha's tonight?"

"No, I have a small stockroom in the back and I can turn that into some sort of living space. I brought a sleeping bag."

"That was good thinking."

"I figured it might come in handy in a ghost town."

The professor watched his aunt go back through the divide. She passed Thud coming the other way and absently patted the dog's head. Elwood could not remember a time when she had ever done that. Perhaps his grandfather's entrepreneurial spirit was in her blood after all.

He walked over to an old player piano covered in cobwebs. There was a stack of music rolls dating from the late nineteenth century up until the 1920s leaning against it. He moved the sliding panels to expose the spool box and was surprised to see a roll in it. He blew the dust away and could read the name of the song. It was "Sahara, Now We're Dry Like You." The date, 1919! He had no idea how to make a player piano work, although he sincerely doubted this one would rise to the challenge in any case. He noticed a pile of picture frames angled along one side of the bar. They were large and he couldn't really see what they were until he propped each one up against the wall and stood back. Thud leaned against him as he surveyed the artwork.

He was relieved that they weren't the oil paintings of nude or tightly corseted women that he had expected. Instead there were four watercolors, all of Fat Chance back when it was still a bustling town. There was no mistaking the stores and the boardwalk. Even though the paintings had faded, the town seen in the pictures still had more color than the sun-bleached city they had all just inherited. Professor Johnson stood, riveted at the sight.

This town really had been alive once.

* * *

Pappy strolled down the sidewalk, lost in memories. It was more than a quarter century ago, when he and Cutthroat Clarence were driving through the Hill Country. Cutthroat was looking to buy some land with rumored hot springs on it. He was determined to cash in on the latest spa frenzy that was sweeping the nation.

With charts and graphs from leading geologists, which pinpointed a few areas north of Austin, they had stumbled upon a road off a deserted highway with a rusted gate padlocked against trespassers. On the gate hung a sign which read Town For Sale.

Padlocked gate be damned, Pappy and Cutthroat had made their way down the trail to the town, which was covered almost entirely in tumbleweeds. Nailed to the ruined forge was another sign, this one welcoming them to Fat Chance, Texas. They wandered up and down the street, poking inside the few buildings that tumbleweeds hadn't barricaded. Pappy knew when Cutthroat had made up his mind about something, and he could see that they would not be leaving Texas without purchasing the town.

"What are you going to do with a ghost town?" Pappy had asked.

"I don't know yet," Cutthroat said. "But you know me—it's all about instinct. My gut tells me that Fat Chance is going to be something someday."

Pappy knew better than to try to reason with him. If Cutthroat Clarence deemed a ghost town worth buying, nothing would stand in his way. Not to mention that Cutthroat's batting average was exceptional. Although Fat Chance didn't have any identifiable hot springs, both men took a fancy to the town over the years, and went about cleaning it up a little at a time. When the A-listers were traveling to Aspen or Paris or Bora Bora, Cutthroat and Pappy would spend their vacations—either separately or together—trying their collective hand at living a simpler life. In time, Cutthroat lost interest in the place, but one day Pappy just couldn't bring himself to leave. He hadn't heard from Cutthroat in years, when a letter arrived in Spoonerville for him, telling him of Cutthroat's dismaying diagnosis and outlining his crazy scheme to turn the town over to these city folks.

Cutthroat must have known that Pappy would not be happy about sharing the town. Pappy had become a recluse. But, while he may have been mayor, sheriff, and banker of Fat Chance, Cutthroat still had the key to the city—and he had decided to unlock it.

# CHAPTER 13

Powderkeg admired the circular saw. It was one of the best. There was also a wall full of screwdrivers, levels, handsaws, and almost any instrument a carpenter could dream of. Considering how dilapidated City Hall was and how broken-down some of the other buildings looked from his quick glances in the windows, he couldn't believe his good fortune. But why was Cutthroat being so generous?

When he first met Cleo, he was collecting his pension from the army and making leather belts to supplement his income. He sold the belts at craft fairs all over the country and was working in Manhattan Beach when he caught his first sight of Cleo. Her hair, a perfect golden yellow, was twisted up on top of her head with long tendrils escaping the bun. Through the years, whenever he thought of her—which was more often than he would like to admit—he thought about that first glimpse. She was so much like her wonderful hair, reined in tight but with a few wisps looking for freedom. She'd bought a belt—tan with a small gold heart for a buckle. They had flirted; their chemistry was off the hook. As a craftsman, he could see that most of her accessories came from Tiffany's, not from local artisans. He figured he didn't stand a chance. But he couldn't quite bring himself to give up. He always attached a small cardboard business label to all his leather goods and he scribbled his phone number on the one attached to the belt he'd just sold her.

She called.

Cleo had been cagey about her background. He knew she was twenty-two to his thirty-two, but any other information was hard to come by. She never talked about her family and always had a reason why she should meet him for their dates instead of having him come to her house. It was Cleo's idea that they elope to Las Vegas. When there was no way to hide from her past any longer, she confessed to being rich. Not just rich, but stinking rich. Unlike many men, who might have felt angry that they had been duped or their manhood threatened by the bag of gold just dropped at their feet, Marshall had naively thought his wife's status as an heiress wouldn't impact their lives.

Then he'd met Daddy.

Cutthroat was furious when he heard the news that Cleo had gotten married. He loved his daughter and wanted her to be happy, but he nevertheless viewed her as a commodity. He viewed everything as a commodity. He was sure he could pick a more suitable husband than this leather worker! Cutthroat had called them to his office instead of his home to announce his terms. He informed them that he had decided to let the newlyweds be, but that he was washing his hands of them entirely. Until Cleo came home without a husband, she was on her own. She accepted her father's terms, took her husband's hand, and walked out the door. She'd cried in the passenger seat of the truck as they pulled out of the office parking lot.

"I miss my mother," Cleo had said. "She always knew how to handle Daddy."

It was one of the few times Powderkeg had heard her mention her mother, who had died when Cleo was in college. It became obvious very quickly that Cutthroat was the overpowering presence in the family.

Cleo gave real life all she had, but it wasn't enough. She was not equipped to deal with flat tires, electric bills, and sacrificing a designer leather bag in order to buy high quality leather for making belts. Their luck was always terrible. Powderkeg jokingly blamed it on getting married in Las Vegas, but Cleo was convinced her father was secretly pulling strings so that they never caught a break. Fairs were overbooked, reservations were lost, money was always tight— he did odd jobs where he could find them, and the only jobs Cleo could ever seem to secure were waitress gigs at truck stops and greasy spoons. After five years, Cleo had had enough. She called her father.

Cutthroat sent his plane.

It was impossible not to hear about the Johnsons over the years. They were hardly a low-profile family. One of them was always cutting a ribbon at a new charity as they opened their doors, or breaking ground on another building, or being honored as a patron of the arts. Cleo had already divorced him when he read that her brother and sister-in-law had died. Cleo had been very attached to her brother. Powderkeg knew she would grieve intensely but silently. There was no denying the Johnsons had shouldered their share of losses, but as Cutthroat always said, "Nobody feels sorry for the rich. Don't let them see you sweat."

Or cry, apparently.

He'd thought about calling her to offer condolences, but things had ended so badly between them. Cutthroat had made sure that there would be no communication between them—that was clearly spelled out in the divorce. Hearing from Powderkeg might make things worse, so he left it alone.

Powderkeg took one of the large levels off the hook on the wall and put it on the workbench. The table was perfectly level. That seemed odd, since the building itself listed heavily to the left. He put the level down on every surface he could find. They were all straight.

Maybe Cutthroat figured his ex-son-in-law needed a little more help than the others to finally make something of himself. Powderkeg opened another cupboard and a cache of leather spilled out. He burst out laughing.

# CHAPTER 14

The jar of tomato sauce crashed against the wall of the grocery store. Wally stood in the middle of the room, preparing to toss another one.

"This is bullshit!" he yelled to the empty room. "BULLshit!"

As he prepared to launch the next jar, he stopped. He could see someone standing in the doorway, but the sun blocked his view. As the figure moved into the room, he could see that it was Powderkeg, his immediate neighbor to the east.

"Something wrong?" Powderkeg asked.

"Yeah, man. This is bullshit."

"Yes," Powderkeg said. "I heard that part. I think we all heard that part."

"What are we even doing here? This might be some crazy old man's idea of a joke, but it's not mine, man."

Powderkeg walked around the store. There were boxes of canned goods stacked to the ceiling, but nothing on the shelves. He ended up behind the counter and checked out the old register. "Here's some good news," he said. "The cash register works."

"Any money in it?"

Powderkeg shook his head.

"Then who cares?" Wally Wasabi said. "It's just more—"

"Bullshit, yes, I know. Why are you so angry? Nobody forced you to come here."

Wally let out a deep sigh and put the tomato sauce down. "That story about my great-grandfather. That's why I came. I don't know how much you know about Japanese culture—" Wally noted a slight raising of Powderkeg's eyebrow and remembered the man had been in Vietnam. "But my family never talked about this. I knew that there was something in our past that my family was hiding. Something that made them ashamed. Then I find out it was all because they lost their store in the forties and nothing was even their fault. It just pisses me off."

"That still doesn't explain why you're here."

"I told my father about Cutthroat's offer. He wouldn't even look at me. He said his father—my grandfather—and my great-grandfather never wanted my generation to know about what happened to the family during the war. My father doesn't believe in that—I remember hearing fights between him and my grandfather about reparations from the government. But he's old-fashioned enough to respect his father's wishes and his father's father before him, so he never told me."

"What did he say? When you told him you knew?"

"He said that he was relieved that I knew the truth," Wally said. "He thinks that I'm carrying around anger for my ancestors without knowing it and that I should make things right."

"But that's not what you think?"

"I don't see why *I* need to make things right! That's ancient history, man! *I* didn't do anything wrong! *My* family didn't do anything wrong." Wally got ready to hurl the next jar of sauce. "It's up to Cutthroat to make amends to me, not the other way around."

"So you're doing this for your family," Powderkeg said, catching the jar of sauce midflight.

"I guess so. I've kind of screwed up a couple times. If my dad wants me to do this . . ." Wally trailed off.

"Time-honored tradition," Powderkeg said. "I don't know your family, so I don't know why they chose to not seek retribution of any kind. Your father honored the wishes of his father and now you are honoring his. I think you've already made him proud."

"Whatever. But now I'm here! I'm probably the first Watanabe who can't run a grocery store! And one is handed to me."

"You'll figure it out," Powderkeg said.

Wally sneered. "How do you know?"

"Because you don't have a choice."

"How do we get mail around here anyway?" Wally asked, abruptly changing the subject.

"I don't have any idea. You expecting some important mail?"

"Maybe."

Powderkeg walked along the shelves, testing them. Most of them wiggled or were lopsided.

"I get a store—with groceries—but the shelves won't hold any canned goods without crashing to the floor."

"I'll make a deal with you," Powderkeg said. "I'll fix these shelves for you if you give me groceries on credit."

Wally thought a minute before answering.

"You seem pretty young to have been in Vietnam," he finally said.

"I was. Youngest soldier drafted for the war is my claim to fame. So, do we have a deal?"

"I guess so."

"You *guess* so?"

"Whatever," Wally said.

But he accepted Powderkeg's hand to shake on it.

# CHAPTER 15

Polly had no idea what to make of the inventory in her hat store. There were rows of featureless mannequin heads and drawers full of ribbon, buttons, elastic, glue, and glitter. An old sewing machine was set up in one corner of the shop. Polly was happy to see it had a mechanical foot pedal instead of a pumping footboard. She would at least know how to use the thing. The shop, the narrowest on the boardwalk, was reminiscent of a railroad car, with wooden floorboards traveling the length of it.

As Pappy promised, there were several cowboy hats on display. Some were straw and some were felt, but all of them were plain. Polly picked up a plain black straw hat, popped it on her head, and looked at herself in the display mirror on the counter. The hat contrasted starkly with her kohl-rimmed eyes and black lipstick—just Polly's style. Although she wore black and dark gray exclusively, she made the most of it. She wore every fabric and texture known to man and technology.

*This hat needs something*, she thought.

She started poking through the vases of artificial flowers and the bolts of lace and fabric propped against the wall. She selected a gray lace with a black scalloped edge and rummaged around in the drawers until she found a pair a scissors. She snipped about a foot-long piece and wrapped it around itself several times, pinching it in the center until it formed a pretty, petaled flower. An oversized pincushion sat on the counter holding an array of antique hatpins. She chose a black jet pin and attached her new creation to the front of the hat.

Still not satisfied with the effect, she looked through all the black ribbon, finding a grosgrain shot through with silver metallic threads.

She added this for a hatband, tucking the edges under the flower. She put the hat on again.

"That's pretty," Old Bertha said from behind her. "I guess we're all going to need hats. That sun is *hot.*"

Polly had not heard the door open. She was embarrassed to have been caught admiring herself. But Old Bertha was all business, walking around the store, trying on one hat after another. She finally selected a beige cowboy hat, an orange ribbon, and some yellow feathers.

"I'll take these," Old Bertha said. "Can you put this together for me?"

Polly had the hat together in moments. She handed the now accessorized hat to Old Bertha and the old woman handed over the debit card she'd received from Pappy.

Polly stared at the card. "I . . . I don't take that. I think."

Old Bertha stared as well. "Yeah, I don't think I take them at the hotel either."

"There seem to be some holes in Cutthroat's idea," Polly said.

"You think? That damn man."

"I could let you take the hat and pay me when you can."

"No, I don't work that way. Let me ask you something. You look like you know what you're doing around all this fabric stuff." Old Bertha eyed the sewing machine. "I heard you tell Pappy you know how to sew."

"Yes," Polly said. "I make my own clothes."

Old Bertha's lips seemed to pucker as she took in Polly's black short-sleeved top with the asymmetrical neckline and her multi-tiered black skirt. "OK, well, nothing fancy, you understand," she said. "But there's a bunch of white fabric. I think it's cotton, but I don't know much about that sort of thing. You can have a room at the hotel if you make me some curtains—and throw in this hat."

"How long can I stay?" Polly asked.

"How fast do you sew?"

"How many curtains do you need?"

"This is ridiculous," Old Bertha said. "You can stay till I throw you out."

Old Bertha left Polly standing in the middle of the store.

# CHAPTER 16

Old Bertha climbed over the footbridge that crossed the creek in front of the hotel. She walked up the crooked, rickety steps into her even more lopsided inn, hanging her new cowboy hat on the hat rack just inside the door. The front parlor was small, with a threadbare red Oriental rug, a pair of worn Victorian claw-footed settees, a rocking chair near a potbellied stove, and a few tiny marble-topped tables. The tables held thin-stemmed lamps with stained-glass lampshades dripping with crystals—except in the places where the crystals were missing.

*The old man filled a hat store with nonsense and whatnots, but couldn't see his way clear to redecorate the hotel?* Bertha fumed. *Oh sure, there are some new sheets and towels, but the place is a wreck! What is more important—hats or a nice place to sleep? Who was more important to him—the daughter of someone he'd never met, or me, his first love?*

Bertha didn't know if Cleo's ex-husband was any good as a carpenter, but if he was, she was going to get him over to the hotel as well. She needed a lot of work done if this hotel was going to be safe. She didn't want Polly to be worrying about falling through the floor like her father did at the World Trade Center. Poor kid.

The hotel had four rooms on the lower level—the parlor and two small, square rooms separated by a bathroom. Bertha planned on making these her bedroom and office. There was a small hotplate and an electric kettle in one of the rooms, but no kitchen. That was OK—Bertha had dedicated her life to business and never was much of a cook. Over the years, she had sometimes wondered if Cutthroat left her because she couldn't make a decent meal. Although she certainly wasn't happy with his dying testimonial—that he had left because he got a good deal on the business—at least he wasn't casting aspersions on her femininity.

The upper level had a long hallway with four bedrooms, two facing the street and overlooking the creek and the other two facing the mountains. There were also two bathrooms—neither of them private.

*Well, Cutthroat didn't have the foresight to set the town up with a plumber, so we'll have to make do.*

Bertha had been a bookkeeper for a business incubator. She worked with many start-ups over the years. Several of her entrepreneur clients had dealings with Cutthroat, but she never let on that she knew him. It would have helped her to get ahead, but she wanted to make it on her own. And she certainly didn't want anyone using her to get to him. Thanks to Cutthroat, she felt used enough.

Over the years, romance had taken a backseat to business. That was fine with her. She'd had to keep her guard up, working in a male-dominated world. When she was younger, there had always seemed to be a holiday party where one of her bosses got drunk and wanted to corner her in the office kitchenette. She'd gotten a name for herself as a tough, humorless, no-nonsense businesswoman. Perhaps she had been. Or perhaps a hand up her sweater in the glare of the kitchenette's fluorescent lighting just didn't do it for her. She turned the bosses down, one by one, year after year, until age and her reputation stopped the propositions flat.

Bertha plugged in the electric kettle and searched the cupboards for some tea. She really did not want to go back out and face that awful Wally Wasabi and barter for a teabag. She opened the bottom drawer of an old, stained desk. She reached inside and pulled out an oblong box. It was a box of Earl Grey—the perfect, simple tea she used to make for Cutthroat when the Closed sign was put in the window of the hardware store in that perfect, simple time.

She could almost hear the Platters crooning "Only You" as she wiped away the tears.

# CHAPTER 17

Evening was settling over Fat Chance, Texas. The group had almost made it through their first day. Titan had made an effort to clear out most of the debris from the forge. Sweat poured from him as he stacked pieces of metal, tools, and lumber. He was exhausted, but had to admit that it was a stellar workout.

*At least I won't miss the gym.*

As he struggled to get the forge in some sort of order, he watched his neighbors across the street. He saw Old Bertha leave the millinery shop with a new cowboy hat topped with yellow feathers. He couldn't wait to get over to that store and see what else Polly had there. Titan tried not to be jealous of Polly. He had always wanted his own store where he could make and sell beautiful things. Dressing actors and singers only went so far. Looking around, he had to admit, there really was no one else in their party who could get the forge running. Maybe Powderkeg would have the strength to pound away on that anvil thing, but he was getting up there in age. Titan heaved a sigh and went back to organizing the forge.

Pappy had called the place "a smithy," shorthand for "a blacksmith's shop." Titan liked the sound of that. "Smithy" sounded much less intimidating. But no matter what you called it, when you stood in the middle of it, it *was* intimidating! There sure were a lot of hammers! Titan started to arrange them by size, but quickly realized that there were as many different *styles* of hammers as there were *sizes*. There were also myriad long-handled pliers, tongs, chisels, and other frightening-looking instruments.

*It looks like the office of a crazed dentist!*

Titan was a bit disconcerted that the forge was not attached to most of the stores in Fat Chance. He wondered if there was some hidden message. Did Cutthroat have something against black people? He quickly dismissed that notion. Cutthroat had been known to fund generous scholarships for the underprivileged. The billionaire was an old-school patriot and a New Age media genius, a firm believer in "helping others to help themselves." There was no need to guess at Cutthroat's philosophy of life. He managed to tell America at least once a week to "Get up, get out, and achieve the American Dream." He'd often been criticized for having no compassion for the downtrodden—he vocally and unapologetically opposed welfare programs—but he always put his money behind his principles.

It didn't take long for Titan to come across the real reason for his isolation. The forge had to be separate because there would be hot embers flying—a real danger to a town made of wood. If Fat Chance had withstood fire for over a hundred years, Titan took it as his solemn responsibility to keep the town safe for at least the next six months.

Titan heard a rustling in the corner of the shop. He looked over to see Fancy flapping her one good wing. He had once worked on a campaign to save the California condor, so he knew a little about the habits of buzzards. With dusk coming on, Fancy was probably settling down for the night. Buzzards had terrible eyesight and hunted by day. Fancy seemed to know she was being watched. Titan could swear the bird gave him the stink eye out of her one blazing orb.

"Want me to tell you a story, Fancy?" Titan asked. "When I left my friend Maurice's show in Vegas, I was making a fabulous Old West costume out of suede and feathers."

Titan realized that his feathered companion might not approve of this.

"Sorry," Titan said. "But the costumes were beautiful."

The bird cocked her head suspiciously.

"I'm not going to throw you out of your home," Titan said gently.

Fancy seemed to take Titan at his word, because she settled down into the dark corner. Titan watched her. Buzzards were social birds who nested in groups in treetops, gathering together an hour before dusk. Fancy was alone and on the ground—living a life totally against her nature.

"If you can do it," Titan said, "I can do it."

# CHAPTER 18

Dymphna was pretty sure her fellow travelers were feeling a little out of their depth, but she felt she had come home. Cutthroat had decided to make amends by supplying her with a snug farmhouse on a little hill above the town. The creek that ran behind the buildings in Fat Chance continued on to her farm. You couldn't see it from the farmhouse, but you could hear it. It emptied noisily into a little pond that she'd named Loudmouth Lake. Behind the farmhouse was a small barn, which would be home to the animals. The animals she had glimpsed from the boardwalk were four Angora goats—excellent animals for making mohair yarn and extremely tolerant of the Texas summer heat. Even so, the barn had an overhanging porch, which would provide much-needed shade.

She'd never raised goats, but Dymphna had always had an instinct when it came to animals. If she was doing something wrong, the goats would let her know.

There was also a henhouse, with several chickens and a mean-looking rooster.

The farmhouse kitchen was stocked and so was the barn. There were also wild strawberries on her farm and a mulberry tree. She picked some berries while it was still light outside. As she ate them, she savored the warmth of the sun still lingering on each berry.

Her farmhouse had one large room in the front that served as the living space. It had two large windows that faced town and an enormous stone fireplace. When Dymphna watched those home-makeover shows, the designers were always going on about a new concept called "the great room," where the living, dining, and kitchen areas were all in one open space. Those designers would be surprised to find that her little one-hundred-year-old cabin perfectly fit this modern ideal. It might not have the granite countertops and stainless steel appliances everyone on TV was asking for, but the place seemed to have been modernized in the 1950s. There were a little stove and refrigerator that would fetch a nice sum on any urban city's designer row. There were also two rooms and an old-fashioned bathroom in the back.

Dymphna worried about her rabbits. It hadn't occurred to her that she wouldn't be able to check in every night, but she knew Virginia would take great care of them. Dymphna missed her friends in Venice Beach, too. It was very quiet out here on the little rise over Fat Chance, Texas. Once she'd fed the animals and herself, there really wasn't much to do but go to bed.

She hadn't realized how tired she was. One thing you had to give to Fat Chance was that it lent itself to slumber. It was very dark and very quiet. Dymphna went to bed and fell immediately into a deep sleep.

She woke to the sound of . . . something. Were those gunshots? Where were they coming from? Town? Stumbling in the dark, she groped around for her robe but couldn't find it. She pulled her blanket around her sleeveless T-shirt and bikini panties and stumbled toward the door. Slipping into a pair of cowboy boots (keeping shoes by the door had become a precautionary habit she'd adopted in earthquake-prone California) she stepped outside.

They were gunshots, all right. She could hear yelling and see shadows on the street. But she was too far away to figure out exactly what was going on. Should she go into town and see? Stay here and protect her animals? Could she even protect her animals?

While she stood in the front yard, two men dashed right by her, splashing across the creek at the bottom of the hill. They flew by her so fast, she saw nothing but two silhouettes in motion, but it was obvious that they weren't anyone she knew. She ran to the barn, feeling along the wall for a light switch. She knew there had to be one—she had seen a lightbulb hanging over one of the stalls earlier. Admonishing herself for not making a note of the location of the light switch, but determined to check on her animals, Dymphna ran back into the house and grabbed her cell phone. Even though she had no reception, she'd plugged it in out of habit and it was fully charged. Returning to the barn, she tapped the flashlight icon and scanned the barn. The animals looked up groggily, then returned to sleep. The animals knew they were safe.

If only Dymphna felt the same way.

# CHAPTER 19

Dymphna opened her eyes when she heard the snap of a twig outside the barn. Had she really fallen asleep? Had the intruders come back? The goats had been snuggled around her, but were now as agitated as she, bleating loudly. She wasn't sure if they were looking to her for protection or if they were protecting her.

*Some watchdog you are, Dymphna Pearl!*

A watchdog! That's what she needed.

Another snap from outside—closer this time. The first trickle of sunlight was coming through the cracks in the barn walls. She jumped as she heard the rooster announce the coming of a new day. Would the rooster be enough to scare the men away? The rooster crowed again. Another twig snapped.

*I guess that would be no.*

There was just enough light for Dymphna to spot a thin coiled rope hanging on a peg by the entrance. Silently, she crept toward the door. By now, her goats were making so much noise she could have stomped over and no one would have heard her.

The thought that no one could hear her sent a tremor down her spine. But she was tasked with safeguarding these animals. She would do whatever it took to keep them safe. The rope was on a hook just slightly out of reach. Dymphna stood on her toes. She just managed to pull it down and tied one end to the bottom of a post on one side of the door. Stretching the rope as low and taut as possible, she tied the other end to a post on the opposite side of the door. Her sleep-deprived theory was that whoever tried to get in, would trip, giving her goats—and herself—time to escape.

As soon as the rope was in place, the barn door creaked open. Dymphna stood back in the shadows. A ferocious growl erupted from the doorway, as a hound from hell leapt over the rope. It landed in the center of the barn and started barking at the terrified goats, who ran to the back of the barn as fast as their little legs could carry them. Dymphna could hear the chickens squawking loudly in the henhouse. Her breathing was ragged as she faced down the animal.

It was Thud.

*What is he doing here?*

"Thud!" Dymphna grabbed the dog's collar. "Stop! Good boy!"

*Good boy? He's terrorizing my goats!*

Another sound made Dymphna turn toward the barn door. She turned in time to see a man's silhouette in the open doorway. She bent down and wrapped her arms around Thud. Here was her watchdog, for good or ill. Dymphna held her breath. The man moved silently through the doorframe. He tripped over the rope as if on cue. The dog pounced.

"Stop it, Thud!"

*Stop it, Thud? How does this man know the dog's name? Unless it's . . .*

"Professor Johnson?"

Professor Johnson was still wrestling with his slobbering bloodhound's kisses. When he finally pushed the dog off and got to his feet, he squinted at Dymphna, who was suddenly acutely aware that she was standing there in her underwear and cowboy boots. She cast a quick eye around the barn for her blanket. One of the goats was lying on it, watching the action.

"I came to see if you were all right," he said. "We had some . . . excitement in town."

"I know," Dymphna said. "I heard the gunshots. Is anybody hurt?"

"No. The gunshots were from Pappy, scaring them off. I seem to have dropped my glasses. Do you see them?"

"Don't move," Dymphna said, realizing it was still pretty dark in the barn. "You might step on them. I have a flashlight."

She grabbed her phone. Hitting the flashlight icon, she started hunting.

"Here they are." She picked up the glasses and bent the wire frames into place. "I hope they're OK."

"I needed to make sure you were all right," Professor Johnson said. "The moon was so bright, I could see the men heading toward your place. Thud and I went after them, but a cloud rolled in and I couldn't see anything. I thought Thud was on the scent, so I just followed him. By the time the cloud cover had passed, I was completely off course. Thud had just gone to the creek for a drink of water. If the creek wasn't so loud where it emptied into that pond, I probably would have fallen in!"

Dawn was filtering through the barn in soft waves. Dymphna tried not to smile, but she couldn't help herself.

"I told you—Thud has other skills. Those guys crossed the creek just behind here. I think they're long gone."

Professor Johnson walked toward her and touched her shoulder. Even in her cowboy boots, she was a head shorter than he was.

"Are you sure you're all right?" he asked. "You're shaking."

Dymphna *was* shaking. But she knew it wasn't from fear.

Thud thrust his enormous head between them. The spell was broken. Professor Johnson's crisp demeanor returned like a swallow to Capistrano.

"I'm glad everything is shipshape," he said.

*Shipshape? Who talks like that?*

"I'm fine," Dymphna said, taking a step away from him. "I'll see you in town later."

"If you're sure. I mean, we could wait."

"No, thank you," Dymphna said, feeling more and more undressed as sunlight filled the barn. "I'm sure everything will be OK."

She could tell the professor was hesitant to leave. And in all honesty, she was a little leery about staying by herself. But she knew she would have to get used to being alone, so she might as well start now.

Professor Johnson went over and inspected the rope that had tripped him. He untied the booby trap, recoiled the rope, and handed it to her. "Suppose I leave Thud with you for the rest of the morning? You can bring him down the hill at your leisure."

Thud seemed to understand he was staying. He leaned against Dymphna as they watched Professor Johnson walk down the hill.

Dymphna kissed the dog on the top of his wrinkled head.

"Who's my hero?" she asked.

It was easier to ask the dog than Professor Johnson.

By eight thirty Dymphna and Thud were headed into Fat Chance. She initially walked toward the creek, thinking that would be a pretty route and more fun for Thud, but then she remembered her late-night visitors went that way. She reversed course and just headed down the hill. As she walked onto the street—she had christened it Main Street, although it was the only road in town—she saw that everyone had gathered on the steps of City Hall.

Dymphna didn't realize how incredibly terrified she had been until she saw the group assembled in the center of the street. Thud bounded ahead toward his master. She saw Professor Johnson and wondered if their conversation was going to be awkward. He strode toward her, Thud at his heels.

"Thanks for lending Thud to me," she said.

"I'm not sure it's a good idea, you living so far from us," he said.

"I can see Fat Chance from my front door. It's not really far at all."

Dymphna thought Professor Johnson was reaching for Thud, who was jumping on her, but his arm went around her shoulder. She flushed. In her wildest dreams, she never expected to be navigated to the middle of their little band of misfits with Professor Johnson's protective arm around her.

Everyone was there but Cleo. Titan had a huge triangular piece of iron in his fist.

"Settle down. You're all safe," Pappy said, trying to calm everyone down as they compared notes.

"Polly and I were terrified," Old Bertha said. "Thank God Powderkeg was there to protect us."

"It was my pleasure." Powderkeg unleashed one of his charming smiles on Old Bertha. He turned to Dymphna. "I saw Professor Johnson and the dog going up your way, so I figured I'd stand guard in town."

"I couldn't get back to sleep last night, so I made this," Titan said as he handed Pappy the iron triangle. "I thought it might help in the case of future attacks."

"We weren't attacked! Y'all need to toughen up!" Pappy said, his arms nearly buckling under the weight—and Pappy was a strong man! "What is it?"

"It's a chuck-wagon triangle," Titan said. "I used to see them in old Westerns when I was a kid. Instead of shooting, next time you need to raise the alarm, you can just clang."

"Clang?" Pappy's voice bristled with outrage. "What fun is there in that?"

"I don't like guns," Titan said.

Pappy ignored the comment as he studied the triangle. "I would have seen the smoke and heard you banging away if you were working on the anvil," he said. "How did you make this?"

"I bent it," Titan said simply.

"You *bent* it?" Pappy was clearly impressed. "I'll be damned."

Titan seemed embarrassed as the group looked at the triangle with renewed admiration. He clearly wasn't one to crave the spotlight.

Dymphna decided to step in and change the subject. "Where is Cleo?" she asked.

"She got up early," Old Bertha said. "I heard the floorboards squeaking in her room about dawn. I looked out the window and saw her go over to the café."

It didn't seem to occur to Old Bertha, but she had just revealed herself as the town busybody.

"Do I smell coffee?" Polly asked.

The group turned as one toward the café as Cleo walked out onto the boardwalk with a large metal coffeepot. She leaned against a sagging pillar and spoke to her fellow townspeople.

"Old Bertha traded me a place to stay for meals in the café," she said. "I started thinking that I might be able to make some deals with the rest of you. Marsh—Powderkeg, I'll need tables mended. Polly, I want seat cushions made. Dymphna, you could supply me with a steady supply of eggs, and Wally, we can work out a deal about groceries. Elwood, you and I will work out how to operate the bar and café side by side. How does that sound?"

"Sounds good," Wally said.

"What about me?" Titan asked. Dymphna patted his massive bicep.

As Wally headed up the steps to the café, he was cut off by Fancy, who stood in the doorway of the café, looking down at them. Cleo screeched and almost tumbled down the stairs with the pot. Waitress training was like riding a bicycle—you never forgot how to do it—and the coffeepot didn't spill a drop.

Titan ran up the stairs, knelt down and spoke to the bird. Dymphna watched, fascinated, as Fancy looked into Titan's face, then lurched off across the boardwalk, flopped down the stairs, and headed back to the forge.

"All right, Titan," Cleo said, regaining her composure. "Two meals a day if you keep your friend on your side of the street—and if you help me around here."

Titan nodded in agreement.

"And you have to include me, too," Pappy said.

"Why do I need you?"

"Protection," Pappy said.

"Because you're also the local Mafia?" Professor Johnson asked.

"Who saved y'all from those outlaws?" Pappy said.

"Outlaws?" Cleo asked. "Did I miss something?"

Everyone was staring at Pappy.

"Let's eat," Pappy said. "I'll tell you all about it over breakfast."

# CHAPTER 20

"Outlaws," Pappy said as Cleo served up dried-cherry muffins and pancakes with warm syrup.

Dymphna shot a quick glance at Titan—Was Pappy nuts? Titan seemed to read her mind and shrugged.

"This is bullshit," Wally said.

"Young man," Pappy said, "you really need to come up with at least one other expression."

The townspeople, all seated at one long table, held their collective breath, waiting for the epithet that they knew was ready to spew forth from Wally's mouth. Wally Wasabi caught Old Bertha's eye and miraculously held his tongue.

"How do you know they're outlaws?" Polly asked. She was in her pajamas, but already had her full Goth makeup in place.

"You think I don't know an outlaw when I see one?" Pappy said. "Back in the day, this place was overrun with lowlifes!"

"It was?" Old Bertha gasped, closing her robe around her throat.

"Fat Chance was a Pony Express stop. Some exhausted rider would be just getting into town, when *bam!*" Pappy smacked the table. "He'd be held at gunpoint. Happened all the time."

"The Pony Express stopped operations in 1866," Professor Johnson said.

"I'm just saying, attacks of this nature are not uncommon around here," Pappy said. "Besides, I know those two. They used to work and live over at the ranch, but they split off. They live up in the hills somewhere. A couple times a week they come down here and cause trouble."

"Split off?" Professor Johnson asked. "From what? Not that I doubt you, but there probably hasn't been a band of outlaws around here in almost a hundred years."

"I know that," Pappy said. "They didn't split off from any band of outlaws; they split off from their league."

"Their *league*?" Titan asked.

"Yeah," Pappy said. "They were part of the ranch's bowling team."

"We're being attacked by a bowling team?" Powderkeg let out a booming laugh.

"Not the whole team," Pappy said. "Like I said, it's just the two of them."

"Why are they coming here?"

"Who knows? They only come around at night and I'm always ready for them."

"Yeah," Powderkeg said, recalling the gun blasts of the night before. "We heard."

"What do they want?" Old Bertha asked. "I mean, there's nothing here."

"You can say that again," Wally said.

"I can't figure that out myself." Pappy pushed his cowboy hat back on his head. "They've been coming around for a couple months. They sneak into town and stand in the middle of the street. The weird thing is, they always come when the moon is up. I can see them clear as day."

"Well, if you can see them clear as day, why haven't you shot one of them yet?" Wally asked.

"You sure have a mean streak, kid," Pappy said. "I don't want to shoot anybody. I put rock salt in my shells. I just want to scare them off. It's my job as mayor."

"It is not your job as mayor!" Professor Johnson corrected. "It's your job as sheriff."

"Whatever," Pappy said, winking at Wally.

Dymphna couldn't believe her eyes, but she saw a slight smile tug at Wally's lips.

Cleo returned with fresh coffee.

"Seems to me we need some sort of plan," Powderkeg said, pulling out a chair beside him. "Cleo, sit down a minute. We've all had plenty to eat."

"We sure have," Dymphna said. "I can't believe how good everything was!"

"Surprised?" Cleo asked.

A chorus of no's made it pretty obvious the answer throughout the room was yes.

Cleo shot a glance at Powderkeg, who silently saluted her. She filled a few more cups, then sat down.

"Shooting to scare them off isn't a good enough plan," Old Bertha said.

Pappy bristled. "Why not? It's worked so far."

"You've got a town full of people now," Cleo said. "You can't go blasting off guns right and left."

"Besides, you're waking everybody up," added Wally.

"If these creeps are stalking around town, I don't mind being awake," Old Bertha said.

Pappy stood up. "Well, if any of you come up with a better idea, let me know." He walked out the door.

The new inhabitants of Fat Chance looked at each other. Had they hurt Pappy's feelings? Did Pappy *have* feelings?

# CHAPTER 21

Cleo put Titan to work cleaning up the breakfast dishes. She had to admit, it was soul satisfying to see her neighbors' eyes light up when they tasted the breakfast she'd offered. While she was able to flex her waitress muscles immediately, it took a little while for her chef's training to come back to her. But she seemed to have been successful.

"Everything was delicious," Titan said, soapsuds up to his biceps.

"Thank you, Titan. I haven't cooked in years, but it was just like getting back on a horse."

*Getting back on a horse? Will I now be spouting Texas clichés at every turn?*

Titan seemed to be doing just fine, and she had other business this morning. If she was going to feed people several times a day, she'd need supplies—and the money to pay for them.

She stood in front of the bank, having taken great care with her makeup and clothes. Her father had taught her to always project confidence and success when dealing in finance. You had to look like a winner! Pappy already knew she only had five thousand dollars to her name (minus the expenses from the trip to Fat Chance), and so she certainly was more of a success story than any of her neighbors.

*Aren't I?*

She realized she actually hadn't achieved anything on her own. Over the years, she had become a dynamo in her community, raising money for important causes, chairing committees for the arts, and funding cutting-edge designers as they made their debut in nonprofit house shows. She always did a good job, but it was her name that got her in the door.

She looked in the bank's window. The word Bank was decorously etched in lacy letters on the glass. Pappy had taped a handwritten sign that said "Pappy's" over it, so it now read Pappy's Bank. Cleo rolled her eyes.

*I might be attempting something on my own for the very first time, but I can handle this lunatic.*

She walked in the door and looked around, surprised to find it was in as bad a shape as the rest of the town. It might even be worse. Sawdust covered the floor, desks were turned over and chairs propped haphazardly against the wall. She assumed if her father were going to restore anything, it would be the financial heart of the place. Well, clearly when it came to second-guessing her father, she'd been wrong before.

"Hello?" Cleo called out to the empty space. "Pappy?"

She walked toward the back of the bank. A cavernous vault with a dial lock took up half the back wall, its heavy steel door ajar.

She thought about what an odd, formal phrase that was—"the door is ajar." But it was one in everyone's consciousness since the advent of the talking car. Cleo thought back to her fleet of cars—correction, her *father's* fleet of cars—in Los Angeles. Would she ever get to hear the robotic voice admonishing her driver that "the door is ajar" again? She doubled her resolve to get what she wanted from Pappy.

She pulled open the door to the vault. The hinge groaned as if being exercised for the first time in a very long while. She walked into the spacious interior. It was surprisingly cool in there. That wasn't the only surprise. There also was no money, no gold bars, and no deposit boxes inside. It was totally empty.

"You looking for me?" Pappy's voice bounced off the steel wall of the safe.

Cleo let out a gasp—she hadn't heard him come in. She turned and looked at him. She wanted to slap that smug smile right off his hairy face. They both knew he had the upper hand.

"I was over at the jail."

"You're a hardworking man," Cleo said.

"It's good to keep busy," Pappy said, ushering Cleo out of the vault.

Pappy looked around the room. He grabbed an upended desk and flipped it effortlessly over onto its carved feet. Cleo thought that if she ever made it out of Fat Chance, she'd want to get her hands on some of this old carved furniture. Everything in town was in terrible condition, but her practiced eye told her that much of it could be restored to its former glory. Maybe she would become an interior decorator who specialized in ghost-town antiques.

Pappy carried two chairs over, placed one behind the desk and one in front. He dusted the guest chair off with his hat, then motioned for Cleo to take a seat. He lowered himself heavily into the chair behind the desk. She sat bolt upright and silent as Pappy took off his glasses and wiped them on his T-shirt—as if that were going to clean anything!

"I know your secret," Cleo said, trying to regain her footing.

Pappy halted for the briefest moment while cleaning his glasses. He looked up at her. Those silver-tinged green eyes reminded her of someone. But as soon as the glasses went back on, whoever it was disappeared. She was back staring at Pappy. The banker.

"And what would that be?" Pappy asked.

"There's no money in this bank," Cleo said.

"That's no secret." Pappy let out a roar of laughter. "You think I would have left the vault open if I had any money?"

"Well, if there's no money, why is this called a bank?" Cleo asked.

"The sign says so," Pappy said, pointing at the window. "What can I do you for?"

"What kind of answer is that? I sometimes think you're just making fun of us."

"You just need to lighten up, Cleo. This isn't Beverly Hills or New York City. What do you need?"

"I want a loan."

"Nope."

"Why not?"

"You said it yourself. I have no money."

"How am I supposed to run a café with no credit?" Cleo asked. "All of us have debit cards, but there are no machines set up in our stores to take plastic. I know there are those little phone-things that swipe credit cards, but we have no cell phone reception, so that won't work either. Are we supposed to barter services back and forth the whole six months we're here?"

"I guess you'll have to figure that out," Pappy said. "The universe is just waiting to see what you'll do."

"Thank you, Yoda." Cleo knocked over her chair and stormed to the door.

"There is one thing that might make you feel better."

Cleo turned around to see Pappy sitting at his desk, hands folded under his chin. "What would that be?"

"They take plastic over at the Rolling Fork Ranch."

"How do we get there? It's four miles away!"

"Well . . ."

"I know, I know," Cleo said. "I'll have to figure that out."

She opened the door. She knew it was childish, but she couldn't resist. "Screw the universe," she called back into the bank.

She could hear Pappy's booming laugh as she stormed back toward the café. She practically ran into Powderkeg on the boardwalk.

"Hey, slow down there," Powderkeg said. "You sure seem steamed up about something."

"Pappy is a crazy person," she said.

"I know. He's awesome."

Cleo turned on her heels and stalked away.

"Where is he?" Powderkeg called after her. "I need to talk to him."

"He's over at the bank," Cleo said without turning around.

"Damn. I need to wait until he goes into the sheriff's office. I have a plan about those outlaws!"

This time, Cleo didn't answer him.

*One lunatic a day is enough.*

Titan was just leaving the café as she arrived.

"You have a wonderful day, Ms. Cleo," he said.

"I'll do my best," she said as she watched his broad back heading away. The buzzard waddled out to meet him and the two of them went into the forge like two old friends.

Cleo was pretty sure she wasn't going to make any friends here, even after providing them all with good food. As she entered, she saw Elwood through the archway that connected the saloon to the café. He'd washed all the glassware and was putting them up, very carefully, on the shelves behind the bar.

She sat on a lopsided stool. "Elwood, give me a martini, no sal—"

"I don't know how to make—"

"Oh, never mind." She jumped down from her stool and headed behind the bar. "Move over."

# CHAPTER 22

After breakfast, before Dymphna went back to the farm, Pappy asked how the animals were doing. Dymphna confessed she was fairly certain she could manage the goats, but she wasn't entirely sure what she should be doing about the chickens. Pappy said she could always call on him for advice, but also gave her a few issues of a magazine called *Backyard Brood*. The magazines were ancient, but Dymphna was grateful for them.

*How much could chicken advice change in ten or twenty years?*

She checked in with the hens as soon as she got back to the farm. All seemed to be well in the henhouse. She'd counted eleven hens, so Dymphna was confident she could supply Cleo with the requested eggs.

"Out of the way, Wobble!" Dymphna said, passing by the rooster, who stood oscillating aggressively in her path.

The rooster stared at her, cocking his head from side to side.

"Yep!" Dymphna said, laughing. "Wobble. That's your new name. Get used to it."

Dymphna was surprised at herself. She had never spoken to any creature in such an authoritative voice before. She'd only been in Texas a day and was already seeing a change in herself. She wondered if her rabbits would recognize her when she got home.

She chuckled when she saw the goats waiting at the pen for her, each little head poking through the slats of the fence. Instinct took over. She let them out of their yard. The goats leapt into the air and pranced their way over to the pond. Dymphna sat on a large rock at the edge of Loudmouth Lake and watched her goats. She remembered a report she'd written in the third grade about what collections of animals were called. Her group of goats were a *tribe*. She thought back to elementary school, wondering how many animal groups she could still name. Some of the more memorable ones were: a company of baboons, a glint of goldfish. While a group of kittens were a litter, cats traveled in a clowder. She loved that an animal as commonplace as the cat had such an imaginative designation. There was also a cloud of bats, a bellowing of bullfinches and a band of gorillas.

*A band of gorillas. A band of outlaws.*

A chill went down her spine as she thought about the two men racing through her property the previous night. Pappy said they were harmless, but did he really know? She tried to put them out of her mind. She watched a flock of ducks overhead and continued to test her memory.

*Ducks in flight are called a flock, but they're called something else when they are in the water. Mob? Gang? Murder?*

Dymphna shook her head. Why was she coming up with these terrifying names? True, they did belong to the animal kingdom—a mob of emus, a gang of elk, a murder of crows—but there was no need to freak herself out!

The smallest goat seemed to sense Dymphna's dark mood, because she came over and settled in Dymphna's lap. Dymphna focused on her tribe, deciding she could distract herself by naming them.

"I'll start with you," Dymphna said to the diminutive goat, her mood lifting immediately.

She studied the serious little face in front of her. The doe's eyes were peeking out from a mop of shaggy hair. They were a startling blue, like a Siamese cat's.

"I'm going to call you Catterlee," Dymphna said. "Do you like that?"

She felt a little guilty giving the goat such a pretty name after christening the rooster Wobble. But this petite beauty deserved a sweet name. The other goats seemed to realize something important was happening, because the three of them presented themselves. Dymphna never realized goats had such solemn expressions! In turn, she named the other two does Udderlee and Sarilee. The buck butted her, looking for attention.

Dymphna studied the buck, which was the largest of the tribe. He was so white, he reminded her of goose down. She knew what she was going to call this guy.

"OK." She patted the buck. "I'm going to call you Down Diego."

The ducks skidded into the water. Ducks in the water were called a team!

*A bowling team.*

Dymphna returned the goats to the barnyard, hurriedly gathered eggs in a basket for Cleo, and then headed down the hill to town. She wasn't sure how she was going to ask Professor Johnson if Thud could spend nights with her, but she hoped she would think of something. She stopped and picked some strawberries, hoping the offering might sweeten the deal. She felt safer as each footstep brought her closer to Fat Chance. As she passed by the inn, she saw Powderkeg lying on the roof, reaching over the eaves, trying to grab hold of the sign that said Creekside Inn.

Dymphna looked up at him and smiled. "There must be an easier way to get that sign down."

"There is," Powderkeg said. "It's called a ladder. But there doesn't seem to be one in Fat Chance."

"You can make one, can't you?"

"Yeah, but I'm hoping the professor gets the Covered Volkswagen running so we can go into Spoonerville and just buy one."

Dymphna was sure she'd heard him wrong. "Professor Johnson is working on the VW? *Our* Professor Johnson?"

The Creekside Inn sign dropped into the dust a few feet from Dymphna.

Powderkeg lowered himself from the roof, wiping his hands on his jeans. "Yeah," he said, picking up the sign. "Pappy said that the thing is always overheating. Professor Johnson has a plan to keep the engine cool."

"How's he going to do that?"

"Do I look like Professor Johnson? You'll have to ask him."

*I'll add it to the list of things I need to ask him.*

She was going to have to climb the trail to where the Covered Volkswagen hunkered if she wanted to speak with the professor. She dropped off the berries at the saloon and took the eggs to Cleo's Café. The café was spotless, but also empty. Dymphna wondered if Cleo was back at the inn, but she wandered into the kitchen, just in case. Cleo was sobbing, sitting at a counter with her head in her folded arms. The index finger of her right hand was held aloft.

*She must have cut herself!*

Dymphna rushed to her, putting down the eggs and turning on the cold water spigot.

Cleo sat up and wiped her eyes. "Oh," she said, suddenly composed but still holding her finger in the air. "I didn't hear you come in."

Dymphna grabbed Cleo's hand and thrust it under the water. She steeled herself to watch the sink fill with pink swirls of blood-tinged water, but the water ran clear. She lifted her confused eyes to Cleo's, which were red-rimmed.

"What are you doing?" Cleo asked as she extracted her hand, keeping the finger bent.

"I saw you crying and I thought you cut yourself."

Cleo's face crumpled. "I broke a nail," she wailed. "I did everything in my power to prepare for this trip to hell, and it made no difference."

Dymphna patted Cleo's back. "Go ahead and cry. This is just transference. It's not about your fingernail. You're out here in the middle of nowhere, where everything is foreign. You're scared. It's completely understandable."

"Thank you." Cleo tried to stop crying, but it was no use. The tears poured down her cheeks. "I went to my manicurist and said 'give me a sport-length manicure, no acrylic' and still . . . and *still!*"

She shook the offending index finger in Dymphna's face.

*My God! It* is *about her nail.*

Dymphna noticed that Cleo's hand was free of the oddly placed ring. Big changes all around.

They were both happy to change the subject. Dymphna gave Cleo the eggs she'd brought.

"These will do," Cleo said. "Thank you."

Cleo took the eggs and put them in the refrigerator. She kept her back to Dymphna, who realized she'd been dismissed. She was relieved to see Cleo had returned to her ice queen persona. Cleo Johnson-Primb acting like a human being, even an insane human being, was unnerving.

As Dymphna left the café and made her way toward the trail that led up the hill out of Fat Chance, she glanced at the forge. Titan, shirtless and with sweat pouring down his washboard stomach, was pounding away on the anvil. She stuck her head in the doorway. The heat made her head swirl. Titan spotted her and stopped working. He wiped his entire head down with a shirt and came out.

"It is hot in there," Titan said. "But I think I'm getting the hang of it. I helped Pappy make a new shoe for Jerry Lee. Now I'm making a bird stand for Fancy. I'm pounding out the iron and welding the pieces together."

"That sounds pretty advanced," Dymphna said.

"It will probably look terrible, but she won't care. I just want to get her off the ground so she'll be safe."

Titan went back to work as Dymphna started the steep ascent to the top of the trail. The trail turned sharply and she stopped to catch her breath. As her breathing returned to normal, she thought she heard the unmistakable shaking of a rattlesnake's tail. She tried not to panic. As a veteran of the hiking trails in Southern California, she had run into a rattlesnake or two in her time. Hikers were taught that if you left a snake alone, the snake would most likely return the favor.

She stood motionless, but the rattling continued. The dead grass along the edge of the trail disguised the snake's brown skin and the rattle seemed to be coming from everywhere. She snapped to attention as she heard a hissing sound. A few inches from her right foot was the snake. She could see straight into the pink mouth, the fangs glinting in the sun. Her heart started pounding. She knew a rattler could strike about two-thirds of its length and she was definitely in the danger zone! She sucked in some air and backed away as slowly and soundlessly as possible. After what seemed like an eternity, the snake slithered away from the path. Dymphna was happy to see it go. She knew her goats were too big to tempt this snake, but she'd seen several wild rabbits on her land—and what about her chickens? Of all the new neighbors, she did not want to get used to this one.

She gave the snake plenty of time to move before she continued. She was already accustomed to hopscotching across the worst of the ruts, and navigated the climb quickly. When she crested the top of the trail, she couldn't believe her eyes. There stood the Covered Volkswagen with the rear hood open, exposing the engine. Professor Johnson appeared to have attached a wooden platform over the bumper and was attempting to attach the base of a rusted old fan, pointing inward toward the engine, to the platform with a screwdriver. Thud snapped at flies.

*And I thought running into a snake was interesting.*

Just like the rattler, Professor Johnson seemed to sense Dymphna's presence. Looking up from his handiwork, he seemed nothing like his serious, buttoned-up self. Grease smeared his cheeks, his glasses perched at an odd angle on his nose, and perspiration had made his carefully combed hair into a mass of ringlets. He looked damn cute.

"I know this appears cumbersome," Professor Johnson said, indicating his creation. "But in theory, it should work."

"Um," Dymphna said, studying the homemade shelf sitting on the bumper, and the fan. "How?"

"The reason the engine overheats is that it's air cooled. And the air here is hot. Of course, the bus is a wreck and that doesn't help matters, but I think if I could find a way to cool the engine, it should at least get us to Spoonerville and back. It's unrealistic to suppose Jerry Lee can carry enough supplies for all of us for six months."

He took off his glasses and held them up to the sunlight. As he lifted up his shirttail to wipe them off, Dymphna glimpsed a remarkably taut abdomen. She looked quickly away and saw Pappy headed in their direction, leading Jerry Lee along the side of the road on which they'd seen the RV and the town car disappear. It seemed a lifetime ago. Dymphna remembered that Jerry Lee was wearing a new shoe and was happy to see the mule walking easily in the gravel. She gasped as the mule got closer—smoke was billowing from both saddlebags. She ran to Pappy, waving her arms. The sudden activity roused Thud, who started barking, but, with one look at Jerry Lee, stayed where he was.

"Slow down, girlie," Pappy said. "Where's the fire?"

"Right here," Dymphna said, pulling at the saddlebags. "Can't you see Jerry Lee's smoking?"

Professor Johnson joined the fray. "Hold on," he said, grabbing Dymphna around the waist and pulling her back. "You don't want to touch that with your bare hands!"

"We've got to get this pack off the donkey!" she said, trying to get away.

"Mule," Professor Johnson said, holding her firmly off the ground.

While the professor and Dymphna tussled, Pappy put on a pair of rubber gloves and took the saddlebags off the mule. Dymphna stopped fighting with the professor as Pappy opened the bags. Smoke billowed out.

"Is this what you were looking for?" Pappy asked.

"Yes," Professor Johnson said as he looked inside one of the bags. "But this should be in a cooler!"

"They didn't have coolers," Pappy said.

"What's going on?" Dymphna asked.

"It's solidified carbon dioxide," Professor Johnson said. "Dry ice. My hypothesis is that if I put a block of it in front of the fan, it will keep the engine cool enough to get us to Spoonerville. While we're there, we can buy enough to get us back."

"Why not regular ice?" Dymphna asked.

Pappy winced. "Oh, don't get him started."

"Carbon dioxide turns solid at a temperature of minus 109.3 degrees Fahrenheit. It's so cold you can't handle it without gloves or tongs. You'd get frostbite! Regular ice is just frozen water that starts to freeze at thirty-two degrees Fahrenheit."

"Oh." Dymphna was at a loss.

"He means so-called 'regular' ice is not as cold as dry ice," Pappy said. "He's just long-winded."

Professor Johnson also put on a pair of gloves. The two men hoisted a block of the dry ice, smoking like a witch's brew, onto the shelf in front of the fan.

"Doesn't the fan need electricity?" Dymphna asked.

"Yes," Professor Johnson started to explain, but Pappy cut him off.

"It has something to do with attaching it to the fan belt. Trust me, you don't have time for an explanation! It took me two-and-a-half hours to get the damn ice here, so let's try this out!"

Professor Johnson placed the ice strategically in front of the fan, secured it, signaled to Pappy to start the engine, and switched on the fan. He hopped in the passenger seat next to Pappy. Dymphna wasn't sure she was invited, but when Thud jumped into the back of the van, Dymphna decided to go along, too. She looked at the mule.

"What about Jerry Lee?" she asked.

"Oh, don't worry about him," Pappy yelled over the engine. "He'll head home. He's a smart one."

"Let's see if this works," Professor Johnson said.

Jerry Lee made a beeline down the trail toward Fat Chance as Pappy took off down the road toward Spoonerville. Dymphna realized she didn't have her purse with her. On the off chance that the bus actually made it to the next town, she wasn't going to be able to take advantage of the situation.

"It usually overheats in about ten minutes," Pappy said.

"It's been eight," Professor Johnson said, looking at his watch.

Pappy started whooping and pounded on the ceiling. Dymphna knew Pappy was going for a nice triumphant banging sound, but the canvas only made a pathetic *whoosh*, *whoosh*.

"Ten minutes," Professor Johnson said. "I think we did it!"

"*You* did it!" Pappy said. "Spoonerville is only twenty minutes away. Let's go for it!"

"I thought you said it's only four miles," Dymphna said.

"Yeah, well," Pappy said. "Even the good roads are bad up here."

Dymphna, sitting with Thud's head in her lap, looked out the window and saw two ATVs riding up a dirt trail to her left. The sight startled her. The country seemed so isolated. She didn't really think about other people actually being anywhere around Fat Chance—nighttime intruders to the contrary. The ATVs whizzed past the Covered Volkswagen. Pappy did a double take. He spun onto the gravel so quickly, Dymphna was afraid they'd go up on two wheels.

*Is Pappy going off-roading in the Covered Volkswagen?*

Professor Johnson had his own concerns. "What are you doing?" he called out, grabbing one of the roof's steel supports. "You're going to lose the apparatus!"

"Hold on tight," Pappy yelled. "Those are our outlaws."

# CHAPTER 23

Polly cleaned all the mirrors in her store. There were three hand mirrors in ornate frames on the center counter and a full-length one near the back wall. The full-length mirror was too heavy to move by herself, but it wasn't doing her any good where it was. She needed it in the front of the store, in the sunlight, so she could use it to clean up the shaved sides of her "undercut" hairstyle. She had her scissors and comb ready to go, but didn't want to attempt the delicate maneuver without the proper light. She was trying to position two of the hand mirrors in a way that she could see the sides and back of her head, when Wally came in.

"Hey," she said.

"Hey," he said.

"Can I help you?" she said, blushing.

She felt like she was faking being a saleswoman. It didn't help that Wally was pretty damn adorable—in a hostile, emotionally shutdown sort of way.

Wally shrugged.

Polly realized she couldn't really get back to her mission of trimming up the sides of her hair with a customer around. She didn't want to appear pushy, so she busied herself with hatpins. She stopped, afraid she looked like a lurking security guard at a department store.

"I have some awesome hats," she said. "And I can customize them."

"Yeah," Wally said. "I saw Old Bertha about an hour ago sweeping her porch. You could see her hat from the other end of town."

*Is that a good thing?*

Wally walked up to the center counter and glanced at the comb and scissors. He picked up the scissors and held them up to the sun, clicking them quickly. "These aren't very sharp. I'm making a list of things I want to order for the store. Want some new scissors? Or a scissor sharpener?"

"I don't know." Polly ran her fingers over the sides of her hair. "What I really wish I had was a straight razor and a barber."

"I think I have a straight razor!" Wally said. "I'll be right back."

Without another word, he was out the door.

"I was kidding," Polly called after the slamming door.

It was no surprise to Polly that Wally had a straight razor for sale in his little store. Cutthroat Clarence seemed to have stocked each store by whim rather anything that made sense. Who would ever use a straight razor in the twenty-first century? And yet she'd just asked for one.

Wally returned with an unopened package, a can of shaving cream and a towel.

"Here's everything we'll need!" he said.

"What do you mean, *we*?" Polly asked in alarm.

"Oh! Were you going to shave the sides of your head by yourself?"

He sounded so impressed, she almost decided she should give it a try. But one look at that straight razor brought her back to reality.

Wally was opening the package as he handed her the towel. "Go soak this in really hot water and wrap it around your head."

Polly thought he'd spoken more sentences in the last ten minutes than she'd heard since they'd met two weeks ago at Cleo's.

She left and came back with the towel around her head. Her Goth makeup was getting a little runny from the steam, but she decided to leave it on. It had been at least two years since anyone had seen her without it.

"Do you know how to use that thing?" she asked, indicating the razor.

"Do I know how to use a straight razor?" Wally looked right at her as if she'd asked the stupidest question in the history of the universe. Then he laughed. "Before I was paroled from my last . . . gig," he said, "I was in the middle of occupational training as a barber. I guess they thought they should make the most of my natural ability."

Polly thought back to when Wally had pulled the switchblade from his back pocket with lightning speed and tossed it out of the RV. Should she tell him she'd changed her mind? That she'd decided to grow out her hair? She thought back to her last haircut. Running her hands over the pear-smooth sides, she'd said to her hairdresser, "I might die out there without a good haircut." Now she might die with one. The irony made her chuckle.

Wally looked at her in surprise. "What's so funny?" he asked, an edge creeping into his voice.

"Nothing," she said, irritated that he'd made her defensive.

Wally seemed to take the comment at face value, because he was instantly back to the task of assembling his implements. He'd added a hair clip from her own store to his tools. He looked around the room.

"There isn't enough light in here," he said.

"Yeah. I hear you."

He indicated that she should pick up the shaving cream and comb and follow him. He grabbed a chair and pushed through the door onto the boardwalk.

"Still not right," he said, almost to himself. "Too many shadows."

He walked into the street, looked up again, and put the chair down.

"This will work." He took the towel off her head and tossed it over his shoulder. "Have a seat."

Polly was mortified to be sitting in the middle of the street with a handsome guy pinning the damp pieces of her long red hair on top of her head. Titan came over from the forge and stood nearby, studying them. Wally flicked open the razor.

Titan gasped and his long fingers fluttered to his chest. "That looks sharp."

Wally ran his finger over the blade. "Hmmm, not sharp enough. I wish I could run this over a leather strop first."

"I was thinking that myself," Powderkeg said, coming from out of nowhere. "Here, allow me!"

Wally handed Powderkeg the razor. Powderkeg nudged Polly off the chair and sat down. Polly juggled the comb, clip, and shaving cream as she watched Powderkeg dust off the bottom of his cowboy boot and draw the blade over the sole.

"What are you doing?" Wally asked in near panic. He reached for the blade, but the look from Powderkeg shut him down.

"I did basic training at Fort Hood, over in Killeen," Powderkeg said. "All the old-timers used to strop their razors on their boots."

"Bad*ass*," Wally said, watching the movements of the blade.

Polly tried not to smile as she noticed Old Bertha sweeping her porch once again. It appeared the Creekside Inn was going to have the cleanest porch in town, if she started sweeping every time there was someone on the street.

Cleo came out of the café and watched the proceedings in a much more direct manner. "What's going on?" she asked.

"Wally Wasabi is going to shave the sides of my head and Powderkeg is prepping the razor on his boot!" Polly said.

"That is a recipe for disaster," Cleo said. "Don't we have enough problems?"

"If you don't like it, you can go away," Powderkeg said without looking up.

Cleo frowned and stormed back into the café.

Powderkeg held the gleaming razor up to the sun. It was an impressive sight. Polly thought it looked like it had a mind of its own and was ready to get to work. Powderkeg returned the razor to Wally and the seat to Polly.

Titan looked at Polly, who was now sitting quietly in the middle of the street with the can of aerosol shaving cream and a comb in her lap. He picked up the shaving cream and studied it. "This isn't the right stuff for a straight razor," he said.

"It'll do," Wally said.

"Shouldn't you be using a shaving brush?" Titan asked. He grabbed the wet towel off Wally's shoulder and dabbed at Polly's makeup, which was starting to run.

"Don't have one," Wally said, studying Polly's head.

"Be right back." Titan dropped the shaving cream back on Polly's lap. Polly watched him practically run back to the forge. In an instant, he returned with a fat, stubby makeup brush.

"A kabuki brush! Why didn't I think of that?" Polly said.

She forgot she also owned one of the most fundamental makeup brushes of all time. She bet Cleo also owned one, but doubted that Cleo's kabuki would ever be offered up for community service.

Wally shot a dollop of shaving cream into his hand. He slathered it onto the sides of Polly's head and rubbed it in with the kabuki brush.

"If we ever figure out how to order supplies," he said, "we'll have to get the right stock. Aerosol doesn't really cut it."

"Let's not use the expression 'cut it'—OK?" Polly asked.

Titan wiped away more of Polly's makeup.

The very air stood still as Wally held the skin behind Polly's ear taut with his left hand. She looked into his eyes—which were inches from her own—and saw the deliberation on his face. She could hear the razor whispering along the skin near her ear. As the tension in his fingers increased, the tension in her body increased. She willed herself to relax. He was entirely focused on her and appeared to know what he was doing. She tried to look at Powderkeg and Titan, but what Wally didn't block, the sun did. He worked quickly and expertly. In minutes, he had finished one side and was lathering up the other. Polly finally caught a glimpse of Titan, who came over and wiped away more makeup. He stood back appraisingly and gave her a thumbs-up.

"You're a brave girl," Powderkeg said. "But I gotta say, this guy seems to know what he's doing. I'm thinking about a shave now, myself."

"Damn it, Powderkeg," Wally said, "I'm a grocer, not a barber."

Polly could tell that the two men were as surprised as she that Wally had just made a joke.

Wally repeated the process on the other side of Polly's head. She was aware of his fingertips on her collarbone for an instant. She felt it would be prudent to try to control the shiver that went up her spine, considering there was a straight razor gliding over her scalp.

When Wally was finished, he sheathed the razor and stood back to scrutinize his work. Without a word, he took the towel from Titan and gently dabbed at the remaining shaving cream. He also wiped away the last of her eye makeup. He took the clip from the top of her head and let the red strands fall over her shoulders. Polly stood up. She was almost Wally's height. They were eye to eye.

She looked around and saw that Titan and Powderkeg had silently faded away. She and Wally regarded each other in the middle of the street without saying a word. Polly touched the sides of her head, shocked at how smooth they were. One thing was certain: She had never had a haircut like this before. She smiled.

Wally spoke. "You look beautiful."

He turned abruptly, disappearing into his store. Polly stood for a minute, gathered the barber tools and put them on the seat of the chair. She hoisted the chair and returned to her own little shop. She caught a glimpse of herself in the mirror—she didn't have on a stitch of makeup!

She looked down the empty street. Was he making fun of her? He couldn't possibly think she was beautiful!

Could he?

*Why didn't I say something to him before he left?* Polly chided herself as she went about putting things back in place. Up until now, the thought of physical contact with any of the men in this bizarre experiment hadn't occurred to her. They were either too old or too lame. She wasn't sure why she'd never thought about Wally before now. He really was the bad-boy type that she sought back in the real world.

She shivered again as she played the intense look they'd shared one more time through her mind. Maybe Wally Wasabi deserved his spicy-sushi-condiment moniker after all.

# CHAPTER 24

The outlaws had taken one look at the jalopy roaring toward them and zoomed out of sight. The old bus didn't last two minutes off-road. Luckily Pappy had gotten the bus *almost* back to the main road before it wheezed its last. Whatever fine construction Professor Johnson had cobbled together to keep the bus cool had scattered within minutes. The landscape looked like a zombie apocalypse, the dry ice smoldering across the ground. Professor Johnson started collecting pieces of fan. Pappy stared at the engine, which was smoking as much as the ground, though it had nothing to do with dry ice.

"Dee," Pappy said to Dymphna, "go on back down to Fat Chance. We're gonna need Jerry Lee."

Dymphna got out of the bus and started down the road.

"Take Thud with you," Professor Johnson said. "Just to be on the safe side."

Dymphna was used to living alone or with other women. She hated to admit Professor Johnson's protective nature appealed to her. As much as she wanted to say "I'll be fine," she found herself saying, "Come on, Thud."

She and the dog made it into Fat Chance before she realized she had no idea where the mule would be. She wondered if she should ask Titan, Wally, or Powderkeg to come lend a hand, but she spotted them huddled together around a chair in the middle of the street.

*Why is everything so weird here?*

She went back to plan A—find Jerry Lee.

She walked behind the false-front structures and saw a small barn on the open expanse of land between the buildings and the creek. The barn was a miniature of the one on her own property, with the slanted roof creating its own little shaded porch area. Jerry Lee was munching on the grass outside the barn. He looked up and took a step backwards. Dymphna stepped closer. She realized the mule was wary of Thud. Grabbing Thud's collar, she approached the mule slowly. The last thing she needed was for him to bolt. She told the dog to sit and he obeyed.

"Hi, Jerry Lee," she said in her calmest voice. "Who's the best mule?"

Jerry Lee seemed to realize he was the best mule, because he walked over to her, putting his nose in her hand. Dymphna kissed his velvety muzzle. Thud whimpered. He clearly didn't like Jerry Lee getting any of Dymphna's attention.

"Ok, Thud," she said in the same soothing tone. "I'm going to let go of your collar. You be a good dog!"

She took her hand off Thud's collar. The dog continued to sit as he stared up at her adoringly. He shifted his gaze to Jerry Lee. Then all hell broke loose. Thud bounded up, shaking spittle in all directions. Some of the slobber whipped across Jerry Lee's nose, which sent the mule racing across the countryside. Thud, tail wagging, raced after him. Jerry Lee outpaced the dog, but Thud bounded on determinedly. When the dog finally caught up, Jerry Lee started kicking. The dog skidded to a stop. Jerry Lee was an accomplished kicker.

Dymphna, panting, finally caught up with the animals. "All right, you two," she said, using her stern voice. "Be friends."

The animals seemed to understand that Dymphna's tone meant they were *not* the best mule and the good dog. She was able to lead them both up the road and deliver them to their respective owners.

Dymphna couldn't imagine what a car passing them on the road would have made of the sight of the Covered Volkswagen. Jerry Lee was towing from the front, Professor Johnson and Pappy were pushing from the rear, and she walked alongside, steering. Thud sat in the driver's seat, occasionally licking the perspiration off her glistening face.

It took a half hour of heaving and shoving until Jerry Lee quickened his pace and Dymphna was able to steer the VW onto the pullout above Fat Chance. Pappy and Professor Johnson collapsed on what remained of the fender.

"Sorry that didn't work," Pappy said, slapping a meaty hand onto the professor's shoulder. "Good try though."

"What do you mean, 'sorry that didn't work'?" Professor Johnson sounded outraged. "If you'd stayed on the road, everything would have been fine."

"Maybe yes, maybe no." Pappy shrugged. "I guess we'll never know."

"Here's something I *do* know," Professor Johnson said, standing up.

Pappy got up quickly once Professor Johnson had upset the delicate balance of sitting on the fender.

The professor opened the engine door and peered in. "This engine is *finished*."

"I agree with you on that one, Prof," Pappy said.

"Don't." Professor Johnson held up his palm. "Don't call me Prof." He stomped down the trail to Fat Chance.

Thud leapt out the driver's window and followed, casting a quick glance back at Dymphna.

"Do you want some help with Jerry Lee?" Dymphna asked as Pappy started to untie the mule.

Pappy suddenly looked very tired. "No, I got this," he said forlornly. "I'm getting old, missy. Days like this used to roll off my back."

"We're all here now," Dymphna said. "Maybe life will be easier."

Pappy looked at her. Neither one of them believed it.

As they started down the hill, Dymphna turned right and left, stomping her feet.

Pappy looked at her sideways. "You all right there, Dee?"

"Yes." Dymphna shuddered. "I saw a snake out here earlier and I just want to make sure he knows we're here."

"Oh, he knows we're here, all right," Pappy said, spreading his hands about four feet apart. "You're talking about a big rattler?"

She nodded.

"That's Big John," Pappy said. "He's legendary around these parts. Moved in here about ten years ago. He'd bite ya as soon as look at ya. If he left you alone, he must be in a rare good mood."

"I thought snakes *always* left people alone as long as they weren't feeling threatened," Dymphna said, moving closer to Pappy.

"Mostly, that's true. But not Big John. You know that expression 'mean as a snake'? That was coined for Big John."

Dymphna looked panicked as she glanced around at the ground. She wasn't eager to run into Big John again.

"He won't be out now," Pappy said. "It's too hot. Snakes are very particular about the weather. Too cold or too hot, they disappear."

"That's good to know," Dymphna said, grateful that Big John had spared her earlier.

"Just be mindful. He's as ornery as they come."

As they approached the boardwalk, Powderkeg came out of his shop. "Where have you been, Pappy? I've been looking all over town for you."

"Looking all over town?" Pappy asked. "How long did that take? Ten minutes?"

Dymphna left Pappy with Powderkeg. She headed up to her farm.

"I don't think the dry ice would have worked anyway," Dymphna heard Powderkeg say to Pappy. "Unless you put it actually in the engine compartment."

"Well, it doesn't matter now," Pappy said. "The engine is shot."

Dymphna was halfway up the hill when she remembered why she'd come into town in the first place: She wanted to ask Professor Johnson if Thud could come to the farm with her. She knew the request was incredibly presumptuous—and she still wasn't sure what she was going to say. Professor Johnson was probably not going to be in a very receptive mood after the dry ice debacle, but he did seem concerned for her safety. She stood in front of the bar, trying to find her courage. Realizing she was never going to find it, she pushed through the double saloon doors. Thud was asleep just inside the entrance, snoring softly. Professor Johnson was behind the bar, head in his hands—the very picture of dejection. She started backing out the door, but Thud decided to rouse himself and bark.

*You are one selective watchdog!*

The professor looked up. "That fan and dry ice *would* have worked. And now the bus is ruined."

"That isn't your fault!"

"It doesn't matter whose fault it is. What are we going to do now? We need a way to get supplies in here."

"We'll think about that tomorrow," Dymphna said.

*Did I just quote* Gone with the Wind?

"We're going to be just as screwed tomorrow," Professor Johnson said gloomily.

Dymphna stood awkwardly in the middle of the saloon. She wasn't quite ready to plunge into her bold request. She looked around the place. It was spare but rather beautiful.

"Do you have a name for this place yet?"

"No, not really. I hadn't given it any thought. Have you named your farm?"

"No," Dymphna said, coming up to the bar. "But I'll make a deal with you. I'll name my farm right now if you name your saloon."

Professor Johnson shrugged. "All right, you first."

"OK. Let me think . . . how about the Fat Farm?"

*Did Professor Johnson just smile?*

"OK," she said. "Your turn."

The saloon doors suddenly swung open and Powderkeg entered. "Hi, barkeep," he said. "What've you got?"

"You heard Pappy at the town meeting. I don't have any alcohol."

"But I heard a rumor that a certain aunt of yours dropped off a little inventory. In which case, I'll take a scotch. Neat."

"I don't have a liquor license!" the professor said, getting out the bottle of scotch and serving the one drink he knew how to pour. "She wasn't supposed to tell anyone!"

Powderkeg downed the drink and slammed the glass on the bar. "She didn't," he said. "Lucky guess. Gotta be quick around an old boozehound like me, Professor."

Powderkeg stepped over Thud and started out. Before he left, he turned around. "Tell you what. I'm making a new sign for Old Bertha in exchange for room and board. I'll cut you the same deal. I'll make you a sign for this place in exchange for a scotch every now and then."

"OK," Professor Johnson said.

"But he doesn't have a name for it yet," Dymphna said.

"Yes, I do."

Something in his tone made Thud sit up.

"I'm going to call it the Boozehound," he said.

Powderkeg patted Thud on the head. He roared his approval as he headed back to his shop.

"I like it," Dymphna said.

"So, now both of our establishments are officially christened," he said.

"Yes."

There was a strained silence between them. Dymphna knew she wouldn't leave until she had said what she came to say, but she couldn't quite get the words out.

"Would you like a drink?" Professor Johnson asked, waving the scotch bottle in front of her.

*I'm going to have to ask him or drink scotch.*

"No, thank you. I actually came in to ask a favor of you."

The professor put the bottle back on the bar. He looked at her over the rim of his glasses.

Dymphna took a deep breath. "I was really scared last night," she admitted. "When those two guys went splashing across the creek. I don't want to sleep in the barn again tonight and I will if I have to, but . . . I . . . well, it was really great having Thud around . . . so . . . I was wondering if maybe . . ."

"I was actually hoping you'd ask. I thought you might take offense if I offered."

"Oh, I was so afraid to ask you," she said. "It's such an imposition!"

"Not at all," the professor said. "Just hang on one minute." He disappeared into the back of the saloon.

Dymphna called Thud to her side. She gave him a big kiss on the head. "You and I are going to be roommates."

Professor Johnson returned from the back room. Dymphna tried not to gasp. He was carrying his suitcase! His sleeping bag was tucked under his arm.

"Pappy said you had two bedrooms," Professor Johnson said. "Thud and I will take the smaller one."

# CHAPTER 25

Cleo walked down to the creek as the sun started to sink behind the west end of town. She knelt down and plunged her arms into the icy water and sighed. Her hands were out of the habit of working and the hours spent dicing, chopping, and whisking had taken a toll. The cool water relaxed her aching fingers. She sat back, running her dripping fingers through her hair. Stretching her fingers, she held them up and studied them in the remaining sunlight. She hardly recognized them— in two weeks, they were already raw and red. Of course, her short, stubby nails didn't help matters. But there was no way to work in a kitchen with the talons she used to wear. The only familiar feature was the thin gold ring she wore midway up her index finger on her left hand. She'd taken it off during the day; while in Paris at Le Cordon Bleu, she'd found it impossible to work wearing any jewelry but tiny stud earrings. Anything that could conduct heat or catch on something spent the day in her jewelry case. Apparently the habit had stuck. She'd almost decided to put the ring away for the duration of her sentence in Fat Chance, but elected to wear it when she wasn't in the kitchen. It reminded her of who she was outside of the town.

She looked across the creek at a small stand of trees. She could see these trees from her back window in the café. During the day, a small, almost imperceptible sparkle would flash from out of the grove from time to time. She might not have noticed it at all if she hadn't put her cutting board and knives right near the window—it had the best light for working. But every once in a while, she would notice a tiny glimmer out of the corner of her eye, and by the time she looked up, it was always gone. The shadows of dusk were marching across the hills. Cleo almost decided she should wait until morning to investigate, but changed her mind.

*What else have I got to do?*

Balancing on stones—*Thank you, Daddy, for the ballet lessons,* she thought—she crossed the creek. She wasn't sure what she was looking for. The stand of trees appeared taller and more ominous as the darkening sky advanced. Losing her nerve to actually enter the grove, she walked around the perimeter instead.

Standing off by itself, on a small rise, sat a tree unlike the others. She recognized it almost at once. Walking over to it, she put out her hand and touched the base. She smiled.

*Nice try, Daddy.*

This tree was going to make all the difference! Should she tell the others or keep it to herself? She didn't know. What she did know was why the outlaw bowlers were coming into town.

She headed back across the creek as Fat Chance wrapped itself in night.

# CHAPTER 26

"You didn't have to make dinner," Professor Johnson said. "If I'm going to live here, I don't expect to be treated like a guest."

*How am I supposed to treat you? Like family? Like a roommate? Are you living here?* Dymphna's thoughts were racing.

She was impressed that Cutthroat had made sure to stock her larder, but he seemed to have missed the fact that she was a vegetarian. Or, as Erinn always said, a 'vegaquarian,' since she ate fish. Dymphna put a plate of corned beef hash from her larder and eggs from the henhouse in front of Professor Johnson and a plate of eggs for herself on the table.

Professor Johnson forgot to bring dog food, so Dymphna opened another can of hash. Thud seemed to sense that he was going to be fed. His whole body tensed.

"Don't just give him his dinner," Professor Johnson said in regard to Thud, who was on high alert and wagging his tail furiously. "He has to sit and stay seated while you put the food on the floor. Then you signal that he should eat."

Dymphna looked hesitant.

"Do you want me to do it?" Professor Johnson asked.

Dymphna was looking forward to feeding Thud—he seemed so excited—but she clearly was going to bungle up the professor's elaborate dog-feeding ritual, so she handed over the plate. The professor stood up and Thud now gave *him* his undivided attention. The dog's tail snapped back and forth like a whip.

"Sit," Professor Johnson said.

The dog sat. Then he lay down. Then he sat back up. He cocked his head to one side, then whimpered.

Dymphna tried not to laugh. Professor Johnson was extremely serious about this.

*What are the odds of that?*

When Thud was sitting quietly, Professor Johnson put the plate on
the floor. The dog stood up, but the professor was not finished. "Stay,"
he said, putting his palm out emphatically.

Thud stared at the food. His whole body quivered, but he put his
butt back on the floor.

"Good dog!" the professor said.

Thud slammed his nose into the plate and started devouring the
hash at warp speed.

Professor Johnson sat back down. He took a bite of hash and
eggs. Dymphna watched him. That old saying that people and their
dogs resembled one another over time was overruled by the maxim
"the exception makes the rule." The professor was restrained while
Thud was spontaneous, thoughtful while Thud was impulsive, brilliant while Thud was—

*Well, that's just unkind.*

Thud, having inhaled his food, turned to Professor Johnson, who
looked at the dog over his glasses. "You know better than to beg."

Thud slunk into the living room.

"He's embarrassed I reprimanded him in front of you. He's a very
sensitive dog."

"I guess so!" Dymphna said, feeling bad. She didn't want Thud to
have hard feelings. He just got here!

"I still have to find a way to get to Spoonerville," Professor Johnson said. "I need to get some real dog food."

"We could walk. I mean—four miles—it could take a little over an
hour each way, but we could do it. Maybe we could shop for everybody—borrow Jerry Lee from Pappy to haul it all back."

"I don't want to deal with Pappy right now, thank you very much."

"Tomorrow is another day," Dymphna said.

*Why is Fat Chance bringing out the Scarlett O'Hara quotes?*

Professor Johnson got up and picked up his plate. Dymphna was
surprised that he picked up hers, too. He took all the dishes over to
the sink directly behind her. She forced herself to stay at the table.
After all, he had said he didn't want to be treated like a guest. She felt
awkward sitting with her back to him, but realized since he was

standing at the sink, if she turned around his back would be to her. She got up and went to the little refrigerator.

"I'm going to have some iced tea," she said. "I brewed it this morning. Do you want any?"

"No, thanks," he said as he continued to wash the dishes.

She noticed how neatly he had rolled his cuffs. She always just pushed her sleeves up past the elbows and of course they never stayed up. The hot water in the sink steamed the professor's glasses. He dried his soapy hands on his jeans, then took off his glasses. He picked up his shirttail and wiped off the lenses, exposing his washboard abs again. Dymphna grabbed a glass and focused on pouring her tea.

She wasn't sure she should be sharing a house with a six-pack like that.

Professor Johnson rubbed his fist over the steam that had clouded the window over the sink. Although Dymphna's house technically had a porch, a gigantic hole in the roof over the porch offered a view of the sky. The moon looked smudged behind a blanket of clouds.

"If the bowlers only come out when the moon is bright, you should be pretty safe tonight," Professor Johnson said.

"That's good." Dymphna hoisted herself up on the counter. She'd always wanted to sit on a kitchen counter but never had. Life in Fat Chance made all the old rules seem silly. What could it hurt?

"To tell you the truth," she continued, "I wasn't really worried, now that Thu . . . you and Thud are here."

Professor Johnson rinsed the last dish and turned off the faucets. "I didn't come up here to take advantage of your hospitality."

"I know."

"So, we're in agreement?"

"Certainly!" Dymphna said. "About what?"

"That we don't need to compound an already awkward situation by adding a sexual element to our relationship."

"Of course," she said, sipping her tea.

She could lie to him, but she couldn't lie to herself. He was a strange one, but Professor Johnson was not without his . . . attributes.

"Because," he said, "I have felt once or twice that we've had some sort of chemistry."

"You're the doctor," Dymphna said feebly.

"Of natural science. Not chemistry. Would you agree?"

"I don't know," Dymphna said, confused. "I mean, it's your degree."

"Not my degree," he said, his cheeks turning a little pink. "About our chemistry."

"Oh." *Should I lie?* she thought. *No. If the professor is willing to go out on a limb, I'll meet him halfway.* "I think . . . there have been moments, yes," she finally said.

*That's just about as halfway as you can get!*

"Good to know we are in agreement," Professor Johnson said.

"So, I guess it's off to bed, then? I mean, separately! Separate beds! You don't even have to go to bed. But I am going. To bed."

She started to push herself off the counter but, with a glass in one hand, found herself stuck.

"Let me help you."

He put his hands on her waist, but instead of lifting her, he froze. He had positioned himself so he stood between her legs.

Dymphna held the glass aloft in one hand. *Well, this is awkward.*

The professor raised his eyes to her. He cradled the back of her neck and bent her almost into the sink, and kissed her. She closed her eyes but peeked to make sure her glass was upright. This was a weird moment, but she didn't want to ruin it by spilling her drink.

The professor released her. "Thud!" he called into the living room. "Let's go to bed, boy."

The dog, groggy with sleep, struggled to his feet and followed the professor obediently. Neither the dog nor the man looked back. Dymphna finished her tea, put her glass down, and got herself off the counter.

The walls in the house were paper thin. Getting ready for bed in the bathroom while a man who just kissed you was sleeping in the next room was irritating. She didn't want to pee or brush her teeth. She had changed into sweatpants and a baggy T-shirt. Wearing bikini panties and a sleeveless T-shirt to bed wouldn't be respectable with a man—especially a man with whom you've just agreed you had chemistry—in the house.

*Old Bertha is going to have a field day when she gets wind of this cohabitation business!*

Dymphna's hair was pulled back in a ponytail, with a cloth headband over her ears, a prelude to her nightly regime of washing her face. As she scrubbed her forehead, she thought back to the kiss. It was awkward and unplanned, but there was no denying it was a great kiss! Maybe there was more to Professor Johnson than met the eye. She patted her face dry. Normally she slept with her hair in a tight braid or ponytail, but tonight she shook her hair loose. She stuck with the sweatpants, though.

With the moon obscured by clouds, her room was dark as coal. She snuggled under the blankets, sure she would be awake all night. But the stillness of the farm settled over her and she felt herself relaxing into sleep.

The weight of his body in bed beside her woke her. Her eyes flew open. She was facing the wall but didn't want to change position and signal she was awake. Her whole body tensed while she waited.

Waited for what?

He was breathing softly, clearly asleep.

*How long has he been here?*

The mattress was old and the springs were shot. His heavier weight made the bed sag and Dymphna had to grab the edge of the mattress to keep from sliding toward him. Minutes passed, but he stayed on his side, not moving. How long had she been asleep? It wasn't morning—the room was still dark. The moon must still be in shadow.

Now she was wide awake and annoyed. Who did he think he was, sneaking into her bed in the middle of the night—chemistry be damned! She flipped over and was met by yet another kiss. This one wet and warm and all over her face.

"Thud!" Dymphna said, tossing out the words she'd expected to say to Professor Johnson. "Go back to your room!"

The dog gave her another slobbery kiss. Dymphna listened to the night. No alarm sounded from the barn, so she knew her animals were safe. She curled around Thud's large, wrinkled frame and went back to sleep.

She must have been sleeping deeply, because she bolted upright in confusion. Sounds seemed to be coming from everywhere. Thud was standing in the middle of the bed, barking. Drool flew everywhere. Dymphna tried to avoid the spittle and lunged out of bed. There seemed to be a lot of yelling coming from town. Professor

Johnson appeared in the doorway. He was wearing striped pajamas and frantically trying to get his glasses to stay on his face.

"Thud," he said, snapping his fingers. "Let's go. Dymphna, you stay here."

*Like hell!*

Professor Johnson and Thud took off as Dymphna jumped out of bed. Tucking her sweatpants into her boots as quickly as possible, she grabbed her cell phone–flashlight and followed the professor and Thud onto the porch. Two men flashed past and Thud raced after them, growling and barking. The animals in the barn raised their voices as well. The farm was a cacophony but the whooping sounds were still coming up the hill. The clouds parted and the moonlight revealed Pappy and Powderkeg giving chase and shrieking.

Dymphna thought back to Powderkeg saying he needed to talk to Pappy about something important. Was this Powderkeg's great idea?

Powderkeg shot by them just as the clouds overtook the moon again. Dymphna grabbed Professor Johnson's arm as they listened to yelling, howling, and growling.

"Get this dog off me," came a voice in the dark.

Pappy wheezed up to the porch. "I'm deputizing you and your dog."

"We're pacifists," Professor Johnson said.

The moon continued to play peekaboo with the clouds. One minute Dymphna could see Powderkeg holding on to a slender man in the middle of the creek while Thud held on to the man's pant leg. The next minute they were in darkness again.

"Where's your buddy?" Powderkeg asked.

"Somebody call off this dog," the man said, in what sounded to Dymphna like a very youthful voice.

"Thud!" Professor Johnson sounded stern. "Come here, boy!"

Thud let go of the man's trouser leg and trotted over to Professor Johnson. The dog panted exuberantly.

"Ain't in a bloodhound's nature to be a pacifist," Pappy said.

"Dude, you made me drop my phone in the creek," the man said to Powderkeg, who loomed over him.

The clouds parted once again and Dymphna could see Cleo, Polly, Old Bertha, Wally, and Titan making their way up the hill together. Wally was still wearing jeans and a sweater, but the others had clearly been woken from sleep. Sweatpants seemed to be the nightwear of choice with Titan and Polly; Cleo was wearing leggings and an over-sized T-shirt and Old Bertha was wearing a lumpy bathrobe and curlers.

*People still wear curlers?*

As if reading Dymphna's mind, Old Bertha started yanking out the rollers and stuffing them in her pockets.

"Dude, you scared the tar outta us," said the young man. "What was with all that noise?"

"I figured you'd gotten a little used to Pappy's routine," Powderkeg said.

"Did you catch the other one?" Titan asked.

"No," Pappy said. "But we'll make this one talk."

"No, you won't," the young man said to Pappy. "I'm not afraid of you."

He seemed to lose a little bravado when Powderkeg's grip tightened around his arm. He looked away from Powderkeg's icy glare but did a double take and quieted down when he saw Titan's massive biceps gleaming in the moonlight.

"Man, can I get my cell phone out of the water?"

Pappy reached into the creek and grabbed the phone from where it was wedged between two rocks, creating a miniature waterfall. Pappy shook it and water vibrated off of it like a dog just out of a lake. Cleo reached for the phone, but Polly cast a practiced eye at it as it exchanged hands.

"Wow," said Polly, "that phone is toast."

"What difference does that make?" Pappy asked. "Can't use them up here anyway."

"I wouldn't be too sure of that," Cleo said.

"What are you talking about, Cleo?" Pappy said.

Even by moonlight you could tell Cleo was smirking.

"You look like the Cheshire cat," Powderkeg said.

"Only slimmer, I hope," Cleo said.

"Goes without saying," Powderkeg said.

"I know what's going on around here," Cleo said as she looked at the young man. "I would have filled everybody in in the morning, but it looks as if my ex-husband decided to take matters into his own hands."

"Well," Titan said to Cleo, "spill!"

"I need to take this man into custody," Pappy said.

"Oh, not again with the sheriff business," Professor Johnson said. "Can't we sort this out here and now?"

"Nope," Pappy said. "This man is a fugitive."

"No, he isn't," Professor Johnson said.

"At the very least he's a trespasser," Old Bertha said.

"They were in the middle of a public street," Professor Johnson said. "That's not trespassing, no matter who you are."

"Loitering?" Titan offered.

"I'm taking him into custody; I don't care what the charges are or what anyone says," Pappy said. "Powderkeg, bring him on down."

"Doesn't anybody want to know why these guys are coming into town?" Cleo asked, sounding disappointed.

"We'll sort it out at his trial in the morning," Pappy said.

Dymphna gasped. "His trial?"

"There isn't going to be a trial," Professor Johnson said.

"That's what you think," Pappy said.

A new sound was added to the raised voices as Wobble the rooster announced morning had broken. Dawn had snuck up on the group. Thud started barking again as another slender young man, who looked remarkably like the one in Powderkeg's custody, came splashing across the creek.

*Twins?*

"Hey," he said to the astounded group. "Me and my brother stick together. If he's going to go to jail, so am I."

"Nobody's going to jail!" Professor Johnson said.

"Oh, come on," Pappy said. "I've never had anybody in my jail before."

"No," Professor Johnson said. "And that's final."

"Oh, all right," Pappy said. "Let's all go down to breakfast then. My feet are getting cold."

"I'm up for breakfast," the young man in Powderkeg's grip said. "What are we eating?"

Powderkeg kept his grip on the man's arm.

"Dude," the young man said, "I give you my word, we're not going anywhere."

"Do you know how long it's been since we've had breakfast?" said his twin.

Pappy and Powderkeg must have exchanged some sort of macho secret signal, because Powderkeg let go of the man's bicep. It appeared the captives were going to be true to their word. Neither young man was going to bolt with an offer of breakfast on the table.

"So what are we having?" repeated Powderkeg's captive.

"Whatever Cleo is serving," Powderkeg replied.

# CHAPTER 27

" A cell phone tower?" Polly asked when Cleo announced her discovery in the woods.

"Yes," Cleo said, putting another basket of muffins on the table. "When those towers were first being built all over California, I complained so much about how ugly they were. So Daddy hired a designer to figure out a way to hide them just to shut me up. As soon as I saw the tree in the woods, I knew that Rodney and Rock must be coming into town to get a signal for their phones."

Introductions had been made on the way down the hill. Rodney and Rock were identical twins with fierce dark eyes and glossy black hair. Rock wore three silver hoop earrings in graduated sizes in his left ear, and one silver stud in the right. He was the sneering, tough one whom Powderkeg had caught. Rodney was his soft-spoken, younger-by-twenty-minutes brother.

They corroborated that they used to work at the Rolling Fork Ranch and were superstars of its bowling team. They broke away and were hoping to move to a bigger city where their talents as bowlers would be recognized and appreciated. In the meantime, they were scraping by—camping in the woods, pilfering gas from the Rolling Fork, and living on their wits and berries.

"Why sneak into town at night?" Powderkeg asked.

Rock sneered. "Why don't you ask Miss Know-Everything?"

"Here's my guess," Cleo said, sitting down across from the trespassers–loiterers–former bowling teammates. "You somehow found out about cell phone reception in town and pinpointed the only place the signal was strong enough to do you any good: the middle of the street."

"Pretty good," Rodney said, but shut up as soon as Rock glared at him.

"What else?" Rock asked sullenly.

"Obviously, you didn't want to be seen, so you came at night. But Pappy said you only come to town when the moon is bright," Cleo said. "What I couldn't figure out is that since phones have lit screens, why you needed illumination."

"What did you come up with?" Old Bertha bristled, annoyed that Cleo seemed to be hogging the spotlight.

Cleo pulled the phone from her apron pocket. She held it out for everyone to see, as proud as a kindergartener at show-and-tell. "My guess is this wasn't your phone's first time in the creek. Here's my theory: Your phone got wet before and the backlight stopped working. But you still had reception, and everything else in the phone still worked. So you needed light. You couldn't risk coming into town during the day—Pappy and that rifle were too unpredictable. So you came at night when the moon was full."

"Sorry, Cleo," Wally said. "That's a pretty lame theory."

"Yeah," Rodney said, helping himself to pancakes. "Except she's right."

Rock snickered. "Except for the creek part."

"Ewww," Polly said. "TMI!"

"She's *right*?" Powderkeg asked. "Wow, Cleo! How did you figure that out?"

"Let's just say I've been there. Of course, all I had to do was go see the geniuses who fix phones. I was absolutely *frantic* when I didn't have my phone . . . so I thought . . . what would I do?"

Thud put his head in Professor Johnson's lap. Rock, glancing quickly at his torn pant leg, stared at the dog nervously. "Don't let the health department catch that dog in here," he said.

"The health department? In Fat Chance?" Professor Johnson asked. "We make our own rules here." He made a big show of feeding scraps from the table to the dog, proving how lawless he'd become.

The townspeople all turned to stare at him. Had that outlandish statement with its tinge of humor and bravado just come from Professor Johnson? Pappy seemed particularly impressed.

Cleo exchanged a look with Powderkeg. When Professor Johnson was a little boy and Powderkeg was still her husband, the couple sometimes discussed how humorless he was. They had tried everything to help the solitary little boy make friends, but he was always a stern adult in a child's body. If people had told Cleo that it would take a compulsory extended stay in a ghost town in the middle of Texas to get her nephew to loosen up, she would not have believed them. Of course, if they had told her anything about Fat Chance, Texas, she would not have believed them.

Powderkeg seemed to be thinking the same thing. He caught Cleo's eye and winked at her. Up until recently they hadn't seen one another in years, but here they were, sharing a private moment in a room full of people, just like they used to do. Cleo shook off the nostalgia and returned her focus to the group.

"I don't really care how or why you came to town," Polly said to Rock. "The important thing is there's cell phone reception, right?"

"Yeah," Rock said, turning his attention to Polly. "But only in the middle of the street. It's super awkward, but it's there."

"I don't understand," Dymphna said. "How could you not know about this, Pappy?"

"I bought a cell phone a couple years ago but it didn't work here." Pappy shrugged. "I completely forgot about it."

"So, Rodney and Rock could get reception, but you couldn't? That might just mean your carrier doesn't get reception," Wally said, then turned a threatening face to the bowlers. "Or you guys might just be lying."

"Maybe we are lying," Rock snapped. "We don't owe you anything."

"You owe this lady for breakfast," Pappy said, jerking his thumb toward Cleo.

Titan absently took his phone out of his pocket and stared at it. As if a great idea was passed from one brain to another, the entire group raced into the street. Fancy was waiting on the edge of the boardwalk for Titan, but when she saw the stampede of people, she waddled back to the forge, casting hostile glances at the townsfolk. Everyone stood in the middle of the street while Titan powered up his phone.

He walked the length of the street, holding the phone up to the sky and then down at the ground, like a metal detector.

"What are you doing?" Dymphna asked.

"Trying to find service."

Wally and Rock appeared to be in a contest to see who could win "most disgruntled" by Titan's lack of techno-savvy.

"Sir," Rodney said to Titan. "Just look at the left-hand corner. If you have some bars, it means you have service. If it says 'no service,' then you're out of luck."

Old Bertha snorted. "Even I knew that."

Titan frowned, first at the phone, then at the group. "No service."

Polly let out a whimper while Wally looked smug.

"What are you looking so happy about?" Rock said, almost nose to nose with Wally. "That doesn't prove anything."

"Calm down, everybody," Powderkeg said. "OK, Titan, who is your carrier?"

"I don't know," Titan said. "I didn't have a phone, so Maurice gave me one. I've been keeping it charged for the flashlight."

"The flashlight!" Dymphna called out, waving her phone in the air. "I keep mine charged for the same reason!"

Everyone stared down at Dymphna's phone as she powered up.

Rodney was standing near her. He looked at her screen. "You've got the same carrier as we do."

Dymphna looked down at the phone. "One bar. That's pretty weak."

"Start walking down the middle of the street," Rodney said. "You have to find the sweet spot."

Dymphna started walking, the group following behind her, quietly in single file.

"Three bars!" she said.

"Make a call!" Polly shouted. "Make a call!"

Dymphna hesitated. These past few days in Fat Chance were unlike anything she'd ever experienced. She felt braver, stronger, and more powerful than she ever had in her life. She faced challenges she would have walked away from at home. She had even kissed a man she barely knew, in her own kitchen! Would this phone, with its offer of a hand back to civilization, change everything before this crazy experiment even started?

But one glance at the hopeful faces lined up on Main Street and her resolve evaporated. Fat Chance would have to face the twenty-first century. She punched at the keypad.

"Hi, Erinn?"

Dymphna had to plug her left ear and press her right ear into the phone as a roar went up. Polly and Wally Wasabi jumped up and down with the realization they were once again connected to the world. They high-fived Rodney and Rock. The euphoria was clearly divided along generational lines as Old Bertha, Powderkeg, Titan, Professor Johnson, and Pappy were not acting as if a life preserver had just been thrown their way. Except for Cleo, who, while more restrained than the younger members of town, was obviously just dying to make a phone call.

"Dymphna!" came Erinn's voice from the other end of the line. "We were getting worried!"

"I know," Dymphna said, not sure how she could explain that no one figured out there was cell phone reception in town. That admission would not inspire confidence.

"How are things going?" Erinn asked.

"It's amazing," Dymphna said, surprised at her knee-jerk evaluation. "I have goats!"

The silence at the other end was so absolute that Dymphna thought she might have lost the signal. "Hello?"

"Yes, I'm here," Erinn said. "I think we might have a bad connection. I thought you said 'I have goats.'"

"I did! I mean, I do!" Dymphna said. "And chickens, too."

"Are you a farmer?"

Dymphna didn't like the alarm in Erinn's voice. She hadn't called to worry anybody. She changed the subject. "How are the rabbits?" she asked, a pang of homesickness sweeping over her. "Do they miss me?"

"I don't actually know the signs of melancholia in rabbits, but I'm sure they are exhibiting them, if one knew what one was looking for. I could ask Mother."

"No, that's all right," Dymphna said. She had forgotten how difficult it could be to talk to Erinn on the phone. "I just wanted to check in. Everything all right with you? The family?"

"We're all fine. Suzanna was just saying the other day that if the baby is just a little late coming, you might be back for the birth!"

Dymphna smiled into the phone. "You tell that baby to hold on. I'll bring home a—"

She was about to say "I'll bring home a goat"—but she couldn't bring a goat to a backyard in Santa Monica. She was already testing Erinn's goodwill with her rabbit cages.

"I'll bring home a cactus," she said instead. "Oh, would you ask Suzanna if I can have some recipes for jam?"

"Jam?"

"Yes. I've got a crazy amount of berries out here."

Neither Dymphna nor Erinn were masters of easy conversation, and their chat came to a halting conclusion.

"We'll take care of the rabbits, so don't worry," Erinn said. "We can't wait till you come home."

*Home.*

Erinn had said she couldn't wait for Dymphna to come home. But what she meant was Erinn's home. She looked up the hill at her farmhouse, where she could just make out the outlines of the little goats. She had been a wanderer most of her life—was *this* home?

Polly pounced on the phone as soon as Dymphna had rung off. "Can I borrow the phone for just a sec?"

Dymphna handed it over.

Polly's face, full of anticipation, fell as she looked at the screen. "That's weird," she said. "There's no new Mimi Millicent story."

# CHAPTER 28

Dymphna, Powderkeg, Professor Johnson, and Wally all had cell phone reception. Professor Johnson called Thud's vet to ask if Thud's new diet of "people food" would have any ill effects. Polly, borrowing Dymphna's phone, wore her Goth makeup and a top hat with a white feather, but her sour façade crumbled as she happily sat in the middle of Main Street using FaceTime and chatting with her friends in New York about the disappearance of Mimi Millicent from cyberspace. Cleo borrowed her nephew's phone as soon as it had enough battery power for her to take her turn standing in the middle of Main Street. She called Wesley Tensaw to make sure her affairs were in order and to ask if the Beverly Hills Flower Show would be able to schedule the annual show without her.

It appeared that Beverly Hills was managing to carry on without her.

Titan asked Wally if he could call his friend Maurice once Wally had checked in with his family.

"I'm not calling my family," Wally said, handing over his phone. "I'll show up in six months and that'll be soon enough for all of us."

Old Bertha sniffed that there wasn't anybody she was dying to talk to either, and by midday the drama of the cell phone reception was old news. Cleo was glowing as she realized that ordering from the Internet was now a possibility.

"Don't forget you've only got limited resources," Pappy said. "Don't go buying any wicker monkeys."

*Why would I buy a wicker monkey?* thought Cleo.

Rodney and Rock were sticking around, much to everyone's surprise. The group had reconvened at Cleo's and the twins plunked themselves down as if they were part of the Fat Chance experiment.

"All our problems are solved. We've got Internet!" Polly said, her white feather bobbing.

Pappy said, "I don't want to throw cold water on that—"

"Then don't," Wally interrupted.

"We've still got to get supplies in town," Pappy said. "That means a trip to Spoonerville. Internet or no Internet."

"You said it's four miles," Old Bertha said. "I can't walk four miles."

"You could make a list," Dymphna said. "And we could shop for you."

"I don't know what they have," Old Bertha protested.

"I'm guessing it's pretty basic stuff," Powderkeg said.

Pappy nodded. "You got that right."

"I really need some pink peppercorns," Cleo said. "What do you think my chances are?"

"Zero to none," Titan said.

"Better go back to the Internet for that one," Polly said. "I volunteer to do all Internet shopping."

"We still have to get the supplies from town back here," Dymphna said.

Realizing she'd had this very conversation with Professor Johnson last night, right before their smoldering kiss, made her blush.

"We can help with that," Rodney said. "I could take Old Bertha on the back of my ATV. And my brother could haul some of the supplies on his."

Everyone looked shocked at the offer. Rock scowled but didn't contradict his brother.

"Why are you being so helpful?" Pappy asked.

"You guys are all outcasts." Rodney shrugged. "So are we. We might as well stick together."

"I'm not an *outcast*," Cleo said.

"Misfit?" Titan offered.

"Don't help," Dymphna whispered to Titan, patting his arm.

"Since you quit the bowling team, I thought maybe you were persona au gratin," Pappy said.

"Persona *non grata*," Professor Johnson corrected sternly.

"I know." Pappy beamed. "I was just making a cheesy joke."

"Good one, Pappy!" Rodney said, bursting out laughing.

"My brother is a total nerd," Rock said to Polly.

"Anyway," Pappy said. "Joking aside, how welcome will you guys be in Spoonerville?"

"As welcome as y'all are going to be," Rock said. "Everybody's heard about a bunch of strangers moving into Fat Chance and they're dying to get a look at you."

"Well then," Powderkeg said, "let's give them a good look."

After much discussion of logistics, the group arrived at the arching gates of the Rolling Fork Ranch.

"OK," Pappy said. "Spoonerville is just down the main road. Everybody just remain calm and stick together."

"Why is this such a big production?" Wally asked. "I don't understand."

"That's right," Pappy said. "You *don't* understand. I figure everybody on the ranch probably already knows we're here, so there's no need to try to sneak into town."

*We were going to try to sneak into town?* Dymphna wondered.

"I don't like the sound of this," Powderkeg said. "What aren't you telling us?"

"Nothing," Pappy said. "Sometimes the folks at the ranch are just a little . . . standoffish around new folks."

"You can say that again," Rock said, but was silenced by a look from Pappy.

"This doesn't sound like it's going to be your basic uneventful trip to Market Basket," Titan said. "Right, Cleo?"

"I have no idea." Cleo pointed at Powderkeg. "I haven't been grocery shopping since I was married to this one."

"Well, there's a first time for everything." Old Bertha sniffed, patting her hair.

Pappy ordered Rodney and Rock to leave the ATVs at the gate. No sense half of them roaring up and the others straggling behind. He said that they should arrive together, in a show of solidarity, but Dymphna suspected that he thought they should stay together in case any of them needed backup. Nervously, the little band started down the road. The land appeared flat in all directions, but after a sharp turn in the road, there stood Spoonerville. Dymphna wasn't sure what she had expected, but Spoonerville looked little better than Fat Chance to the naked eye. The buildings might have been a little straighter and the main road was paved, but for the most part, Spoonerville looked fairly down-at-the-heels. Dymphna actually thought Fat Chance had more charm.

*But Spoonerville has more food.*

Pappy led the way to a store at the very end of the street. The store sat above the road, up a steep set of stairs. At the top of the stairs was a long, wide porch, on which sat several sun-baked men. One of them glanced down at the Fat Chancers as Pappy tied Jerry Lee to a hitching post.

"Is that you, Pappy?" the man called down.

"Yep," Pappy said without looking up.

"We heard you were babysitting a bunch of city folks," the man said, leaning against the rail, his arms folded casually across his chest. "But I didn't know you also took up with Hot and Cold Running Water."

Dymphna knew the man was talking about the twins. She could feel all the men in her group tense. A few hours ago, the twins were the unknown terror on Main Street, but there was no doubt, they were all in this together now.

"Yep," Pappy said. "Recruited them this morning."

"What do you mean, recruited them?" another man shouted down.

"Starting a bowling league," Pappy said.

Dymphna caught Powderkeg's eye. He winked at her. Powderkeg was clearly enjoying this banter, as menacing as this conversation sounded. Pappy nodded toward the steps, and the little group ascended. With an unspoken understanding, each man walked alongside one of the women—Pappy with Old Bertha, Professor Johnson and Thud with Dymphna, Powderkeg with Cleo. Polly was in the lead with an entire entourage; Wally and the twins all seemed hell-bent on protecting her should war break out. Titan walked alone but was watchful of everyone's every move.

"Don't worry," Rodney whispered to Polly, although loud enough for Dymphna to hear. "They look meaner than they are."

"But they are just as stupid as they look," Rock said.

Old Bertha was walking behind Rock and gave him a smack on the back of his head. "Don't start any trouble," she said.

"Just be polite," Titan whispered.

The Fat Chancers went quietly into the store. Nobody stopped them. Dymphna worried that someone from the porch was going to make Thud stay outside, but the dog followed the professor into the store without incident. The men from the porch crept in behind them, feigning nonchalance. Cleo stared one of the men down as she stood in front of the vegetables. He moved away and a few of his friends poked each other in the ribs, trying not to laugh. The cowboy Cleo had dispatched glowered at her and at his friends. The little lady had clearly won a round.

While Wally looked over the post office boxes, the store owner, whose name was Dodge Durham, walked over from behind the counter. His belly strained at the buttons on his plaid shirt.

"You looking to open a post office box?" Dodge asked.

"I am," Wally said. "How often would I get mail?"

"How often do you want to walk over from your ghost town?" Dodge asked.

"I'll walk over when I feel like it. How often does the mail go out?"

"It goes out when I feel like it."

Everyone in the store tensed.

Wally shrugged. "That's fair. It's a deal."

After Wally filled out his paperwork, he was issued a number to a little slot on the back wall, which would become his post office "box"—there was nothing as elegant or modern as a key. One by one, the people of Fat Chance finished their shopping and checked out, relieved that Cutthroat's debit cards worked. Professor Johnson, who'd been talked into strapping Jerry Lee's extra saddle bags on Thud, made an attempt to load the pouches with his groceries, but the dog was not cooperating. Rather than force a battle of wits with a dog whose breed was known for its stubborn streak, Professor Johnson decided to carry the supplies himself—at least until they got out of sight, where he could negotiate with Thud in private.

Old Bertha was the last at the counter. Dodge looked distracted. He was keeping an eye on the twins, Wally, and Polly, who, having already checked out, were all trying on sunglasses from an ancient rack, complete with oblong mirror set about a foot too high.

"Sack all this up," Old Bertha said.

The man started loading Old Bertha's supplies into a paper bag.

"Is that your girl?" Dodge asked.

"Pardon me?" Old Bertha looked confused.

"That your granddaughter?" Dodge asked, nodding toward Polly.

"Maybe," Old Bertha answered. "Why do you ask?"

Everyone in the store was listening to the conversation while pretending not to.

The man leaned in to Old Bertha. "She'd be pretty without that zombie makeup," he said. "You should set her straight."

Dymphna could see Polly cringe.

"Oh, I forgot," Old Bertha said. "I need charcoal."

Dymphna and Professor Johnson were standing together and looked at each other. Did Old Bertha not hear him? Was she going to ignore the comment?

"Large or small bag?" Dodge asked.

"Oh, small will do just fine."

The man put a bag of charcoal on the counter.

Old Bertha paid for the new addition to her shopping list. "Thank you," she said, digging in her purse. She pulled out a set of keys. "This should work."

She plunged her keys into the center of the bag. A black cloud of charcoal dust erupted over the counter. She picked up a briquette and walked over to the sunglasses tree. Wally, Polly, and the twins parted to let her look at herself in the mirror. She outlined one eye in a lavish imitation of Polly's style and turned back to Dodge.

"She's not my granddaughter, but she *is* my girl," Old Bertha said, turning back to the mirror and finishing her other eye. "And I think she looks perfect."

Without a word, she handed the briquette to Wally, who silently drew black smudge lines around his own almond eyes until he looked like a raccoon. One by one, the people of Fat Chance outlined their eyes in charcoal. Dymphna made a mess of her own eyes, but she noticed that Cleo and Titan had actually done a pretty good job with theirs. The twins added lines down their cheeks.

The people of Fat Chance, Texas, left the store en masse.

"What do you want to do with the charcoal?" Dodge called after them, picking up the opened bag.

"You can shove it," Old Bertha called back.

As the little troupe made their way back down the street, they were silent, but it was no longer the silence of strangers.

Polly pressed her fingers to her lower eyelids to keep her tears from ruining her makeup.

# CHAPTER 29

The group was giddy with their showy display of solidarity, although Dymphna fretted that they certainly hadn't come in peace—or at least *left* in peace—to the only source of supplies anywhere near them.

As they walked down the main road to the Rolling Fork main entrance, several of the Fat Chancers kept turning back to make sure they weren't being followed.

"Oh, don't worry about that," Rock said. "They're holding a grudge against Rodney and me—and they've never liked Pappy. But they're happy to have your money."

"It's not just that," Pappy said. "Ranches in Texas have a long tradition of helping each other out. They know that they might be the only help for miles around."

"That's so sweet!" Dymphna said.

"Yeah," Pappy said. "Or, they're just happy to have our money."

At the gate, the twins retrieved their ATVs. As Rodney was helping Old Bertha into her seat, Polly suddenly grabbed the old woman and hugged her. Without a word, Polly hopped on the back of Rock's ATV with two sacks of supplies and they sped off. Rodney grinned at Old Bertha, who smacked at his shoulder ineffectually.

"Go on with you, now," she commanded.

As the two ATVs literally left the rest of them in the dust, Wally kicked at a rock in the road.

"OK, the two main reasons we're standing here looking like contestants in a drag-queen contest just drove away," he said. "Now we just look like a bunch of jerks."

"Speak for yourself," Powderkeg replied. "I think I still look like a contestant in a drag-queen contest."

"No, you don't," Titan said. "Trust me."

As they trudged back, Professor Johnson hit on a plan with Thud. Every mile or so, he had someone in the group distract the dog while he slipped an item into one of the pouches. By the time the group straggled into Fat Chance, Professor Johnson had filled the saddlebags.

The road back was long and most of the charcoal had sweated off or, worse, left black rivulets on their cheeks. The twins were standing in the middle of the street when the group arrived. They had their heads together, staring into a phone.

"What are they looking at?" Wally asked, outraged. "Their phone is broken! They must have stolen one of ours."

"I gave them mine," Dymphna said. "I knew they would get back to town before we did. Might as well let them use it."

Dymphna could tell Wally was loath to let his anger go.

"Hey, boys," Pappy called to the twins. "I'm gonna pasture Jerry Lee, then I want you to meet me at the jail."

The twins looked up from the phone.

"I just told you," Dymphna said. "I said they could use it."

"You stay out of this, Dee," Pappy said. "This is between me and the boys."

"What if they make a run for it?" Powderkeg asked. "Want me to keep an eye on them?"

"Nope," Pappy said. "That's up to them."

Fancy was waiting at the forge door. Titan grinned when he saw her.

"There's my girl," he said as he split off from the group. He spoke to the buzzard as he approached the forge. "Did you miss Daddy?"

As the group fragmented, Dymphna stood awkwardly with Professor Johnson and Thud.

*Is he going to take his supplies into the Boozehound or up to my place?*

"I suppose there's no danger now that our marauders turned out to be the twins," Professor Johnson said.

*He doesn't want to come back.*

"That's true," Dymphna said, hoping he couldn't hear the disappointment in her voice.

"On the other hand," he continued, "you never know what might be lurking around the next rock."

"That's also true," Dymphna said, now trying to disguise the excitement in her voice.

"Then perhaps Thud and I should continue to reside at the farm after dark."

"All right then," Dymphna said. "I'll see you later. I have to get up there and take care of the animals."

Professor Johnson nodded solemnly, called Thud, and headed toward the Boozehound to drop off his four cans of beer.

Down the street, the twins were waiting for Pappy in front of the jail, as requested. Pappy saw Wally sitting on the bench in front of his store, obviously waiting to see what Pappy was going to do with the twins. Pappy motioned for the boys to come inside.

"You still have Dee's phone?" he asked, closing the door behind him.

"Yes, sir," Rodney said. "But she said—"

"I know what she said. So, let's talk about you boys staying here for a while."

Rock glowered. "What for?"

"You got someplace else to be?" Pappy asked.

"Anyplace is better than jail," Rock said.

"OK. I just thought you might want to be in town instead of camping out. And, you know, the reception is a lot better here in town, I'm told."

"You mean . . . not actually *going* to jail?" Rodney asked. "Just . . . hang out here?"

"I figured I'd deputize you two," Pappy said. "And you can oversee the place. I'm still the sheriff, though."

"Deal!" Rodney said.

"Yeah," Rock said. "Just let that Wally step one foot out of line."

"No abusing your position," Pappy said sternly. "And you make sure you take better care of Dee's phone than you did your own . . . and you charge it before you give it back to her."

"Yes, sir," they chorused.

"All right then," Pappy said, opening the top drawer in the desk. "Here are the keys to the jail cell and the front door. Not sure which is which or if they even work."

He handed over the keys to the twins, got up from his desk, and headed toward the door.

"I bunk down behind City Hall if you have any questions," Pappy said.

"Wait," Rock said. "You forgot to deputize us in the name of the law."

"You watch too many westerns, kid," Pappy said. "I just need to *think* you're my deputies and it's a done deal."

# CHAPTER 30

Cleo looked at her watch. It was four thirty in the afternoon. Titan had left a spotless kitchen this morning, so she was ready to start prepping for supper. Through her wheeling and dealing, she knew Titan, Bertha, Polly, Pappy, and *Powderkeg* would all be coming by for a meal. Dymphna and Wally seemed to prefer to fend for themselves in the evenings and she had no idea what was going on with the twins. She had assumed her nephew would be at the café in the evenings, but now that he seemed to be staying with Dymphna, she wasn't sure what to expect. Since there was no way to pinpoint the number of guests, and her options were limited anyway, she opted for spaghetti. The fact that she only had boxed grated cheese hurt her, but she took solace in the fact that she had overcome worse obstacles in the last few days.

*I never thought I would say this, but I can live with boxed Parmesan.*

She could see her nephew through the archway that connected the café and the saloon. She wished they had the kind of bond that would allow her to ask about his relationship with Dymphna. She watched him playing with Thud. Thank God for that dog; caring for the bloodhound seemed to be the only time the man let his guard down. She blamed herself for not trying harder during his childhood, but also patted herself on the back. After all, she was the one who had bought him the dog.

"Are you coming for dinner, Elwood?" Cleo yelled into the saloon.

The professor stopped roughhousing with Thud. Cleo pretended not to notice his sheepish expression.

"I'm not sure," he said tentatively.

"Because you might go up to Dymphna's?" Cleo asked, hoping her nephew would see that she was leaving a door open for conversation.

"I'm not sure," he repeated.

You could almost hear him closing the door.

Powderkeg suddenly burst through the front entrance of the café. Professor Johnson took this as his chance to escape and went back to tending to his saloon, with its supply of his aunt's liquor.

"What's for dinner?" Powderkeg boomed.

"Spaghetti," Cleo said. "And not for another hour."

"OK," Powderkeg said. "I was just over at the inn and Polly and Old Bertha are going to pass on dinner. Today wiped them out, I guess."

"Two less mouths to feed," Cleo said, feeling vaguely rejected but not wanting to show it. "Fine."

"But the twins want to know if they can come instead."

"I suppose that would be all right—this one time. Until I cut some kind of deal with them."

"Pappy gave them the jail," Powderkeg said. "So I'd stay on their good side if I were you."

"Can you just *give* someone a jail?"

"No!" Professor Johnson yelled from behind the bar in the Boozehound. "But that has never stopped Pappy, has it?"

Professor Johnson and Thud left the Boozehound. Cleo and Powderkeg could hear the professor locking the door behind him.

"Why is he locking the door? What good is that going to do?" Powderkeg said. "There are holes in the building big enough to climb through."

"I have no idea." Cleo smiled. "Old habits die hard?"

"Is he going up to Dymphna's?"

"Did you hear him tell me where he was going? How should I know?"

"You're his aunt."

"What does that mean?" Cleo asked hotly.

"It means—you're his aunt."

Cleo sat down at one of the tables and put her head in her hands. "He's practically a stranger to me," she moaned. "I don't know him any better than I do these other lunatics."

"Hey, hey." Powderkeg came up behind her and massaged her

slumped shoulders. "I didn't mean anything by that. Just in the habit of getting your goat."

"You haven't seen me in years."

"That's true," Powderkeg said. "But I haven't forgotten you."

He picked up her left hand and kissed the oddly placed ring on her index finger.

"And you haven't forgotten me," he continued. "Remember when I found that ring when we were packing up from that craft show in Seattle? You stuck it on your finger—it was way too small, but you liked the way it looked, so you kept it. You said it was like us—a weird fit, but perfect in its own way."

"I can't believe you remembered!" Cleo said, stretching. "And I remember these killer massages, too. You certainly haven't lost your touch."

"Well," Powderkeg said, slowing down the massage to long, sensuous strokes along her back. "Like you said, old habits die hard."

Cleo sat up straight and looked at him. "Do you realize you and I know each other better than anyone else? How sad is that?"

Powderkeg continued to massage her shoulders, not saying anything. The time for conversing was over.

Cleo got the message, relaxing as she closed her eyes.

"You know what the hardest part of being in Fat Chance is?" she eventually asked. She'd never been good at the non-conversing part.

"What?" Powderkeg asked in a whisper, as he stroked her back.

"All this time to *think*," she said. "Elwood is just the tip of the iceberg. I look back on my life and all I see is one mistake after another."

"We've all made mistakes, Clee," he said, using a sobriquet he hadn't thought of in years. "And besides, it wasn't *all* bad, was it?"

He remembered a spot, just behind her ear, that was especially sensitive. He touched it lightly with his index finger, tracing light circles from her ear to her collarbone.

"No," Cleo breathed. "It wasn't all bad."

# CHAPTER 31

As soon as Old Bertha returned from Spoonerville, she'd taken a shower and washed off her charcoal makeup. Before she got in the shower, she'd caught a glimpse of herself in the mirror. Of course she appeared thoroughly insane with her eyes rimmed in charcoal, but she suddenly saw the appeal. She felt wholly unlike herself. It was as if she were wearing a mask and could be anyone she wanted to be.

The sun was just starting its slow descent over the town when Bertha made her way to the front porch swing. She had a big pot of chicken soup cooking on the stove and the smell from the kitchen wrapped the whole porch in comfort. Sipping a cup of tea, she rocked the ancient swing back and forth with her foot. Powderkeg had checked the swing, tested the support beams, added a few sturdy molly bolts, and declared it strong enough to hold her weight. She trusted him.

It had been a long time since Bertha had trusted anyone. She thought back to their trip to Spoonerville earlier that day. They had left Fat Chance as eleven individuals and returned as a team. She was happy to be a part of it. She didn't want to think of this group as a family . . . but she did declare before God and Spoonerville that Polly was "her girl." Was this what Cutthroat had in mind when he sent them here? Didn't sound much like him. But this was as good a guess as any.

Polly poked her head out the door. Her face was freshly scrubbed and she was already in her nighttime uniform of sweatpants and T-shirt. She had taken an even longer nap than Old Bertha had. Today had exhausted both of them.

"Can I come sit with you?" Polly asked.

Bertha shifted her weight so she was only taking up half the seat.

Polly came out of the house and tugged on the chain holding up one side of the swing. "Do you think this will hold us both?"

"If it doesn't, we'll crash and burn together."

"Just like in Spoonerville," Polly said as she sat down.

"Soup will be ready in a few minutes. You want some?"

Bertha could just make out Polly's nod.

"I really appreciated what you did, you know," Polly said. "That took some nerve."

"I've always had nerve," Old Bertha said. "Not sure where it's got me . . . except to Fat Chance."

"I know! This is probably the craziest thing I've ever done in my life."

Old Bertha chuckled. "Me too. And I've been on this planet a lot longer than you."

From the porch of the Creekside Inn, they could look directly down Main Street. They could see that dinner was just finishing up at the café. Titan and Wally walked together down the boardwalk, stopping in conversation in front of Wally's store before parting ways. The twins were standing in the middle of the street, faces illuminated in the glow of a cell phone.

Old Bertha looked at Polly. "You want to head into town and use a phone?" she asked. "I can keep the soup on."

"No," Polly said as they watched Pappy leave the café and wave goodnight to the twins. "I'm happy sitting here with you."

For several minutes the splashing of Loudmouth Lake and the creak of the swing were the only sounds on the porch.

"Can I ask you something?" Old Bertha said.

Again, the almost imperceptible nod.

"Where is your mom?"

"She's around," Polly said. "It's just that after my dad died, she couldn't handle anything, you know? She kind of gave up on life— and that included me."

Bertha's instinct was to condemn the woman. But then she thought back to the day she'd realized that Cutthroat had left town—and her. She'd never really recovered from that. Listening to Polly talk about her mother, a woman who lost her heroic husband in a tragedy, Bertha felt nothing but compassion for the woman.

"I'm sure your mother did the best she could," she said, surprising herself.

"Oh, I know she did. It was just hard. It's still hard, you know?"

It was Bertha's turn to nod without speaking. But she didn't know. She had absolutely no idea. She knew debits and credits. But she knew nothing about the kind of anguish that would make a mother lose track of her little girl's life and terrible makeup choices. Old Bertha wondered if this is what Cutthroat had in mind when he sent her here—to examine her own meaningless life.

*But he loved me. He said he did.*

Polly's voice cut into Bertha's thoughts.

"Mom and I used to cry all the time. One day, I was playing with my mom's makeup. I was twelve. I saw a model in a magazine and I tried to copy her. I spent about two hours in front of the mirror. When my mom came home from work, she found me and she started to cry—again. Usually, as soon as Mom's tears started, mine followed. But I had worked so hard on my makeup! I reached up and pressed on my lower lids to keep the makeup from running. It worked. So I just started to wear crazy makeup, 'cause I knew I could stop my tears. I know it sounds nuts, but it works. I never cry anymore."

"Do you think if you cried all the tears you needed to cry, you might not need that makeup anymore?" Bertha asked.

"I don't know."

Bertha put her arms around Polly, and she sank into the old woman's pillowy bosom.

"Let's just see," Bertha said, gently rocking Polly back and forth and stroking her hair. "You go ahead and cry those tears."

The building creaked in harmony to Polly's sorrowful song. Bertha could tell the soup was going to burn on the stove, but she just held the trembling, sobbing girl.

Maybe *this* was what Cutthroat had had in mind after all.

# CHAPTER 32

Dymphna was not sure what to make of Professor Johnson. He arrived in time for dinner, announcing that he didn't want to be an inconvenience as he took a seat at the table. She was happy to have him there for many reasons, including the fact that she had canned meat to get rid of. Tonight she had made a vegetable stew and added some cut-up Spam to Professor Johnson's bowl. She gave the rest of the Spam to Thud.

"I bought some dog food in Spoonerville," Professor Johnson said. "But Thud could only carry so much. I'll order a month's supply now that we have access to the Internet. I'm concerned he's going to get so used to people food he won't go back."

"It's Spam," Dymphna said as they watched the dog eat. "I don't think you need to worry."

Professor Johnson insisted on cleaning up after dinner while Dymphna took Thud outside.

"Want to tuck in the goats and chickens?" Dymphna asked Thud.

She knew no one was listening, but she felt herself flushing. If she were going to make a go of it in Texas, she'd have to learn the terminology. She was pretty sure hardcore Texas ranchers didn't 'tuck in' their animals. The hens in the henhouse seemed to take care of themselves. She left the barn doors open during the day, but closed the goats up at night. Pappy told her that goats didn't really even need a barn, but she felt better knowing they had shelter.

The three does came running up to her when they reached the barn. Dymphna assumed that Down Diego must be avoiding Thud, but as she looked around the pen, she couldn't see him. Her heart started to beat faster. Down Diego was nowhere to be found.

"Thud," Dymphna said. "Go get your dad."

Thud bounded around the yard, scattering the does, chickens, and Wobble.

*OK, he's not exactly Lassie.*

"Professor Johnson!" Dymphna called.

The professor came out of the house, his shirtsleeves still rolled up to his elbows. "Is there a problem?" he asked, coming quickly through the gate.

"I can't find Down Diego!" Dymphna said frantically.

"Who?"

"My buck!"

"Your what?"

"My male goat!" Dymphna said. "He's missing!"

Thud starting barking furiously.

"Not now, Thud," Professor Johnson said sternly. "We have a crisis."

"We do?" Dymphna said.

"Don't we?"

"I hope not!"

Thud continued to bark. Dymphna watched him. He was focused on the roof of the barn and jumping as high as he could before collapsing on the ground. Dymphna looked up. Down Diego was on the roof, staring down at them.

*My gosh! You* are *Lassie!* thought Dymphna.

"How in hell did he get up there?" Professor Johnson asked.

"I have no idea. But how do we get him down?"

"I guess we go into town, get your phone back, and google it!"

"What if he falls in the meantime?" Dymphna asked.

The professor looked up at the goat. "He appears pretty sure-footed."

"But it's almost dark," Dymphna said.

"Does that bother goats?"

"I don't know."

"I guess we'll have to google that, too."

"I'll get my phone."

Before they could head into town, Down Diego was suddenly in the yard with the other goats.

"I guess what goes up, must come down," Professor Johnson said, as they stared at the goat.

Dymphna sighed and hurried the goats into the barn for the night. She gave Down Diego a pat on the head.

"Maybe I should have called you Houdini," she said. "Goodnight, you guys."

By the time she was back in the farmhouse, Thud was asleep in the living room. Dymphna saw a light outlining Professor Johnson's door. She felt a mixture of relief and disappointment. As she walked to her room, Thud staggered to his feet and climbed into her bed. She fell asleep curled around Thud's warm, wrinkled mass.

As soon as Wobble made his acerbic announcement that a new day had arrived, Dymphna awoke to find Thud already standing at the door. She dressed quickly. Time to collect eggs! As she closed the front door, Thud at her heels, she heard Professor Johnson turn on the shower.

Heat colored her cheeks.

*Do not think about that man in the shower.*

She walked resolutely to the barn. Wobble flew up to the top of the fence, letting Thud into the yard but keeping an eye on him.

The goats, Udderlee, Catterlee, Sarilee, and Down Diego, were let out of the barn. She was relieved to count all four of them—and happy that she could finally tell them all apart. Their white coats, black faces, and drooping black ears had made them almost indistinguishable at first—but little differences in their personalities made each one an individual. Udderlee was shy; Catterlee, with her brilliant, knowing eyes hiding under her crazy hairdo, was haughty (it was as if she knew she had the prettiest eyes); Sarilee was playful; and Down Diego was a watchful old man. They romped joyfully around the yard, stretching their little goat legs—or at least what you could see of their legs under their impressive long white coats.

Thud and Down Diego ran around the yard, engaging in some sort of animal tag. Dymphna was sure Thud thought the game was all in good fun. But the goat had such a serious face. She didn't know him well enough to tell if he was chasing the dog or playing with him. She figured as long as neither got hurt, it was OK.

When Dymphna stepped back inside the farmhouse, Professor Johnson also appeared in the kitchen, fully dressed and cleanly shaven. He seemed preoccupied and was tucking his wire-rimmed glasses behind his ears, when he spotted Dymphna putting the berries she had collected into a bowl. He seemed surprised to see her.

"Ah!" he said, "You're here."

*It's my house.*

"Yes," she said. "I am."

*Why can't I get better at this?*

She started washing the berries in the sink for something to do. To make conversation, she said, "I was afraid to run the hot water. I've lived in old houses before and if you tried to run the water in the sink, the water in the shower would get cold."

She concentrated on the berries as she realized this conversation pretty much said "I was thinking about you being in the shower," which was not exactly what she had planned on projecting this morning.

"That was very kind of you," he said.

Dymphna turned off the tap and looked at him. "May I ask you a question?"

"All right," he said. "Although I may not have the answer."

"Why don't you ever smile?"

The professor frowned. "I don't know. Do I *never* smile?"

"Pretty much never."

"I guess I have nothing to smile about."

Dymphna dried her hands on the dish towel hanging on a nail by the sink. She walked over and stood in front of him. He stared down at her. She turned and looked at the dog, who was staring at the two of them.

"Don't look, Thud," she said.

Standing on tiptoe, she put her arms around his neck, closed her eyes, and kissed him, praying that the kiss didn't land off center. She wasn't really very good at this sort of thing. She let herself off her toes, and slid her arms back down to her sides.

Professor Johnson smiled.

*What am I doing? We don't know anything about each other!*

Thud barked.

They looked at the dog, who was scratching at the door. The mood in the little kitchen snapped like a ripe green bean, and Dymphna let the dog into the yard.

She knew that getting involved with Professor Johnson was not a good idea. If they had met any other time in any other place, they clearly would have no interest in each other. She wasn't the type to start a relationship out of convenience, so she shouldn't start now. On the one hand, six months seemed like forever, but on the other hand, they had to go back to the real world after that—and they would go back separately.

It was evident Professor Johnson was having the same thoughts. By the time she came back inside, she found him with his backpack already over his shoulder.

"If you're completely sure you are out of danger," he said, "perhaps it would be better if I stayed in town."

"Of course."

"But Thud should stay with you every night, if you would like a little extra security."

"I'd like that," Dymphna said.

By the time they headed into town, it was obvious that by mutual consent and fake amnesia, they had forgotten that he had kissed her and that she had kissed him.

They were even—the slate had been kissed clean.

# CHAPTER 33

As Professor Johnson, Dymphna, and Thud made their way down the hill, they were greeted by the chuck wagon triangle clanging impressively. Powderkeg was alternately ringing it and calling out that the whole town was invited to breakfast.

"I wonder if Aunt Cleo knows about this?" Professor Johnson said.

As if in answer to his question, Cleo appeared in the doorway, threw her arms around Powderkeg, and kissed him. Professor Johnson and Dymphna stopped dead in their tracks. Not everyone in Fat Chance took the high road last night, apparently.

Inside the café, Powderkeg and Cleo had put all the tables end to end. The idea must have been to have the entire population of the town sitting at one long table; however, the fact that some of the tables were round, some square, some oblong, and all of varying heights, didn't give it the symmetry that would land it in a *Rustic Living* magazine spread. Dymphna handed her basket of eggs to Cleo, who beamed at her.

"Good morning, Dymphna," Cleo said. "These are just beautiful eggs. Thank you."

Dymphna took a seat next to Polly, who was wearing considerably less makeup.

"Did I miss something?" Dymphna whispered to Polly.

"You might have," Polly whispered back. "But I didn't. Good thing Old Bertha is a little deaf. Those two were at it all night."

"Aren't they a little old for that?" Dymphna asked, studying Cleo's new featherweight step.

"No, they are not," Old Bertha said, leaning across Polly to look

Dymphna right in the eye. She turned to Polly. "And I'm not *that* deaf."

Dymphna and Polly both giggled. Titan came by with a misshapen bowl of pastries. He offered the bowl to Dymphna. She took it and almost dropped it. The bowl must have weighed ten pounds. Titan caught it before it hit the floor.

"Oh, sorry," Titan said. "I still have some bugs to work out of the design. I thought I might try making hand-forged tableware. I think I'd have a corner on the market."

"I bet you would." Dymphna grabbed a bear claw out of the bowl. She wondered if you'd have to have a bodybuilder accompany each bowl.

Polly took a muffin and bit into it before continuing her conspiratorial conversation with Dymphna. "So," she whispered, "anything interesting happen up at the farm last night?"

"My buck got up on the roof."

"That's not what I meant." Polly smiled, flashing a quick nod in the professor's direction at the other end of the table.

"I know," Dymphna said, following Polly's gaze. "You asked if anything interesting happened."

"Oh," Polly said as enlightenment dawned. "Sorry."

"Don't be. We're both too mature to jump into something just because we're trapped here."

Dymphna was serving herself some eggs and it took her a moment to realize the conversation had ceased. She looked up as she passed the platter of eggs to see Polly and Wally exchanging smoldering glances across the table.

Polly snapped out of her trance as she took the platter of eggs. "What did you say?" she asked.

"Never mind," Dymphna said.

Dymphna noticed one chair at the head of the table was empty, just as Pappy came through the doors.

Cleo jumped out of her chair and rushed to him. "I was wondering when you were going to show up," she said, ushering him to the empty chair. "Sit down. I was just about to make a toast."

By the look on his face, Pappy seemed as startled as the rest of the town by the change in Cleo's behavior. He sat, flanked on one side by Rodney and on the other by Rock. Rock held out a fist. Pappy hesitantly made a fist and Rock bumped it. Dymphna could barely hear the conversation at that end of the table, but she could make out Rodney asking if their jurisdiction extended to Spoonerville.

"No," Pappy said, buttering some bread. "Why?"

"We just thought we could kick some Spoonerville ass," Rock said.

Rodney and Wally laughed, but Pappy looked at them sternly.

"You keep your noses clean," he said.

The boys sobered up. Pappy seemed dead serious. None of them knew Pappy well, but this was a side they hadn't seen before. Cleo, still in her own world, missed the exchange. She stood behind Pappy's chair with a small juice glass and a spoon. She hit the glass with her spoon and the juice jumped with the chime.

"I'm so glad you could all join me here this morning," Cleo said. "I just want to say how much we appreciate this dedicated man. Pappy, we are all so grateful for all your hard work. We came here a disorganized mess and look at us now! Without you, none of this would have been possible."

Cleo held her glass up into the air, smiling all around the table. Dymphna could imagine Cleo giving this exact speech at Beverly Hills fundraising breakfasts a hundred times before. In stunned silence, the group clinked their glasses.

"Pappy," Cleo said, "say a few words."

She put down her glass and started applauding. The little assembly followed suit.

Pappy stood up. "Well, I don't know why this is happening. I didn't do anything special. But, as long as you're all here, it's as good a time as any to tell you. I'm leaving Fat Chance. So—thanks."

Pappy pushed his chair back and started to the door. Dymphna thought he must be joking and it took a few seconds for the reality of Pappy's little speech to hit home. Everyone jumped up at once, following Pappy outside. His suitcase was already on the sidewalk. As the group bombarded him with questions, he held up a meaty hand for silence.

"You can't leave us just like that!" Old Bertha said.

"You'll be fine," Pappy said. "Wally, I'm leaving Jerry Lee in your care. Don't you let anything happen to him or you can just head for the hills when you hear I'm coming back."

"This is bull—" Wally started, but caught himself. "I don't know anything about mules!"

"You'll figure it out," Pappy said. "You're a nasty SOB, but you're quick on your feet."

"I really wish you would reconsider," Cleo said, her voice quivering. "What will we do without you?"

"Well, little lady," Pappy said, picking up his battered suitcase, "you're about to find out."

The group stood on the boardwalk and watched him until he disappeared around the bend in the trail leading out of Fat Chance.

# PART THREE

# CHAPTER 34

Pappy came back to town five months later, arriving as unceremoniously as he had left. Wally Wasabi was washing windows in front of his store, so he was the first to spot him coming down the trail.

Pappy was still wearing his hiking boots, but had reversed his attire. He had replaced the Hawaiian shorts and white T-shirt with white shorts and a Hawaiian shirt. With a begrudging nod to the cooler January weather, he'd added a blue hoodie. He wore a Panama hat over his long hair, which was tied back in a ponytail.

"You back?" Wally asked.

"Yep," Pappy said. "How's my mule?"

"Good," Wally said.

"Good," Pappy said.

Titan came running out of the forge. "I thought I heard a familiar voice!" Titan gave Pappy a bear hug, which Pappy tolerated.

Pappy looked at Titan's wrist, which was sporting a leather brace laced up from fingers to elbow. "You hurt yourself?" he asked.

"Oh no," Titan said. "Powderkeg made this for me. I've trained Fancy to use it. Come see!"

Pappy left his suitcase on the bench outside Wally's store as Titan pulled him across Main Street to the forge.

"You got Fancy to fly?" Pappy said in a reverent tone.

"Of course not, silly," Titan said. "She has a broken wing! But watch this!"

Fancy was sitting up on her wrought-iron perch. She peered at Pappy with her one eye, cocking her head sideways to get a better look at him.

"She's so happy to see you!" Titan said. "She thinks you look very handsome in your new outfit, but she wonders where you've been all this time."

"She's one wordy bird," Pappy said.

Titan realized he wasn't going to get any answers and shifted gears. "OK, watch this!"

He held out his leather-bound wrist to Fancy and she climbed on his arm. He held Fancy aloft. "Ta-dah!"

"That's it?" Pappy said.

"What do you want from a buzzard with a broken wing?" Titan sounded crestfallen.

Pappy looked around the forge. Titan had shelves stacked with hand-hammered bowls, trays, and utensils. Even more surprising, a support beam held at least a hundred nails, each one holding a pair of earrings. Some of the earrings were made of metal, but at least half of them were combinations of metal and beads, lace, or feathers.

"I've been working on jewelry with Polly," Titan said proudly, setting Fancy back on her perch. "We're selling them at the store over in Spoonerville."

"In Spoonerville?" Pappy's eyebrows shot up so high, his hat almost fell off.

"Yeah. Dymphna convinced us we needed to make nice over there if we were going to survive over here. The twins agreed to go back to the bowling league—I think they were looking for an excuse to go back to the game anyway—and that was pretty much all it took. We never did convince a delivery company to bring stuff here, but now we just have our Internet orders sent to Spoonerville. It's working out just fine!"

"Maybe it's good that I left," Pappy said.

"Oh, that's not what I meant, you big grouch. Anyway, Powderkeg wants me to work on some belt buckles, but I haven't had much luck with a design yet. My friend Maurice says—"

"Hmmm," Pappy said, cutting him off and picking up a pair of silver earrings with turquoise stones in the middle. "I'll take these. Put them on my tab."

Pappy put the earrings in his shirt pocket.

"You don't *have* a tab," Titan called as Pappy walked out the front door.

Once his eyes adjusted to the sunlight outside the forge, Pappy noticed a carved sign nailed to the right side of the forge's entrance:

Titan's Treasures. Pappy bent to examine it. If he had to guess, he would say that, while the name was pure Titan, the workmanship was all Powderkeg.

While the inhabitants of Fat Chance weren't putting the town on the map, they were clearly making a go of things.

Pappy looked down Main Street and saw the difference that five months had brought about. Someone had replaced the broken or warped slats on the boardwalk and cleared the stacks of tumbleweeds that had huddled in the corners of every crevice. Most noticeable were the hand-carved signs over each building. More of Powderkeg's handiwork? Pappy walked down the boardwalk. Looking up at each wooden sign, he noticed that the workmanship got better with each one. Wally's simple *Groceries*, Powderkeg's own *Carpenter*, the *Jail*, *Bank*, and *City Hall* signs gave way to the more ornate *Cleo's Café*, *The Boozehound*, and Polly's *Tops, Hats & Tails*. Pappy couldn't make out the carving on Old Bertha's inn, but a sign clearly hung over the porch there as well. Frankly, Pappy thought that the *Bank* sign took away from the calligraphy on the front window, but nobody had asked him. In all fairness, he hadn't been here to ask.

One of the twins came out of the jail.

Pappy was as surprised to see him as he was to see Pappy.

*Is this Rodney or Rock?*

"What are you doing here?" Pappy and the twin asked simultaneously.

"I live here," the twin answered.

From the scowl, Pappy was fairly confident he was talking to Rock, but since the kid's hair was covering his ears and there was no way to see the parade of earrings, Pappy played it cool. "I heard you and your brother moved back to Spoonerville."

"You heard wrong," the twin said.

This *had* to be Rock.

"We just decided to go back and bowl," the twin said. "But we live here. Besides, it's not even bowling season."

"Good to know," Pappy said.

"You stayin'?"

"Who's askin'?" Pappy said, congratulating himself on this approach to finding out the twin's identity.

"I am."

Powderkeg came flying out of Cleo's Café, followed by a skillet.

Powderkeg dove onto Main Street as the skillet went flying over his head. He stood up and dusted himself off as Cleo appeared in the doorway. She had a bucket in her hands.

"I'm warning you," Powderkeg said. "You throw that water on me and we're through."

Pappy watched mesmerized as Cleo stood with the bucket. "Ten dollars says she throws it," he whispered to Wally, who had joined the spectators.

"You're on."

As if she saw a flag signaling the start of a race, Cleo heaved the water with all her strength. It fell short of the mark, barely lapping the tips of Powderkeg's boots.

"I warned you," Powderkeg growled as Cleo headed at a full tilt down the boardwalk, Powderkeg at her heels.

"I've only got Cutthroat's plastic," Wally said as Cleo came running toward them.

"You can owe me," Pappy said.

When Cleo saw Pappy, she stopped short. Powderkeg, racing behind her, almost knocked her down.

"Pappy!" Cleo said. "When did you get back?"

"Not long ago." Pappy turned to Powderkeg. "I saw the Covered Volkswagen up on blocks at the top of the hill. Happy to see she might stand a fighting chance of working again. You do that?"

Powderkeg shook his head. "That was Professor Johnson. He put the bus up on blocks and disconnected the battery. Not sure it will do any good considering the shape of the engine, but—"

"I can't believe you think you can just leave us and then waltz back in any time you feel like it," Cleo said.

"Well, I just did." Pappy picked up his suitcase and headed toward City Hall.

Cleo had more to say, but Pappy wasn't going to listen to it.

"Nice signs, Powderkeg," he said, indicating the carved signage as he continued on his way down Main Street.

"Thanks," Powderkeg said. "But don't bring it up around Old Bertha. She's a little sensitive."

Pappy was about to take the bait when Polly roared up on the back of an ATV driven by the other twin. Pappy gave a look over his shoulder to see the brother he'd been talking to, and Wally watching the ATV approach. So, Polly had chosen Rock after all.

*Funny, I was almost sure I was talking to Rock.*

The ATV came to a stop in front of Pappy.

"I thought I saw you heading to town," Polly said, jumping up and throwing her arms around Pappy. "I told Rodney to head back right away! I'm so glad to see you!"

*Rodney?*

Polly still wore her blazing red hair shaved at the sides, but other than that, she looked like a different person. She wore almost no makeup and only had small hoops in her ears. The nose ring was gone, replaced by a tiny stud which sparkled in the sun. Pappy wasn't sure which made more of a statement—her new look or her new fella.

"Does Old Bertha know you're back?" Polly asked, dragging him toward the Creekside Inn.

"Not yet," Pappy said. "I thought I'd throw my bag back at my place first."

"Oh no, Rodney can take your old bag. You've got to come home with me right now!"

It was not lost on Pappy that Polly referred to the inn as "home." As Rodney slapped Pappy on the back and took his suitcase, Pappy let himself be dragged over to Old Bertha's lopsided domicile.

"Oh, one thing," Polly said as they neared the inn. "Don't mention the sign. She's a little weird about it."

Polly ran inside to find Old Bertha as Pappy looked up. The workmanship on the sign was first-rate. It was outlined with delicate carvings of leaves, flowers, and vines. A perfect likeness of the tilted hotel was carved into the left corner. The calligraphy of the lettering was assured, although oddly sloping to one side. Pappy bit his bottom lip as he read the words: The Creakside Inn.

He vowed to ignore it as Old Bertha came out on the porch, wiping her hands on her apron.

"Decided to come back, did you?"

"I did," Pappy said. "I picked up something for you."

Old Bertha looked suspicious, but made her way down the stairs. Polly stood on the porch and watched as Pappy reached in his pocket and pulled out the earrings.

"You picked up something for me at Titan's?" Old Bertha asked.

"Yep," Pappy said, beaming. "How do you like them?"

"You are unbelievable!" Old Bertha said, but Pappy was relieved when she accepted the earrings.

He took that as a good sign, and as she turned around to head back up the stairs, he swatted her bottom. She turned around, red faced.

Pappy threw his hands in the air. "Just for old times' sake!"

Old Bertha dropped the earrings in her pocket and sashayed up the stairs. Pappy caught Polly's thumbs-up signal, which she flashed before Old Bertha could see her. Pappy suddenly thought he heard music. He strained to hear. The tune was familiar but one he had not heard in a very long time.

The music he was hearing was coming from the player piano in the saloon. It was the song called "Sahara, Now We're Dry Like You," a music scroll he and Cutthroat had gotten the player piano to play before it had seized up before their very eyes. And now the player piano was working again!

As Pappy hurried down the street toward the saloon, he thought there was something elusive about Fat Chance. It was always down, but never out.

Maybe that's why somebody way back when had named it Fat Chance, Texas, instead of No Chance.

# CHAPTER 35

Powderkeg raised his hand to give Professor Johnson a high five. The professor awkwardly turned it into a handshake.

"I never thought we'd get this old piano working again, but I've got to hand it to you," Powderkeg said. "'Sahara, Now We're Dry Like You' never sounded better."

"Really?" Professor Johnson asked. "You've heard it before?"

"No," Powderkeg said. "That was a joke."

Thud came bounding out of the back room as Pappy opened the front door of the saloon. The dog put his paws up on Pappy's shoulders and licked his face. Professor Johnson insisted the hound sit down, but Pappy shooed the admonishment away. When the dog finally settled down, Pappy had a chance to look around the saloon. While the bar was still the focal point of the place, Professor Johnson had taken out all the stools and tables. In their stead were display cabinets filled with a wide-ranging assortment of bric-a-brac, including old postcards, antique glasses, a newspaper called *The Carbon Paper* dated 1906, a stained lace handkerchief, and four glass marbles.

"What's all this?" Pappy asked.

"Since I don't have a liquor license, I decided to concentrate my efforts on creating a museum."

"The Boozehound Museum?"

"Yes," Professor Johnson said. "My personal feeling is you can get high on history just as easily as alcohol."

"You'd be alone there, son."

"I've been researching the history of Fat Chance, and it's fascinating. You were right about this being a Pony Express stop."

"Tell me something I don't know!" Pappy said.

"After the Pony Express ceased operations, this place still hung on. First, the ranchers came. By the late nineteenth century, ranchers and farmers were already at war with each other—not to mention the Comanches. The town was originally called Fork Creek, because the creek forks left from the Rolling Fork Ranch—which I found very interesting, because I thought the fork in Rolling Fork was a utensil."

"Me too," Powderkeg said. "Especially since the town is called Spoonerville."

"Spoonerville is the joke, not the fork," Professor Johnson said.

"Don't encourage him," Pappy said to Powderkeg.

The professor continued. "Anyway, the town never had much more than five hundred occupants. Fork Creek got hit with not one but two devastating twisters. The first was in 1908, then in 1915. After that, everybody left. The last resident, a woman named Mabel, was asked by a reporter if she thought the town would ever come back. She said 'fat chance.' Fork Creek has been called Fat Chance ever since."

"Where's my drink?" Pappy asked Powderkeg, but Professor Johnson was not ready to release the men.

"But Mabel was wrong," Professor Johnson said. "Now called Fat Chance, the town hung on until 1950—people looking to ranch again, or farm, or looking for oil or hot springs. I haven't found out what happened after that. Apparently everybody just . . . left. Any hope of Fat Chance surviving seemed to have died, until Cutthroat came in. That's as far as I've gotten with my research. I found a bunch of old registers and ledgers in the attic. They're pretty beat-up, but they might help."

"I can't help you with the mysterious demise of the town in the fifties," Pappy said. "But I can fill in any blanks once Cutthroat came along."

"One step at a time, Pappy," Powderkeg said, tossing his arm around Pappy's shoulder and leading him over to the bar. "Professor Johnson still has an odd bottle or two back here. Let's celebrate your return. You *have* returned, haven't you?"

"For now," Pappy said. "I'm not big on making long-range plans."

"We noticed." Powderkeg pulled out a bottle of whiskey from behind the bar.

Pappy was never much of a busybody, but he noticed that the door to the back of the saloon was open. He could see clothes, books, and a reading lamp through the doorway. Obviously the professor was no longer staying up at the farm.

Powderkeg waved the bottle in front of Pappy. Pappy nodded and Powderkeg put three shot glasses on the table.

"Come on, PJ," Powderkeg called over to the professor, who was polishing the player piano. "Get over here and relax a minute."

"No, thanks," Professor Johnson said. "I relaxed once already this year."

Powderkeg and Pappy shrugged, toasted, and knocked back their shots. As they slammed their glasses on the bar and growled, Dymphna came through the front door carrying a basket. Thud jumped up for a kiss.

"I was just coming to borrow Jerry Lee for a trip to Spoonerville and Wally said Pappy was back in town," she said, putting her basket down and embracing Pappy. "I'm so happy you came back. I was worried you were angry at us."

"No. If I was mad at you, you'd have known."

"That's what I said," Professor Johnson said, dusting his hands on his jeans and joining the conversation. "I mean, you were never exactly coy."

"You doing OK up there on the farm?" Pappy asked.

"It's great!" Dymphna said. "Thud stays with me at night. We're roommates!"

"I just feel better knowing she has Thud to watch over her," Professor Johnson said. "Especially with Big John on the loose."

"That rattler bothering you?" Pappy asked Dymphna.

"I've seen him a couple times," she said. "He's a real stinker, but he doesn't like the look of Thud."

"That snake could take Thud out in half a second," Pappy said.

"That might be true," Dymphna said, "but Big John keeps his distance if he knows the dog is around."

Pappy shrugged, then asked, "How are the goats?"

"They're so cute, now that they have their winter coats! We sheared them in the fall. Everybody helped! I'm storing the mohair until I get home and can work on it there. Every once in a while, I stand in the middle of Main Street and look up acreage that I might be able to buy that's within driving distance of Santa Monica. I'm hoping I can buy something where I can have all the goats and the chickens and my rabbits."

Pappy looked stern.

Dymphna's smile vanished. "The goats are mine to keep, aren't they?"

"Hadn't thought about it," Pappy said. "But, yeah, I guess so. Already making plans, huh?"

"Well, we'll be leaving in a month," Dymphna said.

"You were heading over to Spoonerville?" Pappy asked Dymphna as Powderkeg poured each of them another shot.

"Yes," she said. "I've been making jam. I'm stocking Wally's Groceries and Cleo's Café, too, but I have enough to get us through till we leave and still have some left to sell in Spoonerville."

Pappy frowned again.

"Is something wrong?" Dymphna asked.

"Town meeting in half an hour," Pappy said, then slugged back his shot and grimaced. "Let everybody know."

Pappy stormed out of the Boozehound. Dymphna, Powderkeg, and Professor Johnson stood staring at the swinging doors. Thud whimpered.

"It's OK, boy," Professor Johnson said, patting Thud's head. "It's not you, it's him."

Powderkeg rang the chuck-wagon triangle and summoned everyone to City Hall. Rodney and Rock weren't sure if they were supposed to attend, but Polly insisted they go. Pappy had changed back into his tea-colored T-shirt and Hawaiian shorts. Everyone stared back at him while Pappy's flashing eyes wandered over the tiny group.

"You all know as well as I do that Cutthroat Clarence left this town to you so you could make something of yourselves. Rodney and Rock, I know you were latecomers, but you've gotten in the spirit of the town pretty quick."

The group exchanged smiles. Dymphna had her thriving farm and jam business, Polly and Titan had started a jewelry line and each had found love—Polly with Rodney and Titan with his paternal protectiveness for Fancy. Cleo had rekindled her talent for cooking—and her relationship with Powderkeg was certainly passing the time. Professor Johnson had immersed himself in the town's history, Wally had discovered he had a flair for business, Powderkeg was enjoying a renaissance of his artistry both as a woodworker and as a leather artist. Old Bertha's heart had softened, and Rock, while a little heartsick at losing Polly to his brother, had to admit that living in a town full of eccentrics had made him feel less alone.

"Thank you, Pappy," Dymphna said shyly.

"Don't thank me," Pappy roared. "Jerry Lee and Thud have more sense than the lot of you!"

Thud put his paws over his ears. He didn't like to hear his name used in that tone of voice.

Old Bertha bristled. "What are you talking about?"

"You think Cutthroat would see this as a success?" Pappy spread his hands wide to indicate the town. "You've created a brotherhood, not a thriving town. This is not what he meant. He could always see things in a different light—how to pounce on an opportunity no one else saw."

The group looked at each other. They each honestly had made the most of their time here.

"If Cutthroat had some vision about his dusty little town, why didn't he realize it himself?" Wally asked, the old sullen tone returning to his voice.

"I'm not a mind reader," Pappy said. "But I knew the man, and I know that he was hoping you'd do something . . . great."

"Is that why you left us?" Polly asked. "Because you thought we'd fail?"

"No," Pappy said. "I left you so you could see the town for what it was without leaning on me. I needed to make sure you guys wouldn't kill yourselves or each other or starve to death, but once that was done, you needed some time to figure things out on your own. I will say, you've done just fine without me, but that's not enough."

"Actually," Powderkeg said, "it is enough. We get our money no matter what. We fulfilled our part of the bargain. We've only got to see it through for another month."

"I think I achieved greatness," Titan said. "I've made Fancy happy."

Dymphna put her arms around Titan.

"I think we've done a fine job," Cleo said. "Daddy didn't leave any kind of blueprint."

"He didn't want to leave you a blueprint," Pappy said. "If the idea was that you *had* to achieve something or you wouldn't get the money, that would be one thing. There's money at the end of the tunnel—but what he wanted was to give you a chance to really go for something nobody else could see. And from what I've seen, you've failed."

"Who are you to judge us?" Wally asked. "You haven't exactly set the world on fire."

"No," Pappy said. "No, I haven't. And I wouldn't wish that feeling on anybody."

The group looked embarrassed to hear this heartfelt admission, but Pappy seemed just to be stating a fact, not asking for sympathy.

"My brother and I aren't here for the money," Rodney said, as he got up from his chair. "So I think we can be a little more objective."

"You might be speaking for yourself, bro," Rock said.

"Anyway," Rodney said, shooting his brother a glare, "I think Pappy has a point. What have any of us got to lose by trying something . . . awesome? We've got a month. Let's go for it."

"Go for what?" Cleo asked.

"I don't know, man," Rodney said. "Anything outside of the box."

Dymphna and Titan huddled, whispering to each other through Rodney's speech. Then Dymphna stood up.

"We have an idea," she said. "Let's have a Wild West Weekend!"

Titan and Dymphna looked around the room, waiting for a response.

"That idea sucks," Wally said.

Old Bertha sniffed. "Why would we do that?"

"It would be out of the box, for sure," Dymphna said. "And didn't Cutthroat see what no one else saw? Everyone in the world, including us when we first got here, saw a faded little town with nothing to recommend it."

"So now we're going to celebrate Fat Chance?" Titan asked.

"Exactly!" Dymphna said. "We can call it the Spirit of Fat Chance."

"Fat and Wild?" Wally snickered.

"That sounds like a reality show," Old Bertha said.

"I think we should call it Cowboy-Up," Polly said. "It means muscle through, doesn't it? And that's what we did. Plus it's the only cowboy term I know."

"But," Cleo said, "we're not cowboys. That's the point. I think we need a name with some sophistication—some sizzle."

"Fandango?" Titan offered.

"Fandango-Up *In* Fat Chance!" Dymphna cried.

"It's ridiculous," Powderkeg said. "I'm in."

"Who'll come to see it?" Old Bertha asked.

"The people from the Rolling Fork and Spoonerville," Dymphna said.

"Our whole bowling league," Rock added.

"My friend Erinn might be able to get us some publicity," Dymphna said.

"And Maurice can get the word out in Las Vegas," added Titan.

"I might have a contact or two," Wally said.

Everyone stared at him.

"What?" he asked. "You think I don't know anybody?"

Suddenly there was a chorus of voices as everyone threw out ideas.

"We can attack the town!"

"We don't have any horses."

"We can use Jerry Lee!"

"Dude, we don't want to get laughed at."

"We can attack on our ATVs!" Rock said.

"I think Polly and Wally should attack with us," Rodney said. "You know, the outlaws."

"And Titan," Rock added. "Dude, you should be with the outlaws, too!"

"But these people are my friends," Titan said.

"It's all in fun," Dymphna assured him.

"What would we wear?" Titan asked.

"We'll figure something out!" Polly said, pumping her fist in the air. "I can't wait!"

"If Old Bertha can lend me a hand, I can make the food," Cleo said.

"Maybe we could have booths, too, to sell some of the stuff we've been making," Powderkeg said, then winked at Cleo. "Like the old days."

"You used to be able to sell leather to a cow," Cleo said, poking him in the ribs.

"It's going to be a lot of work getting this right," Powderkeg said. "We're gonna have to order a bunch of stuff—and it would sure be helpful to get the Covered Volkswagen running. This is going to take everything we've got."

"Maybe we should try the dry ice thing again," Professor Johnson said.

"I told you, that won't work," Powderkeg said. "We could try putting water bags over the vents."

"I'm telling you, the dry ice concept will work, it just needs a few kinks worked out," Professor Johnson argued.

"May I borrow your phone?" Cleo held out her hand to Dymphna.

Dymphna turned it over without a word, but followed Cleo out onto the street.

"Do you think a Wild West Weekend is anything like your father had in mind for us?" Dymphna asked.

"Maybe not. I agree that we should attempt it, but frankly, it was always impossible to make Daddy happy, so I wouldn't start worrying about it now." Cleo punched at the buttons on the phone.

Dymphna stood back as Cleo turned her attention to the phone call.

"Wesley, darling, it's Cleo. Be a dear, would you, and send me a Volkswagen engine?"

Cleo paused and furrowed her brow. "I am very aware I don't have the capital for that; that's why I'm calling you."

Dymphna pretended not to listen, but it was impossible. Thankfully, Titan came out to the boardwalk. They both pretended not to listen.

"Wesley, darling, I'm going to be a very powerful woman in less than a month. I suggest you figure out a way to get a Volkswagen engine and deliver it to Fat Chance, Texas, this week ... No, darling, just to the top of the hill will be fine. Be creative! *Of course* I'm not threatening you ... but call me when the engine is on its way. Kisses ... oh, and send a new set of tires—the bus was built in 1972, I believe. Buh-bye."

She snapped the phone closed, but Titan was right behind her, waiting for the phone. He stabbed at the keypad and while he waited, he looked at Dymphna, crossing his fingers in a "here's hoping for the best" gesture. While Dymphna had no idea what they were hoping for, she crossed her fingers, too—both hands.

"Hello, Maurice. Is there any way I can borrow those Wild West costumes for a few days at the end of the month? Oh, thank you! We're putting on a show! I'm going to be an outlaw! Send them all, but especially that gorgeous cowboy hat with the rhinestones and feathers! It's going to be fab!"

Titan and Cleo went back into City Hall, heads together, plotting ideas for the show. Dymphna stared at her phone. What had she gotten them into?

# CHAPTER 36

Everyone in Fat Chance was standing at the top of the trail, look-ing at the Volkswagen bus, which stood proudly on four glossy new tires. Tools, discarded cans of oil, and a large gas can littered the turnout. Powderkeg, Professor Johnson, and the twins knelt shoulder to shoulder, looking inside the engine.

"That should do it," Powderkeg said.

Fancy perched on Titan's sheathed arm, but looked down threat-eningly at Thud, who periodically jumped up to see her.

"I can't watch," Titan said to Dymphna and Polly, covering his eyes with his free hand.

"They seem to know what they're doing," Dymphna said.

"The bus only has to get us to Spoonerville and back to pick up supplies," Polly added. "It's not like it has to be perfect."

"I don't think that's how an engine operates," Cleo said. "It either works or it doesn't."

"I just don't want to hear any more arguments about that damn dry ice," Old Bertha said.

Professor Johnson looked up at Wally, who was leaning against the bus, and gave him a nod.

"OK, Pappy," Wally yelled to Pappy in the driver's seat. "Start her up."

As if reacting to a secret signal, everyone backed away from the bus. Pappy cranked the engine. It started with a clatter and then a roar, which sent Thud running down the hill and Fancy crab-walking up Titan's shoulder.

"Ouch, ouch, ouch," Titan said, coaxing Fancy back onto the leather sheath.

The rest of the Fat Chance occupants danced around the bus, hugging and high-fiving each other. Polly and Rodney shared a kiss, then another, then another.

"Get a room," Wally said sourly.

"Dude," Rock said. "Seriously."

Powderkeg whooped and hollered, throwing a startled Cleo over his shoulder in a fireman's carry and spinning her around. Dymphna spontaneously threw her arms around Professor Johnson. Mid-hug, she realized this was the first physical contact the two had shared since the professor moved back down the hill. She was relieved to find the hug didn't send him scampering down the hill after Thud.

"I can't believe you got that old thing going," Old Bertha said.

"Back at ya," Pappy said.

"Pardon?" Old Bertha asked, confused.

"You got *this* old thing going," Pappy said, pointing to himself.

"I haven't been harassed this much since the nineteen fifties," Old Bertha said. "You should try a new approach."

"Would a new approach get me anyplace?" Pappy asked.

Old Bertha started to shake her head but stopped. She stared at him. "It might."

Pappy, a tint of scarlet in his leather cheeks, called out, "Everybody who's going to Spoonerville, be ready to roll in twenty."

Everyone wanted to go to Spoonerville in the resuscitated vehicle, but it only held four passengers and the driver, since the center seat had been removed long ago.

While a carnival atmosphere surrounded the resuscitation of the Covered Volkswagen, there was no reason to go insane. It was still a cantankerous vehicle. Rock, Rodney, and Polly agreed to follow the bus on the ATVs, just in case the bus broke down. Powderkeg suggested he walk over with Jerry Lee and his saddlebags, since the supplies for Fandango-Up in Fat Chance were coming in. Even an empty VW wouldn't hold everything. Professor Johnson volunteered Thud's services as a pack animal as well. Dymphna quickly did the math. If she walked to Spoonerville, that would leave just four—Titan, Old Bertha, Wally Wasabi, and Cleo—to ride in the bus.

"I'll walk over, too," Dymphna said, casting a sideways glance at Professor Johnson. She couldn't tell if the news made him happy, annoyed—or if he didn't care at all. She knew Thud would be happy to have her along.

"Since I'm heading over on foot," Professor Johnson said to Powderkeg, "I can handle Jerry Lee if you want to ride over in the bus."

Dymphna bit her lip to hide her smile. Maybe this meant he wanted to walk with her and her alone.

"Just in case something goes wrong," Professor Johnson said. "Might be good to have at least one of us riding along."

Dymphna's hopes were dashed. The professor and Powderkeg exchanged a manly handshake as Powderkeg took a seat on the floor of the bus.

"Oh, Wally," Dymphna called into the bus. "Can I grab some of my jam off your shelves to sell in Spoonerville? I'll replace them tomorrow."

"Whatever," came the response.

Dymphna and Professor Johnson stood on the turnout watching the bus clatter down the road, while the ATVs roared up and down the hills, Polly waving from the back of Rodney's vehicle.

"We should have a parade," Dymphna said to Professor Johnson.

"That might be difficult, since everyone just took off."

"Not now," Dymphna said. "For Fandango-Up in Fat Chance. Don't you think that would be fun?"

"I have no idea. I tend to deal more with the tangible."

"Parades are tangible."

"Not at this stage of the game. Get back to me when you have the Grand Marshall."

*Was that a joke?*

They headed down the hill to harness Jerry Lee and Thud. Dymphna let herself into Wally Wasabi's grocery store. She thought he kept a few baskets behind the counter, but she couldn't find any. She looked around the store, and then wandered into the back room. She spotted a beat-up rattan basket on the floor beside a desk. The desk was tidy, but there was a letter and torn envelope on it, as well as his computer, which sat open. The envelope was addressed to Wallace Watanabe at his Spoonerville P.O. address. She smiled. Everyone in town gently ribbed him about his obsession with going to Spoonerville for his mail. She couldn't read the letter without moving the envelope, and she thought that was an invasion of his privacy. But the envelope had a black rose as part of its New York City return address. She had to admit, her curiosity was piqued. Was he in some steamy pen-pal correspondence?

*Seems a little old-school for Wally.*

As she bent to pick up the basket, she jarred the desk and the computer screen came to life. She hadn't meant to look, but she was so surprised to see sentences filling up the screen that curiosity got the better of her. She knew he had no signal in this part of town, so whatever this was, he must be just using the word processing program—which in turn meant—he was *writing.*

> He carefully lifted the hair off the back of her neck and kissed her throat near her right ear, softly moving her pearl-drop earring out of the way with his tongue. Her small breasts rose and fell with each breath. She was wearing a sundress the color of the sky, with spaghetti straps, which were thin and worn from too many washings, tied at the shoulders.

*Wally Wasabi knows the term "spaghetti straps"?*
She kept reading:

> He untied one string, which fell away from her shoulder in a whisper. Her breathing quickened. He ran one finger along her delicate collarbone and then untied the other.

"Jerry Lee and Thud are ready to go," Professor Johnson called from the front of the store.

Dymphna bolted upright. She had no right to read this. But what exactly was she reading? She took one final glance at the header. It read:

*The Cowgirl in the Ride-'Em-High Boots*

Dymphna grabbed the basket and ran from the room.

For the first time since meeting Professor Johnson, she was glad he wasn't much of a conversationalist. Dymphna didn't want to spill Wally Wasabi's secret, but she was afraid if they started talking, she'd spill the beans.

Polly had announced her devotion to Mimi Millicent's romantic texts in the RV and then again when they first got to Fat Chance. Was it possible he hadn't heard her declaration either time?

*Not likely.*

And you would have to be blind not to know Wally was smitten with Polly. He must be writing a romance to impress Polly. The more she thought about it, the less sense it made.

"Is everything all right?" Professor Johnson's voice broke into her thoughts.

"Yes. Why do you ask?"

"You're carrying an empty basket. That struck me as a little odd."

Dymphna looked down at the battered basket.

*I forgot the jam.*

# CHAPTER 37

Dymphna, Professor Johnson, Jerry Lee, and Thud rounded the bend in the road that led to Spoonerville. The tiny town looked like a busy retailer before Black Friday. The ground around the Volkswagen was covered with boxes of every shape and size. Cleo and Old Bertha had their heads together and were going through a checklist with their pens. Rock was standing with a few young men Dymphna didn't know—the bowling team, no doubt. All of them shot admiring glances at Polly from time to time. Polly, oblivious, sat on the ground, digging into a box of lace trims and holding them up for Rodney to see. Titan stood beaming, running his massive hands over two antique steamer trunks covered in decals, probably Maurice's costumes. Dymphna could see Powderkeg off in the distance, staring at the ground. She had gotten used to the sight of him picking up interesting pieces of wood to turn into utensils and bowls.

*At least Powderkeg isn't spending any money.*

While she was pleased that her neighbors had embraced Fandango-Up in Fat Chance, she knew that many of them were going out on a limb financially to make it a reality. There was no denying that it was going to be expensive. While Cleo was game to front the money, Wesley was prepared for her call this time, and had cut her off. However, Cleo's successful strong-arming of one of the most powerful attorneys in Los Angeles opened the floodgates of fancy financial wheeling and dealing. Old Bertha, with her background in finance, sat down with Dodge and laid out their plan. Between everyone's credit cards and Dodge's agreement to finance the balance until the Fat Chance inhabitants got their money, Fandango-Up was proceeding full speed ahead.

"We need nine hundred people to attend over the course of three days to break even," Old Bertha said.

"There aren't nine hundred people anywhere around here," Pappy said. "They'd have to come from Austin, and that's asking a lot."

"Dodge says he can all but guarantee nine hundred people himself," Cleo said. "He has friends and family all over Texas who are just looking for something to do."

"If Dodge can bring in the folks," Old Bertha said, "there's no reason this shouldn't work."

"I wouldn't be trusting Dodge Durham," Pappy warned. "Back in the day, him and his daddy could have given Cutthroat a run for his money—no offense, Cleo."

"No offense taken," Cleo said. "I don't recall Daddy objecting to *everyone* making money. He was very democratic that way."

"I'm with Pappy," Powderkeg said. "I don't trust him."

"Oh, you don't trust anybody," Cleo said.

"And we can all reach out to friends and family," Dymphna offered, turning to Professor Johnson. "What do you think?"

"I think it all sounds like magical thinking."

"Most of us have pretty much survived on magical thinking to this point," Powderkeg said. "Let's go for it."

Feelers to the outside world were not going well. Erinn would be on a shoot, Virginia had to stay in Santa Monica to take care of the rabbits, and Suzanna's baby was due any day. Titan was hoping his friend Maurice could make the trip from Las Vegas—maybe even bring some show members—but while Maurice was generous enough to send Titan some costumes, he really didn't visualize himself in Fat Chance, Texas. Cleo absolutely refused to tell any of her Beverly Hills friends where she was, let alone ask them to come—and the rest of the group didn't have anyone to ask.

Planning for Fandango-Up had the inhabitants of Fat Chance in Spoonerville almost as often as in their own town—supplies being ordered, supplies being delivered, wrong orders being sent back.

They all knew that nine hundred people attending a Wild West Weekend would neither set the world on fire nor turn Fat Chance into an instantaneous destination spot in Central Texas. But in their own way, they would make the statement that they had been there—and that they had mattered. It would be a salute to Fat Chance, even if this was probably not *exactly* what Cutthroat Clarence envisioned for them. And if fate was with them, they'd turn a profit!

Now that would be exactly what Cutthroat Clarence had had in mind.

It had been almost a century since anything resembling Fandango-Up in Fat Chance had taken place in this part of the Hill Country. Rodney and Rock were working on a bowling exhibition. Powderkeg was helping them design an outdoor bowling lane in a prime spot of real estate between the Creakside Inn and Polly's Tops, Hats & Tails.

On this umpteenth trip to Spoonerville, Dymphna looked around for Wally. He was sitting on the porch of Dodge's store, tapping away on his phone. Dymphna studied him. Could the surly Wally really be capable of such passionate prose? Perhaps there was another explanation. As if Wally sensed her interest, he looked up and gave his chin a slight tilt, his trademark ultracool greeting. Dymphna couldn't stand keeping secrets. While she wasn't proud of the fact that she'd been inadvertently snooping, she felt it was in Wally's and her best interests if she confessed.

*If only he were a little a more approachable.*

Losing her nerve, Dymphna went to plan B. She'd go into the store to buy something. She racked her brain, trying to think of what items Dodge kept for sale near the post office wall. She'd already been snooping—would it compound the crime if she tried to see what was in Wally's post office box?

As she climbed the stairs, she saw Dodge come out of the building and hand Wally Wasabi an envelope. She was close enough to see the black rose on the label.

*So much for plan B.*

Did the black rose have anything to do with the writing? What kind of correspondence couldn't be accomplished by e-mail? Granted, when they first got to Fat Chance, they didn't know they could communicate with the outside world, but that was eons ago. Whatever was up with Wally had been going on since they first came to Spoonerville and he'd ordered a post office box. Perhaps there was something more threatening going on than she suspected. Was the passionate prose some sort of code? One thing was clear: If he wanted her to know, he would have told her. Wally slid the envelope into his back pocket and Dymphna slid back down the stairs.

As the residents of Fat Chance headed down the road in the wagon and on foot, back to Fat Chance, Dodge pulled up in a cloud of smoke. He leaned his head out of his big pickup.

"Anybody want a ride back to Fat Chance?" he asked, looking directly at Cleo.

"We've got the animals," Powderkeg said from the road, where he was walking with Jerry Lee.

"What about you, ma'am?" Dodge asked Cleo.

"Don't mind if I do!" Cleo pulled open the passenger door and hopped in.

The pickup roared away, leaving a startled Powderkeg, Professor Johnson, Titan, Wally, and Dymphna in its wake.

"I would have taken a ride," Titan said.

Dymphna shot a glance at Powderkeg, who looked stormily after the pickup truck.

"What was that about?" Powderkeg said.

Wally snorted. "Dude, looks like you got some competition."

*There is no way Wally Wasabi wrote about "drop earrings and spaghetti straps,"* Dymphna thought to herself.

An hour later, as Fat Chance came into view, Dymphna caught her breath. The place looked like a real town. In the time it took her and the others to walk back, the rest of the group had carted box after box down the trail and were piling everything on the boardwalk.

*We haven't even had the festival, and we've already brought this crazy place back to life.*

Powderkeg broke into her thoughts. "I guess Dodge only took Cleo as far as the turnout," he groused, noting Dodge's absence. "Probably didn't want to haul his fat ass down the trail."

"That's the spirit," Titan said. "It's important to look on the bright side."

Dymphna smiled. She loved how Titan saw the positive in every situation.

Dymphna watched Pappy cover his eyes to block the sun. He was on the lookout for the group heading into town with the animals. Dymphna knew Pappy played the tough guy, but she also knew he always wanted to make sure Jerry Lee was all right.

"About time you got here," Pappy said. "Get those saddlebags unloaded. It's gonna take all of us to get Titan's trunks down here."

Old Bertha put her foot down at making one more trip up the trail.

"You can get those trunks without me," she said, heading back to the Creakside. "I'm done."

"You going to bail on us, too, Cleo?" Powderkeg asked. "You must be worn out from your road trip with Dodge."

Cleo let out a throaty laugh as the group headed up toward the Covered Volkswagen. "I just wanted to make sure I've still got it," she said.

"You need a man like Dodge to prove that to you?"

"I don't see a lot of options around here. Besides, you know that old saying, 'Keep your friends close, and your enemies closer.'"

"I don't get it," Powderkeg said.

"If we don't pull this off," Cleo said seriously, "we're going to owe that man a lot of money."

"What's it to you?" Wally asked, not even pretending they all weren't listening. "You're gonna be a gazillionaire."

"It's not about me," Cleo said. "It's about us—all of us. Don't forget this little experiment is *my* father's idea. I need this to work!"

"You do?" Professor Johnson sounded surprised.

Dymphna was glad he asked. As Cleo's nephew, he was the only one who could pose the question. Cleo did seem to be making the best of things since she got here, but Dymphna never thought she really *cared*.

"Yes, I do," Cleo said. "I don't . . . I don't want Daddy to have misplaced his faith in us."

Dymphna wanted to hug her. While this was the most personal statement Cleo had made the entire time they had been in Fat Chance, she was still not giving off any indication she'd like to be comforted. Titan obviously didn't pick up on this, because he swept Cleo into a bear hug, lifting her off her feet.

"Fandango-Up is going to be the greatest party ever," Titan said. "Don't you worry."

"All right, all right," Cleo said rigidly, as Titan put her back on her feet. "I'll try. Thank you, Titan."

As the group made their way to the VW, Dymphna stood back and watched them. Cleo was not the only one worried about Fandango-Up in Fat Chance. It had been her idea, but they had all gone 100 percent into this endeavor. None of them had looked back and she knew none of them would blame her if the festivities didn't come off as planned. But Cleo was right. If they didn't succeed, it would be a failure not only financially, but a failure of the heart.

Of all their hearts.

Could that many broken hearts ever be repaired?

Dymphna shook herself out of her contemplation. While Wally, Rodney, and Rock struggled to yank one trunk from the van, Titan pulled the other one out by himself.

"How are you going to get these down the hill?" Polly asked. "They weigh a ton."

"Maybe Jerry Lee can take them down?" Professor Johnson offered.

"That would be too much for him," Pappy said, shaking his head. "That much weight would really piss him off, and I don't like to piss off my mule."

"Words to live by, Pappy," Powderkeg said.

"What about dragging them with the ATVs?" Rock suggested.

"One of the reasons we drive ATVs is because we've got to drive up and down the hills around here—we've never been able to navigate that trail," Rodney said. "So there's no way we could haul trunks."

"Besides, the trunks would be beat to shit if you dragged them down the trail," Wally said.

"Maurice wouldn't like that," Titan said quietly.

"Maybe some sort of pulley system would work," Powderkeg suggested.

"Like the ancient Egyptians?" Professor Johnson asked.

"Whatever," Wally said.

"I have an idea," Titan said.

"Lay it on us, big guy," Rock said. "We got nothing so far."

"Why don't we just unpack them up here?"

The group stared at the trunks. The suggestion was so beautifully simple, it was almost impossible to comprehend. Titan positioned the first one in the dirt in front of him, creating a monster dust cloud. The trunks opened in the middle, more like a book than a suitcase. When the dust settled, Titan knelt and rattled the combination lock. Everyone groaned.

"I forgot about this," Titan said.

"I got a hacksaw in the bus," Pappy said.

"None of you, by any chance, would know how to pick a lock,

would you?" Professor Johnson asked Rock, Rodney, and Wally Wasabi.

Dymphna winced. This was not going to go well.

"No, man," Rock answered hotly. "Why would we?"

"Because you're—"

"Young," Dymphna cut in, hoping nobody called her on this, since she was not even a decade older. "You know, gym lockers, skating rink lockers, that sort of thing."

"Sorry," Rodney said. "We don't."

Wally shrugged. "Me neither."

"Actually," Polly said, "I do."

Dymphna blinked in surprise. Now that Polly wasn't hiding behind layers of paint, it was easy to forget the tough façade Polly wore when she first came into town. Polly had changed. While it was impossible to credit this current Polly with a casual knowledge of basic larceny, Dymphna wondered if the mask would go back on once they left Fat Chance, or if the world might have somehow gotten kinder in the months they'd been away. Dymphna realized that everyone was staring at Polly.

"I can't tell you how many combinations to my skating rink locker I lost," Polly said with a sly smile.

"Oh, I almost forgot," Titan said, reaching in his pocket and retrieving a scrap of paper. "Maurice sent me the combination."

"Damn," Rodney said. "I really wanted to see Polly spring that baby."

The group waited patiently as Titan rotated the dial on the lock, to no avail. Dymphna saw Powderkeg make an impatient move toward him, but Cleo put her hand on his arm and shook her head—very slightly—no.

*We've all changed.*

The group was so intent on watching the combination dial move back and forth, that when it finally sprang open with a whisper, it startled everyone. They leapt back, as if Big John had darted out of the bushes.

Titan opened the trunk and pulled the sides apart. It stood there, openmouthed, like a book on steroids. The inside of the trunk was lined with drawers. Titan opened one and pulled out what looked like a beaded bikini bottom.

"What's that?" Rock asked.

"It's part of a costume," Titan said, handing it over to him.

"A very *small* part, I hope," Rodney said, looking at the thong over his brother's shoulder.

"Oh yes!" Titan said, struggling with the combination of the other trunk. "The chaps and hats are the showstoppers. They must be in here!"

Titan snapped open the other trunk, which looked like it had been stuffed with feathers. Titan reverently removed an enormous black hat. The headband was brilliantly beaded in orange, white, and gold and had at least six perfectly matched white feathers, studded with gold flashing stones on the side.

Polly couldn't resist—she reached for it. Titan handed it over and Polly placed it on Rodney's head. Everyone regarded Rodney, standing there in his T-shirt, jeans, and boots. The wind rippled the feathers slightly. With his tanned skin and soulful eyes, Rodney looked as if he had stepped out of the pages of history.

"You're gorgeous," Polly said.

"Whatever," Wally said, annoyed.

"No," Dymphna added. "It's true, Rodney. You look amazing."

"Yeah, thanks," Rodney said. "But I'm not attacking Fat Chance in a swanky hat and a thong."

"Yeah," Powderkeg said. "Those thongs on the ATVs would be a killer."

"Let's get everything down the hill and take inventory," Polly said.

"I'm pretty sure we have room for everything at the forge," Titan said.

"I think it would be better to keep everything at Tops, Hats & Tails," Polly said. "Don't you? The forge gets pretty smoky."

"Plus, you don't want Fancy to think it's a family reunion with all these feathers," Rock said.

"Titan," Cleo said. "Why don't you start handing us costumes?"

Titan started with the hats. There were five of them, one more lavish than the next. Rodney, Rock, Polly, Titan, and Wally each put one on their heads . . . it was more practical to wear them than to try to carry them down the trail. Next he distributed jewelry, embroidered leggings, chaps, and boots. They headed down the hill, each festooned with the best faux-outlaw gear Las Vegas had to offer.

"These are totally awesome," Rodney said, adjusting his hat. "We should definitely invite Mom to Fandango-Up."

"Not if we're wearing thongs," Rock said.

# CHAPTER 38

The inhabitants of Fat Chance got 'er done. With only two days until Fandango-Up in Fat Chance, everyone's checklists were complete. Cleo, the self-appointed chairman of the nonexistent committee to oversee the festival, issued the order for a full dress rehearsal of the parade in twenty-four hours.

Titan wasn't the only person in town with connections. Cleo called in a favor from one of her father's friends, a retired costumer from the golden age of movies. She was now wearing a beaded black dance-hall girl outfit with a jet black choker and high button shoes.

Cleo was just putting a few bobby pins in her hair to hold a plume of feathers and ribbons Polly had made for her, when Powderkeg came into the café. All the men who were assigned the roles of "the townies" had grown handlebar mustaches, but Powderkeg's was the most impressive. It was lush, auburn, and neatly skimmed his full upper lip. Powderkeg looked every inch the dandy in his silk shirt and vest, sleeve garters, and shiny black boots. His belt was one of his own creations. It was dark leather, hand-tooled and attached to a small work of art that was a buckle made by Titan.

"You look good, cowboy," Cleo said.

"I'm not a cowboy," Powderkeg said. "I'm a gambler. No self-respecting cow would be seen with the likes of me, little lady."

"All right, then." Cleo returned her attention to the feathers.

"So, Cleo," Powderkeg said.

Cleo shook her head to make sure the feathers would hold. "So, Cleo, what?" she asked absently.

"Have you thought about what's going to happen when this is over?"

"Well, if Fandango-Up is successful, there'll be a lot of cleanup,"

Cleo said. "I've made a chart that outlines everyone's responsibilities."

"That's not what I mean," Powderkeg said.

Cleo sensed the seriousness of his tone. She stopped fussing with her hair and took a seat at one of the café tables. "Then what *do* you mean?"

"In a few days, we'll all leave Fat Chance," Powderkeg said. "Everybody going their separate ways. I was just wondering—if you've given any thought to that."

"Of course I have," Cleo said. She put her hand over Powderkeg's. "Marshall, we can't really have a serious conversation about this dressed as Miss Kitty and Wyatt Earp. Let's just leave it alone. Everything will work out, I promise."

"If you say so." He walked to the front of the café and looked out the window. "It's funny. I know your dad meant for us to do something important here. I just thought of the whole thing as a big joke. I came because I had nothing better to do and I knew my being here would make you crazy," he said, his back to her. "But I think we really did something important after all."

"Don't jinx it," Cleo said. "The festival is still two days away."

"I wasn't talking about that." He turned to face her.

Cleo stood up as he rushed to hold her. He kissed her with a passion she had not felt since—she couldn't remember when. Then she did remember. She hadn't felt passion like this since she'd been married to him.

"Stop! I already can't breathe in this damn corset," Cleo said. "Besides, I have work to do before the rehearsal—and if I checked my list right now, I bet I'd find out you do, too."

"Yes, ma'am." Powderkeg saluted. "But there is one more thing on my mind."

"And that would be?"

"Dodge."

"Oh please, Marshall," Cleo said, all flirtation gone from her voice. "You haven't grown up at all, have you? You always were jealous."

"I'm not jealous," Powderkeg protested. "Well, I am, but that's not what's bothering me."

"Then what *is* bothering you?"

He pulled up a chair. "It just seems a little too neat, don't you think?"

"What are you talking about?" Cleo returned to her own seat, crossing her arms.

"When we first got here, everybody in Spoonerville was suspicious of us—Dodge especially. Add to that, the twins had taken a powder on their bowling team and took up with us. Then suddenly the twins are welcomed back, no hard feelings, no questions asked, and Dodge is Mr. Goodwill Ambassador, doing everything he can to make sure we have enough credit to buy everything we need, making sure we get all our deliveries—no small feat out here—and rounding up everybody he can. And there's that little stunt of offering you a ride."

"A stunt?" Cleo gasped. "What is wrong with you? If it weren't for Dodge Durham, this whole weekend would be a fiasco."

"It doesn't add up," Powderkeg said. "Just ask yourself—why?"

"Because it's good business," Cleo said. "Even the little stunt of being nice, if you can't imagine that he's attracted to me, is good business. You wouldn't understand, because you have no business sense. Or any sense."

"But you do?"

"I am my father's daughter."

"Yes, you are." Powderkeg stood up, knocking over the chair on his way out the door.

Cleo felt hot tears forming and she pushed on her lower eyelids to keep them at bay. She had to admit, it was a pretty good trick Polly had taught them. She put her head in her hands and breathed deeply.

*Damn jealous fool.*

# CHAPTER 39

Polly had worked hard on the little hats for the goats, but as soon as Dymphna took her eyes off Down Diego, he ate them all. Dymphna brought her goats down the hill and installed them in their pen, a home away from home, compliments of Professor Johnson.

Dymphna wore a plain white blouse and checkered skirt, with an apron made from an old sheet. She loved seeing her friends in their fantastic costumes, but she was a simple girl running a farm, and this outfit suited her. Polly had insisted on making an authentic-looking bonnet for her. Dymphna had to admit, those prairie women knew their stuff. The floppy brim took some getting used to, but there was no denying, the cotton bonnet worked as well as any space-age fiber to keep the sun off.

Thud stood at the gate to the petting zoo in his bolero tie. Polly had no better luck with the dog's acceptance of a hat than she had the goats, although Pappy said Jerry Lee was wearing his. Professor Johnson, dressed as a honky-tonk piano man, met her at the pen, a worried expression on his face.

"I was just looking at the bowling lane Powderkeg laid down for the twins' exhibit," he said. "I don't think it's regulation."

"Oh?" Dymphna said.

"I suppose I shouldn't mention it," he said.

"I wouldn't." *Why are men so damned competitive?* Dymphna thought.

"Unless you think I should mention it."

"No, I don't think so." *Is this still about the dry ice?*

"You might be right," Professor Johnson said. "He's very touchy about being proven wrong."

*Oh my God, it is about the dry ice!*

"I think it will be OK," Dymphna said.

"Well, all right then." Professor Johnson turned to head back to the Boozehound. "I'll see you at rehearsal."

Thud stood up and followed the professor. Dymphna watched them go. She could feel her eyes brimming with hot tears. She pressed her fingers to her lower lids to stop them, as Polly had taught her. In a few days, Professor Johnson would go back to his real life and she would go back to hers. She didn't even know where she would end up. She had to find a place for the goats, the chickens, and the rabbits. But she did know one thing—she was going to miss that man.

And that damn dog.

# CHAPTER 40

Old Bertha stared at her reflection in the mirror in her second story bedroom and sighed. Whoever said you could make a silk purse out of a sow's ear was full of malarkey. If you were your basic sow's ear, the best thing you could hope for was to distract folks with a good pair of earrings. Luckily, thanks to Pappy, she had those. She held them up to her ears and sighed again. They didn't really go with her suede gaucho pants and fringed jacket. She heard someone coming up the path to the Creakside Inn and looked out the window to the walkway below. It was Pappy, dressed as a sheriff with a tin badge, cattleman's coat, holster at his hip, and a broad-brimmed hat. Pappy had trimmed his beard but kept his mustache, which was now waxed into an arching handlebar. Bertha hurriedly tucked her earrings into a pocket and went down the rickety steps.

"I don't have a lot of time," she said, meeting Pappy at the door. "Cleo runs a tight ship."

"Oh, don't I know it," he said, lumbering up the stairs to the porch. "But I thought you might have time for this . . ."

He produced two root beers from inside his jacket. "I stole 'em from Wally's coolers in the creek."

"Is that any way for a lawman to act?" Bertha admonished, but she took the root beer as she sat down on the porch swing.

Pappy sat down next to her, casually throwing his arm over the back of the swing, inches away from having it around her shoulder. Bertha stiffened for a moment, but relaxed into the back of the swing as she drank the cold root beer.

"Crazy that this is all almost at an end," Pappy said.

"It is," Old Bertha said.

"Gonna be quiet when you all head out."

"You don't have to stay here, you know. It doesn't matter where you are, whatever you're hiding from, it's going to come up one day, like that snake—Big John—and bite you."

Pappy drained his can of soda pop and crushed the can in his fist. He stood up and headed down the steps. He turned and looked at her.

"You don't know the first thing about snakes," he said.

Old Bertha put her fingertips to her lower eyelids.

# CHAPTER 41

Polly stood in the middle of her store, critically eyeing the outlaws that were in full costume in front of her. Four men in hats, worthy of the Country Music Awards, took every inch of space in the tiny shop. But Polly had no complaints—they were all gorgeous. Rodney and Rock had chosen the most conservative costumes and most elaborate hats. Every detail, jeans strapped into buckskin chaps, the leather vests over bare chests, the sequined bandanas knotted at their necks, all worked perfectly with their copper-colored skin.

Titan had opted for the chaps/thong combo and matching hat.

"Could you add a few more feathers to the hatband?" Titan asked. "I saw a show where one of the cowboys had feathers going all the way from his hat to past his tailbone."

"You'd never get to sit down," Rock said.

"I'll suffer to be beautiful," Titan said.

Polly tried hard not to stare at Wally. While smaller than the other three half-naked men in her store, Wally could hold his own. Taut, wiry, ripped, Wally's body was a revelation. It was the kind of body she used to read about in those steamy text-romances by Mimi Millicent, before she dropped off the planet. While Polly was very happy with her choice in Rodney, the most stable of the young men in Fat Chance, there was no denying the chemistry she and Wally shared. She had a history of getting involved with anyone who interested her, and hoped the time in Fat Chance would help her curb that instinct. The impromptu haircut months ago in the middle of the street certainly got her attention—and she thought about it more than she should. But she knew herself. If she wanted to make things work with Rodney, she'd probably have to let her hair grow for the rest of her life!

# CHAPTER 42

Pappy was muttering about Old Bertha as he headed toward the other end of town. He saw smoke coming out of the smithy. Looking at his watch, he knew that Titan was going to be needed for the parade rehearsal in less than an hour, so what was he doing working in the forge? Pappy had never met Titan's friend, but from the sound of things, Maurice would never forgive Titan if he scorched one of his costumes.

It took a minute for Pappy's eyes to adjust to the low light in the forge. Titan's hat was laid neatly at the entrance. He had his glittering bandana tied around his forehead like a sweatband. He'd pulled a long coat with the arms cut off over his thong and chaps. Pappy wasn't sure if it was for modesty or protection from the embers. Fancy, on her perch, peered at Pappy with her one eye. Pappy took a step back— Fancy at eye-level was an intimidating sight.

Titan, drenched in sweat and pounding on the anvil, looked up.

"What're you doing, Titan?" Pappy said. "Cleo will skin you alive if you run out on the dress rehearsal."

"Oh, I'll be there. I've just been working on this cage and I'm afraid I won't get it done in time."

"What cage?" Pappy asked. "In time for what?"

"A cage for Fancy." Titan wiped sweat from his brow. "I have to take her with me when we leave Fat Chance."

Titan lifted the hammer to strike the hot metal on the anvil, but Pappy stopped him mid-blow.

Titan looked at him in surprise. "What?"

"Titan, you can't . . ." Pappy faltered, looking at Fancy, who cocked her head at him. "You can't take Fancy out of Fat Chance."

"Why not?"

"She belongs here," Pappy said.

"You mean, she's yours?" Titan said, confused.

"No no," Pappy said. "She's yours. There's no denying, Fancy is your buzzard. You two are a team."

"Then why can't I take her?"

"Because, son," Pappy said, putting his hand on Titan's arm, "she won't make it out there. She'll die."

Titan put the hammer down and stared at the ground.

"You know I'm talkin' true, Titan," Pappy said gently.

Titan continued to look at the ground, but he nodded his head in acknowledgment.

Pappy patted the big man's shoulder. "I'll leave you alone for a few minutes. Then you pull yourself together and come on out for the parade, you hear?"

"Yes, sir," Titan said softly.

Pappy turned from the doorway. Titan hadn't moved.

"I'm proud of you, Ray," Pappy said. "You grew up to be a fine man."

"Thank you, Pappy," Titan whispered.

By the time Titan looked up, Pappy was gone. Titan put his fingertips to his lower eyelids, but it did no good. The tears came hot and fast.

# CHAPTER 43

After endless rehearsals, Fandango-Up in Fat Chance was ready to roll.

The sky was perfect—a brilliant blue with clouds that looked as if they'd been blown in by a benevolent god who'd attended art school. The town itself was swept and polished. Powderkeg had completed the Herculean task of making stands for all the handmade inventory the people of Fat Chance had worked so hard to create.

The twins, on their ATVs, were parked at Dymphna's farm so they could see all of Main Street. The ATVs had gone through a renovation. Instead of sitting on seats, Polly and Wally would now stand on pegs behind the drivers, making a more theatrical presentation as they rode into town, whooping their signal that an attack was imminent. Titan stood beside them, the feathers attached to the back of his hat flowing almost to his waist. Titan insisted that Fancy be part of the festivities, so Polly had added beading to his leather wristband. It coordinated with the rest of Titan's costume. Polly only beaded around the edges, so Fancy wouldn't have to deal with a lumpy perch as she tried to stay on Titan's wrist while he attacked Fat Chance on cue. Polly thought the bird was looking longingly at the forge with her one good eye. Since Titan was on foot, he was going to get a head start on the ATVs before the raid.

While Powderkeg had done what he could to camouflage the attackers, if anyone in the audience were to look up to the farm, it was pretty obvious that *something* was going on. Their Vegas costumes shot off sparks in the sun.

If the guys looked like something out of a romantic rendition of early frontier history, Polly could have stepped out of a men's magazine's salute to a New Age Annie Oakley. She wore a buckskin dress, slashed to her thigh. The dress laced up the front and sides, giving her more cleavage than she sported in real life.

In town, Dymphna was busy trying to keep her goats calm. The goats had not remained orderly during the parade rehearsals. Powderkeg floated the idea that instead of containing the Angoras, why not let the goats run through the streets—a Texas version of the running of the bulls in Pamplona. Pappy had nixed that. He said Texans would laugh them out of town.

"It's *our* town," Powderkeg argued.

"Doesn't matter in Texas," Rock said.

It was decided Dymphna would lead Catterlee on a leash in the parade. The rest of the goats would just be available for petting. They appeared to have had an informal goat meeting and agreed that they would cooperate with this plan, since Dymphna had had no trouble with them for the last few days.

Even dressed as a saloon girl, Cleo's steely determination showed through. She pulled an antique stopwatch out of the pocket of her ruffled skirt and frowned at it, then snapped it shut.

"Elwood is ten minutes late," she said. "The parade is already too small; we can't start without him."

"What difference does it make?" Powderkeg asked, sitting on the stoop in front of the bank. "Nobody's here."

"They'll be here," Old Bertha said. "Dodge said he was still hearing from people yesterday."

"I need a drink," Pappy said as he straightened Jerry Lee's hat.

"It's ten o'clock in the morning," Old Bertha said to Pappy.

"I'll see what's holding up the professor," Dymphna said, closing the pen's gate behind her.

Maybe a few minutes without human intervention would calm the goats. Who knew what might calm Cleo.

Dymphna walked into the Boozehound. She patted Thud, who was sitting just inside the doorway. Professor Johnson was sitting at one of the glass display cases Powderkeg had made for some of his historical pieces, staring at a ledger, so deep in concentration he didn't hear Dymphna come in.

"Professor," she said. "Your aunt is waiting for you. I'm not sure if she's more upset that you're not on time or that nobody has arrived yet, but—"

"Come look at this," he said urgently.

Dymphna came over and looked at the book on the counter. The writing was old and faded. "What am I looking at?"

The professor stabbed at a passage in the middle of the page. "This. I found out what happened to Fat Chance between 1950 and when Cutthroat bought the town."

Dymphna read quickly. Her throat felt like someone was cutting off her air. She hadn't realized how closely she was standing to the professor, but when she looked up, she was staring into his troubled eyes. "I'm not sure I understand exactly what this means."

"Neither do I," Professor Johnson said. "But it doesn't look good."

A rap on the window made them both jump. It was Old Bertha, waving them outside. Dymphna took a deep breath. She was aware of a motor, first as a faint hum, now getting louder and louder. She knew it couldn't be a car, because none could navigate the trail, so it must be a group of ATVs coming on the off-road trails from Spoonerville. As she and Professor Johnson came outside, they saw Old Bertha, Pappy and Jerry Lee, Powderkeg and Cleo, standing at the edge of the boardwalk in front of the café, watching a single ATV making its way toward them. Dymphna reached for Professor Johnson's hand. He took it.

They stood just inside the doorway, watching as Dodge drove through town, kicking up dust behind him. Pappy stepped forward as Dodge fishtailed in front of them, causing even more dirt to fly.

"Oh, great," Cleo said to Powderkeg. "It will take twenty minutes for that dust to settle."

"What's happening, Dodge?" Pappy said.

"Not much, by the look of things," Dodge said, looking around.

"Where are . . ." Cleo's voice sounded strained. She took a deep breath, put on her calm Beverly Hills Voice and began again. She beamed a charming smile. "Where are the multitudes?"

"Oh! You mean all those people who are supposed to show up for your pathetic little shindig?" Dodge asked casually. "They aren't coming. Nobody is coming."

Dymphna took a step out the door, but Professor Johnson pulled her back. He put his fingers to his lips. Thud stood up. He was headed out the door, but Dymphna grabbed his collar and he sat at her feet.

"What . . . what do you mean they aren't coming?" Old Bertha asked. "You said everything was right on schedule."

"Everything is right on schedule," Dodge said. "Right on schedule for me."

"Let's cut the crap," Powderkeg said. "What's going on?"

"Let's just say, it seemed like it was in my best interest not to help y'all out," Dodge said.

Old Bertha lost her balance as the weight of Dodge's words hit her. She, better than anyone else, knew that they were now heavily indebted to this man, who had obviously set a trap for them. How could she not have seen it? This was the first time she'd let a man dupe her since Cutthroat Clarence all those years ago.

Pappy caught her before she hit the boardwalk. He helped her sit on the edge of the boardwalk, then they both returned their full attention to Dodge.

"I don't understand," Cleo said.

"You don't have to," Dodge said. "I was going to just call you and let you know, but I couldn't be sure one of you fools would be standing in the middle of the street looking for reception. Besides, I kind of wanted to see your reaction for myself. It's been a long time coming."

"What has?" Cleo asked. She looked at Powderkeg and Pappy, hoping that neither had listened to her and had brought their guns after all, but it was clear there was no weapon on Main Street other than the Colt holstered on Dodge's hip.

"Retribution, Ms. Johnson," Dodge said.

"Ms. Johnson-Primb," she corrected, although she realized this was a stupid time to be standing on ceremony.

"Retribution for what?" Powderkeg asked. "What did any of us ever do to you?"

"Any of *you*?" Dodge laughed. "What could any of you do to *me*? Although I should thank you. Without your half-assed attempt at rehabbing this godforsaken town, I might not have gotten my bowling team back together. So thanks for that."

"Let's back up," Pappy said. "Come on, Dodge. You and I go way back and we've had our disagreements. What's the point of all this?"

"I don't think you're in any position to ask questions, Pappy." Dodge gloated. "And I'm just not in the mindset to answer just now."

"You don't have to," Professor Johnson said, coming out of the Boozehound. "I have the answers."

Everyone turned to the professor, who signaled Dymphna to stay put. As Thud prepared to follow Professor Johnson, Dymphna grabbed his collar to keep him with her. She wasn't sure if it was for his safety or her own reassurance, but she wasn't about to let the dog go.

"Do you, now?" Dodge asked. "Well, go on. Tell us what you think you know."

"I know the Durham family . . . your family . . . worked this land, starting around 1900. I'll forgo the history lesson, but farming—especially tenant farming—was a tough road."

"Tenant farming is nothing to be ashamed of," Dodge said hotly.

"Then why are you ashamed of it?" Professor Johnson asked.

Dodge sat up taller in his seat. Dymphna felt a growl start low in Thud's chest, but she soothed him. Professor Johnson seemed to have a handle on things. She hoped she was right. Brilliant judgment calls—on any of their parts—were not the order of the day.

"Go on," Dodge said, settling back.

"Those were the big days of the American Dream. If Cutthroat had been a little older, he would have had a field day out here! Anyway, when hard times hit, when the twister of 1908 came through, the town was destroyed. But your grandfather saw an opportunity to buy the land cheap. It was a gamble, but he made it. He prospered. Built up the town and had his own tenant farmers."

"He was a tough old coot," Dodge said. "But he never missed an opportunity, I'll say that for him."

"From what I see, he wasn't very popular."

"Very few successful men are," Dodge said.

"Nobody can argue with that," Cleo said.

"As badly as his family was treated when they worked the land for someone else," Professor Johnson said, "you might think he would have had more compassion for his own workers."

"Yeah, well, you'd be wrong," Dodge said. "You can't be weak and get ahead. It's a dog-eat-dog world."

"Then the twister of 1915 came through," the professor said. "His tenant farmers started clearing out, without looking back. Hell, your own grandmother Mabel said it made no sense to stay, but he did. He should have listened to Mabel."

"It was just one bad break after another," Dodge said.

"No doubt," Professor Johnson agreed. "But by 1950, the last families moved out. There wasn't anything for your father to do – nobody wanted to buy the land. He couldn't sell it and he couldn't hang onto it. The bank took it over. Your father got a job on the Rolling

Fork, always dreaming of buying this land back. By the time you were a grown man, you had no choice but to get a job running the store over at the Rolling Fork. Quite a step down for the Durhams."

"But I would have bought the land back," Dodge said. He turned to Cleo. "I almost had enough money saved, when your damned father came in and bought the place! And it just sat there! Every day, every month, every year, I've had to watch this place go further and further into decay, because that rich bastard wouldn't sell."

"You asked Cutthroat to sell it to you?" Cleo asked.

"More times than I can count," Dodge said. "Of course, I never got to talk to him directly, but his—what do you call them out there in California—his *people* said he had no interest in selling at any reasonable price. They gave me a dollar amount, but there was no way I could ever get that much money together."

Pappy coughed, but all eyes remained on Dodge.

"It must have hurt when you saw us all moving in," Powderkeg said. "Is that why you set us up?"

"I don't have time for games," Dodge said. "No. I set you up because I needed to break you."

"Why?" Old Bertha asked. "We were only staying for six months."

"When you came to me with your little fairy tale about wanting to *celebrate* Fat Chance, it was all I could do not to laugh in your faces. But then I realized, with your help, I'd have enough money to buy the town after all."

"Oh my God," Old Bertha said, putting her head in her hands. "I've ruined us."

Dymphna saw a shadow out of the corner of her eye. She turned to see Titan setting Fancy on the corner of the boardwalk. From the troubled look on his face, he had clearly heard everything. He caught Dymphna's eye, but instead of joining the others, he disappeared.

Cleo stalked over to Dodge. "Don't be naïve. I can buy and sell you. I'll pay off all these debts—and you'll be back to square one."

Dodge laughed in her face. "Oh, really?" he said, pulling his cell phone out of his pocket and casually scrolling through it. "Do you want the world to know that Cutthroat Clarence's daughter fell for a scheme like this—and dressed as a dance-hall girl, no less? You know as well as I do you'll let this go."

Dodge quickly held the cell phone up. "Say cheese," he said, snapping a picture of Cleo.

Before Powderkeg could grab Dodge's phone, Dodge gunned his ATV. He raced down Main Street. A sound like the wail of a siren seemed to come from nowhere as the twins, with Polly and Wally on the backs of the ATVs, came barreling down the hill. Titan wasn't far behind, leaping and whooping, waving his feathered hat. Titan must have filled in the outlaws. Dymphna hoped he had passed along the comment about the bowling league to the twins.

Talk about retribution.

# CHAPTER 44

Dodge was heading right toward the charging outlaws as they came rushing, full throttle, down the hill. He spun around and headed back the way he'd come, scattering the professor, Pappy, and Powderkeg. Old Bertha and Cleo stood right in his path, ready to take him down, but Dodge steered out of their way with seconds to spare. The men on foot didn't stand a chance of catching him, but the outlaws were right on his tail as Dodge raced into the hills.

Dodge was trapped on both sides. The twins forced him back toward town. Wally and Rock changed places while still in motion. Wally was now driving and Rock was standing on the back, lasso in hand. As Dodge's ATV reached Main Street, Rock whirled the lasso over his head. It hit its mark, landing around Dodge's middle. Before Dodge could shake it off, Rock pulled the rope taut and yanked Dodge onto his ass in the middle of the street. Dodge's ATV reared up, then stalled a few feet away.

The outlaws joined the rest of the inhabitants of Fat Chance. They all stood in a circle around Dodge, who sat with the lasso around him in the middle of the street.

"I don't think he looks so dangerous," Pappy said.

Cleo was silent. They might have won the battle, but she was pretty sure he'd won the war. Dodge sprung himself from the lasso. Rock grabbed the rope.

"I wonder if we might find some other use for that rope," Pappy said. "Anybody here know how to tie a really strong knot?"

Dymphna was fairly sure Pappy didn't mean to hang Dodge, but she was glad she wasn't a betting woman.

"There's nothing you can do to me," Dodge said, getting up. "This isn't the Old West."

"Don't push your luck," Powderkeg growled.

"Just let him go," Cleo said.

"But he's a no-account liar," Old Bertha said.

"But a no-account liar who happens to be telling the truth," Cleo said. "There isn't anything we can do to him. At least not right now."

Dodge smirked and broke through the circle. He headed toward his ATV, but Powderkeg stepped in his way.

"There is *one* thing we can do," Powderkeg said. "We can make him walk."

Wally sat on Dodge's ATV and crossed his arms. Everything about him said "Just try it."

Dodge's maddening grin broadened as he sauntered out of town. Thud suddenly let out a deafening yowl, broke away from Dymphna, and raced toward Dodge.

Dymphna tried to stop the dog, but he was gone in a flash. Dodge turned around to face the charging animal, looking scared. As he reached for his Colt and Professor Johnson yelled, Thud leapt past Dodge. He was close enough that Dodge hit the ground, his gun flying out of his hand. Everyone ran toward them, confused about what was happening. Dodge was back on his feet, but the people of Fat Chance had no interest in him.

What was Thud doing if he wasn't chasing Dodge?

There was no mistaking the sounds that followed. A rattle, a hiss, a sickening whelp from Thud. As the group moved closer, they saw Thud shaking a huge snake in his powerful jaws. With a savage growl, he tossed Big John's once powerful, now lifeless body, into the air. The snake landed at Dodge's feet. Thud ran off, crying, zigzagging and stumbling through the hills. Professor Johnson ran after him.

Wally grabbed Professor Johnson's arm, pulling him to a stop. "You'll never catch him on foot."

"We'll take the ATVs," Rodney said to Professor Johnson. "You can ride with me."

Dymphna put her hand on Professor Johnson's back. He was staring into the distance. There was no sound coming from the hills.

"Your dog saved my life," Dodge said, a touch of wonder in his voice as he looked down at Big John. "Thank you."

Dodge put out his hand for a handshake. Professor Johnson turned and stared at the man as if he'd never seen him before. He pushed Dodge so hard, Dodge was back on his butt for the third time that day. Professor Johnson knelt on the man's chest.

"If my dog dies for saving your sorry ass," Professor Johnson breathed inches from Dodge's face, "I'll kill you myself."

Wally, already on Dodge's ATV, fired it up. He roared up to Titan, who climbed on the back. Rodney and Rock mounted their own, Professor Johnson on the back of one, Powderkeg on the other. Pappy grabbed Jerry Lee and hurried after them. Dymphna realized that everyone was still in costume. The modern day posse of cowboys and outlaws, now working together, on their ATVs instead of horses, headed off to find a beloved dog that had just been bitten in a heroic battle.

Dodge looked at Old Bertha.

"Should I go help?" he asked. "The dog saved my life."

"Yes, we know," Old Bertha said. "You said that. I don't think anyone wants or needs your help."

"Just go," Cleo said.

"The dog saved . . . ," he began.

"Just go!" Cleo barked.

*The good guys and the bad guys*, Dymphna thought as she watched Dodge slink off. A few things might have changed since the Old West, but not everything.

Sundown came. The women had changed into their regular clothes and hauled in all the merchandise from the sidewalk. Dymphna returned her goats to her farm, fed the chickens, and returned to town as quickly as possible. There was no sign of the Wild West women they had been just a short time ago. Every hour or so, one of them would look out the window of the café, but they saw neither men nor dog. To keep their minds off the search—and the possibility of a tragic outcome—they discussed Dodge.

"He's just hateful," Old Bertha said.

"I can't believe we all fell for his lies," Polly said. "He just played us all!"

"Some of us more than others," Cleo said, remembering his offer of a ride to Fat Chance. "I was kidding when I told Powderkeg about keeping your friends close but your enemies closer. But I guess Dodge really was the enemy."

It appeared Dodge had kept a close eye on his enemies, as well.

"Can we fight him?" Old Bertha asked Cleo.

Dymphna knew this meant, "Will you, as the only one with any real money, fight him?"

Cleo looked out the window and was silent for a long time.

"When we first came here," Cleo said with her back to the others, "if Dodge Durham had been honest with me, I might have made a deal with him. Not only did I not give a fig about Fat Chance, I absolutely hated it."

She turned to face the women. "But now I love this town."

"So . . . we'll fight for it?" Dymphna asked, knowing this wasn't exactly what Cleo had said.

Cleo shook her head and turned around and faced them. "I can't. He's right. If word got out that I let this happen, my reputation would be shot. Dodge proved that hard feelings can run deep—passed down from one generation to the next—and it's no different in my world than it is in his. My father's enemies would have a field day with this. We'll all move out." She bit her lip. "And I'll sell Fat Chance to Dodge."

Dymphna saw Old Bertha stifle a sob. Dymphna knew the old woman felt responsible, having pushed so hard for the festival. Dymphna herself felt guilty for having come up with the idea in the first place. Looking back, it was crazy.

She had to admit, she understood what Dodge was feeling. Fat Chance had a way of making you believe in yourself. It was a feeling you didn't want to let go of—no matter what. Was Dodge any different?

*Of course he is! He is a rat!* Dymphna had to get a handle on her empathy. The man was trying to destroy them!

"Of course I'll cover all of your losses," Cleo said, realizing how upset the women were.

"No," Old Bertha said. "Never took a handout in my life. Don't intend to start now."

"But we invested heavily in this," Cleo said. "I don't want Fat Chance to have been a waste of your time."

"It wasn't," Polly said. "Fat Chance wasn't ever our town, it was yours, Cleo. We always knew we were leaving. I mean, we obviously made a mess of your father's idea, but as far as this being a waste of time, no way. This was the greatest six months of my life."

"I think I hear the guys coming," Dymphna said.

The women raced to the window. Cleo opened the door of the café and the men straggled in. When Thud didn't bound in with them, they looked to see if Professor Johnson was carrying him. He wasn't.

"We couldn't find him," Professor Johnson said, falling heavily into a chair.

Cleo ran to get the coffeepot. All the men, still in costume, greedily reached for mugs. They were soaked to the bone from hours of looking up and down the hills.. The twins, Titan, and Wally, still in their skimpy costumes, were shivering.

"I'll be right back with some blankets," Old Bertha said, obviously relieved to be able to lend a helping hand at last.

Dymphna sat next to Professor Johnson. "What do we do now?" she asked.

"Pappy says this is what dogs do," Professor Johnson said.

"They get bit, they run off," Pappy said.

"But Thud is from Los Feliz!" Polly objected.

"That doesn't matter," Powderkeg said. "If the dog has the instinct to go after a rattler, he's sure as hell going to find a cave to—"

"To go and recover," Cleo said, glaring at Powderkeg.

Old Bertha arrived with a pile of beautiful new blankets, which she'd purchased for the Fandango.

"Oh, I don't want to use this," Titan said. "My costume is soaked. I'll ruin it."

"Use it," Old Bertha said. "It isn't going to do anybody any good otherwise."

"Thanks." Titan pulled the blanket around him. "I hope Maurice feels as kindly when I tell him we wrecked all his costumes."

"We'll start looking again in the morning," Powderkeg said.

"Do you think we'll find him?" Professor Johnson asked Pappy.

Pappy stared into his coffee cup. "No way to know, son. But we'll do everything we can."

"If he's OK," Professor Johnson asked, "when will he come out of hiding?"

"Seventy-two hours," Rodney and Rock said together.

Titan beamed at them, but Rock cut him off.

"No, this isn't knowledge passed down from years on a ranch," Rock said.

"We Googled it," Rodney added.

"Seventy-two hours sounds about right," Pappy said, getting heavily to his feet. "I've got to see to Jerry Lee. That mule earned her grub today."

"I better go, too," Titan said. "I want to make sure Fancy got home OK."

Dymphna started to say that she'd seen Fancy toddle into the forge earlier that evening, but thought Titan needed his rest anyway, so she kept quiet.

"Wish we could have thrown Dodge in the can for at least a night," Rock said, as he and Rodney made their way to the jail.

"I'll be ready first thing in the morning, Professor Johnson," Wally said, draining his coffee and standing up. "We'll find your dog."

Dymphna was reminded once again of the side of Wally that no one really saw.

Powderkeg started clearing coffee cups, but Cleo stopped him. "I'll take care of that, Marshall," she said curtly. "Why don't you escort the ladies back to the inn?"

Dymphna couldn't believe what she was hearing. Cleo seemed to have made a complete reversal from the cold Beverly Hills socialite she was when she first arrived.

Powderkeg saw it, too. "All right," he said stonily. He turned to Polly and Old Bertha. "Ladies, shall we?"

Cleo grabbed several cups by their handles and headed to the kitchen, leaving Dymphna and Professor Johnson sitting at a table alone.

"Do you know why I decided to get a degree in science?" he suddenly asked.

Dymphna was taken aback by the question, but merely shook her head. Wherever this was going, she didn't want to make even the tiniest of missteps.

"Because I wanted to believe in a world that made sense," he said, looking around the room as if he'd never seen it before. "Now I'm in Fat Chance, Texas, and a rattlesnake has probably killed my dog."

"You don't know that," Dymphna said soothingly.

"I have a PhD in natural science from Harvard," he said hotly. Dymphna could see tears welling up in his eyes. "I don't shrink from facts. I live by facts. And the fact is that my dog is probably dead."

Dymphna stood up and put her arms around him. He encircled her waist with his own arms and buried his head between her breasts. She kissed the top of his head and willed herself not to cry.

"I loved that dog," he said. "I loved that damn dog."

# CHAPTER 45

Everyone looked for Thud over the next seventy-two hours, but they didn't find him. With each passing hour, the little band of people who had pulled so hard together, returned to the separate, solitary people they had been when they first arrived. Rodney and Rock quit their bowling league again, in solidarity with the townspeople, but returned to living in the hills.

"It's just too weird here," Rock told Dymphna.

She couldn't argue with him.

Pappy brought Big John's body into town and hung him from a post in tribute to Thud's bravery, but the city folks were disgusted and Pappy took it down.

Fat Chance, Texas, and its inhabitants were broken.

Cleo walked through the archway that connected the Boozehound with the café. Professor Johnson was sitting at the bar, unshaven, eyes closed. He'd been looking for his dog nonstop. The strain showed. He woke when he heard Cleo rummaging around beside him.

"Where's the scotch?" she asked.

"It's seven o'clock in the morning," he said, looking blearily at his watch.

"Too bad. Where is it?"

"Powderkeg finished it off," Professor Johnson said, stretching.

"It's all over, you know," Cleo said, pouring a shot of vodka.

"The seventy-two hours? Yes, I know."

"Not just that," Cleo said, trying not to be too sharp with her nephew, who was clearly suffering.

"If you mean between you and Powderkeg, yes, I know that, too," Professor Johnson said. "Forgive me if I don't join you in the celebration."

"Not that either," she said.

"What then?"

"I'm going to tell everyone at breakfast," she said.

"We haven't had breakfast together in . . ."

"In seventy-two hours. I know. But I think everyone should know, don't you?"

"Know what?" Professor Johnson asked, exasperated, as his aunt marched out the door.

Cleo left her half-empty glass on the counter. Professor Johnson watched her through the front window. She picked up the clapper to the chuck-wagon gong. As she rang it, he knocked back the remains of her drink.

Dymphna heard the clanging and tried to ignore it. She hadn't been down the hill since it was clear Thud wasn't coming home. Professor Johnson was steering clear of her; their dance of moving toward each other then running away had moved into uncharted territory with the addition of their grief. Dymphna had no idea what to do or say— and clearly, neither did he.

It was obvious Cleo was not going to stop her racket until each and every one of them came into town. Dymphna finished feeding the animals and headed down the hill. She smiled as she saw the twins coming out of hiding, pulling up to the café on their ATVs.

Cleo had made a generous spread of homemade breads, eggs, Dymphna's jams, and strong coffee. Even so, as Dymphna studied her, she realized this no-nonsense, brittle and humorless Cleo was more like the woman Dymphna had met at the mansion six months ago than the fiery Cleo who had thrown a frying pan at Powderkeg.

"I have an announcement to make," Cleo said, her practiced, luminous smile in place. "I know we have all been searching for . . . well, we've been searching the past few days, and time has gotten away from us."

"Pass the bread basket, please," Pappy said.

"Pappy, please!" Cleo snapped, then the mask returned. She smiled as if she were addressing the Rotary Club. "Well, I just wanted to inform everyone that, well, our sentence in this loathsome town is complete."

The group sat stunned.

"You mean, our six months is over?" Polly asked.

"Yes, indeed," Cleo said gleefully. "I've called Wesley and he's sending the jet. I'll give you all a ride as far as Los Angeles."

"I can't believe it's over," Titan said.

"I wish I had champagne," Cleo said. "We could toast to our . . . efforts."

"I'm not leaving," Titan said. "I don't want to leave Fancy. If she can't come with me, I'm going to stay here."

"Dude," Wally Wasabi said, "I don't want to leave either. I don't really have anything to go back to, and I'm doing really good work here."

Dymphna's ears perked up. *Work?*

Wally took a deep breath. He looked at Polly. "Please don't laugh," he said to her. Then in a more threatening voice, he said to Rodney and Rock, "You either."

"OK, we promise," Polly said.

Wally gulped down some coffee before continuing. "When I was in jail a while ago, I started sexting some girls. Just to pass the time. But it turned out, I was really good at it. I got a little following, and then a bigger following, and then a bigger following."

Polly gasped. "No way."

"Yeah," Wally said, sounding miserable. "I'm Mimi Millicent."

"But you stopped writing!" Polly said. "I've been looking for you since we got here."

"I know. But when I thought we didn't have reception, I started writing a novel instead. I mean, my word processing program still worked. I wrote three chapters and sent a thumb drive to a couple publishers. Black Poppy Publishing offered me a deal."

*A black poppy, not a black rose*, thought Dymphna.

"If Titan stays, maybe I should stay, too," Polly said. "We could work on our jewelry line—maybe start a website or something."

Polly didn't add that if Rodney and Wally Wasabi were both in the area, she had no desire to leave. Dymphna watched Professor Johnson, hoping he might be next to volunteer his desire to stay. Privately, she'd wondered if she could make a go of this place. She could bring her rabbits here and have a real farm. A real home. She could see it, but what she couldn't see was a future without Professor Johnson in it.

But Professor Johnson was silent.

"Seems like I could see my way to staying—if Polly would sell my stuff on her website," Powderkeg said, winking at Polly.

"I'd like to stay, too," Old Bertha said. "If you think you all might still need an innkeeper."

"Couldn't imagine the place without you," Powderkeg said.

"I think y'all are forgetting," Pappy said bleakly, "Dodge is going to own this town."

"Now, let's all be realistic," Cleo said, her smile getting more and more determined. "You can't stay here. Dodge or no Dodge. It doesn't make any sense. You have to get back to your real lives."

"But," Titan said, "I think this *is* my real life. Don't you think your father would be happy if we wanted to stay?"

"My father wouldn't care," Cleo said. "I know that sounds cruel, but it's the truth. He only did this to assuage his own guilt. He was toying with us."

She looked around the room. She had everyone's attention again. "Look," she continued, "nobody can say we didn't give this little experiment our all. But it's finished."

"Where will you go, Pappy?" Rodney said. "I mean, you can come stay at our campsite, if you want."

"Don't worry about me," Pappy said. "Jerry Lee and I will figure something out."

"I can certainly take care of Pappy," Cleo said, looking around the room as if accepting an award.

"I don't need your help, thanks," Pappy said. "I'll make do. I always have."

"I feel as if you are all looking at me as if I'm the bad guy," Cleo said. "I didn't take your town, Pappy. Dodge did."

"That's right," Dodge said from the doorway. "I did take your town."

The men all stood up from their chairs.

"You're either mighty brave or mighty stupid coming here before we all left town," Powderkeg said.

"Well, I think the events of the last few months prove I'm definitely not stupid," Dodge said.

The men started toward him.

Dodge held up his hands. "Hold on, hold on. I've come in peace. I just forgot my white flag."

"Say what you came to say," Pappy said, "and get out. You don't own Fat Chance yet."

"That's what I came to say," Dodge said. "Things get passed down, generation to generation. In my case, high cholesterol, a receding hairline, and the crazy idea that I had to get Fat Chance back come hell or high water."

"Whatever you came to say, you're taking a long time saying it," Powderkeg grumbled.

"Times change," Dodge said. "I take medication for my high cholesterol and have come to terms with my receding hairline. And, well, I guess I can come to terms with never owning Fat Chance."

"If this is another one of your tricks, dude . . . ," Wally said.

"It's not. I can't get that crazy dog out of my head. He saved the life of a man who set out to ruin all of you."

"Dog never did have any sense," Old Bertha growled.

Dodge turned to Cleo. "I'm ready to let bygones be bygones. I can't cancel all debts, 'cause I don't have that kind of money, but I'm happy to have y'all make payments as they come in. Code of the West."

He put out his hand and Cleo shook it.

"All right," she said.

"Can I stay for coffee?" Dodge asked, seating himself at the table. "I know we're never going to be friends, but y'all are still going to have to come to Spoonerville and I'm still gonna have to deal with all of you, so we might as well make the best of it."

"I . . . I'll get a cup," Cleo said, in stunned confusion.

"And I expect you boys back on the bowling team and back at work first thing in the morning," Dodge said to the twins.

The twins shrugged and nodded.

"Code of the West, my ass," Pappy whispered to Dymphna, who shushed him.

While the mood of the café had lifted considerably, Dymphna was very aware that Professor Johnson had not declared that he wanted to make a life in Fat Chance. She realized that he probably would never be able to see the place as anything but the town that took his dog from him.

"One more thing, just to show my good will," Dodge said, heading to the door. He opened it, and Thud bounded in. "Found him on the ranch two days ago. He was one sick pup. Wasn't sure he was going to make it."

Professor Johnson and Thud met midair.

Cleo heard all the noise and rushed back in. She jumped into Powderkeg's arms.

Professor Johnson had to yell over Thud's whimpers to be heard. "You knew two days ago that Thud was alive?!"

"Yep," Dodge said, puffing out his chest. "It was touch-and-go for a while. I couldn't take my eyes off him. I even had the vet take a look at him. Something I am not inclined to do under normal circumstances."

Thud had knocked Professor Johnson to the ground, licking him until the professor's glasses were smeared with saliva. Professor Johnson got back on his feet. He wiped off his glasses and stared at Dodge.

"But don't worry about it," Dodge said. "You don't have to thank me."

"Oh, I do," Professor Johnson said, as Thud started making the rounds for kisses and hugs.

Dodge extended his hand as Professor Johnson approached. The professor smiled and spread his arms as if waiting for a hug. Dodge shrugged, then opened his arms.

Professor Johnson decked him.

Old Bertha threw a pitcher of water on Dodge to bring him to. Professor Johnson looked down at him until he saw Dodge's eyes focus.

"Next time," the professor said, "you come tell me my dog is alive. Understood?"

Dodge got to his feet and then wheeled on Professor Johnson. "I save your dog and give you your piss-ant town back, and this is the thanks I get?" he said, rubbing his jaw. He pointed a finger at Rodney and Rock. "I still expect to see you boys at work tomorrow. Enough of this horsing around," he declared, and then stalked out the door.

"Thank you," Professor Johnson called out as Dodge stormed down the boardwalk.

# CHAPTER 46

The people of Fat Chance celebrated their good fortune. It was impossible to believe they had their town back and that Thud was among them once more. Cleo finally shooed everyone away. As she hung the last pot on the rack, she turned to find Powderkeg standing in the doorway, his arms folded across his chest, smiling wickedly at her.

"This was quite a day," he said.

"I can't remember anything quite like it," she said.

Powderkeg came into the room and stood in front of Cleo. Smoothing her hair, he took her face in his hands and kissed her gently. "Stay here with me," he breathed softly into her neck.

He released her and looked into her eyes.

"Don't be silly, Marshall," she said. "You know I can't stay."

"What are you talking about? Your father put us both here because he thought we should give it another shot!"

"I know that. Look, Marshall, we're all wrong for each other. We fought as much as we . . . well, as much as we didn't fight. All this proves is that Daddy wasn't right about everything."

"I can't believe this. You're leaving me—again?"

Cleo shrugged. Powderkeg turned abruptly and walked out the door.

Dymphna stood in the middle of the street, talking to Erinn on the phone. She relayed the entire story of planning the Fandango, losing the town, losing Thud, getting the town and Thud back, and Professor Johnson punching Dodge.

"I'm confused," Erinn said. "Who does the town belong to now?"

"It belongs to Cleo."

"So, Cleo is the landlady?" Erinn asked.

"I think Pappy is the landlady—landlord. The on-site manager, anyway. Cleo is going back to Los Angeles tomorrow."

"But most of you are staying to try to make a go of it?" Erinn asked, wading into forbidden territory.

"Yes," Dymphna said, aware that both of them were skirting the big question. "With Dodge giving everybody time to pay off their loans, we'll all have enough money from our settlements from Cutthroat to really try to make something of the place."

"We? Did you say *we*?"

"Did I?" Dymphna asked guiltily.

"I think you did."

"I didn't mean to say that. I didn't mean not to say it, either."

"That's a double negative," Erinn said. "Which means you did mean to say it, which means you want to stay."

"Does it?"

"You tell me. Dymphna, it should be easy. Just ask yourself, where is my heart?"

That was easy. Her heart was here.

Rodney and Rock snuck off the ranch to meet everyone at the top of the trail. It was going to be rough saying good-bye to Cleo and Professor Johnson, who were headed back to Los Angeles.

Everyone was on time and assembled at the top of the trail as the limo pulled up. The Covered Volkswagen stood proudly, like a kindergartener who hadn't gotten the memo that he wasn't the cutest kid on the planet as the real cutest kid on the planet rolled in. As the driver's door swung open, Dymphna was hoping to see Jeffries, but Wesley had hired a local driver to take Cleo and her nephew to the airport.

Powderkeg was all bravado and fake cheer, kissing Cleo on the cheek and wishing her well. "I guess this is it," he said.

"You know I'll be back to visit," Cleo said. "You can't get away from me that easily."

She patted Powderkeg on the shoulder, hugged Titan, dodged Fancy, kissed Old Bertha and Polly, kissed Dymphna twice, playfully boxed with the twins, and came up short as she looked at Pappy.

"You take care of my town," she said.

"I always have and I always will."

"May I ask you something?"

"It's a little late," Pappy said. "But shoot."

"Do I know you?" she asked. "Every once in a while . . . I don't know . . . I just feel as if I know you."

"No," Pappy said. "You don't know me at all."

Cleo looked at Professor Johnson, who was going through his own good-byes.

"Don't take too long, dear," Cleo said. "We may own the jet, but a schedule is a schedule."

Cleo disappeared into the limo. As if by some unspoken signal, the group faded into the background, so only Professor Johnson and Dymphna had their farewells to exchange. True to form, the two of them had avoided each other as the time for departure drew near.

Professor Johnson furrowed his brow. "I have to leave. I hope you know that," he said. "I have a contract for another year at the university."

Dymphna didn't know that. And she had to admit, keeping a player piano running and giving tours of his museum really weren't much of an incentive to stay.

"I hope you'll come back and visit sometime," she said. Worried that she sounded like she was nagging, she added, "You know, if your aunt is coming or something."

"Are you not listening to me? I have to fulfill my contract at the university."

Dymphna's heart started pounding wildly. Was he saying what she thought he was saying? "That depends on what you're saying," Dymphna hedged.

"I am a cautious person by nature," the professor said. "And not the easiest person to get to know."

*I've been trying to get to know you for six months!*

"I've probably handled everything badly," he said.

"Oh no," she said. *Yes.*

"You'll be very busy in the months ahead," the professor said. "I know your rabbits will be arriving and they'll need some time to adjust. But I was hoping . . . I was hoping that when my contract is over, I might come back here and see what I could make of my museum."

"That sounds fine," Dymphna said, restraining herself from jumping into his arms.

"Perhaps we might do some research together."

Dymphna threw her arms around him, restraint be damned. They shared a long kiss. He touched his forehead to hers.

How Professor Johnson made research sound incredibly sexy was beyond her.

He looked around. "Where's Thud?"

He whistled and the dog came running up the trail. He was wearing a new snakeskin collar, compliments of Powderkeg.

"We're going to miss him," Dymphna said, sniffling at first, then breaking down in sobs. "We're going to miss him a lot."

She was well aware that the professor knew she was talking about him as well as Thud, but it was a good excuse not to embarrass them all. Who could say if Professor Johnson would still be in the mood to return in a year?

"He's going to be very bored in Los Feliz," Professor Johnson said. "He's a wild thing now."

"He'll just have to tough it out," Dymphna said.

"Elwood." Cleo rolled down her window and admonished her nephew. "We have to leave, dear."

Professor Johnson nodded quickly, then returned his attention to Dymphna. "What would you say if I asked you to take care of Thud for me until I can get back here? It would mean the world to me."

Dymphna felt another wave of tears coming. She pressed her fingers to her lower lids, but stopped. So what if he saw how much he meant to her? Wasn't that a good thing? Wasn't that what relationships—even this one, one that was starting just as he was leaving—were all about? "I'd be happy to take care of him," she sputtered.

"Good." Professor Johnson kissed her again. "And he'll take care of you, too."

"Elwood, darling," Cleo said sternly.

"Coming, Auntie," Professor Johnson replied.

Dymphna watched as he opened the passenger door. Before he stepped inside, he turned to face her one last time. "You know I have a PhD in natural science from Harvard," he said.

She bit her knuckle to keep from crying. All she could do was nod.

"Stupidest degree in the world," he said, then disappeared into the limo.

Dymphna knelt and watched alongside the bloodhound as the stretch limousine disappeared. She turned to look at the dog and said:

"Welcome to Fat Chance, Texas, Thud."

Be sure not to miss Celia Bonaduce's

### *THE MERCHANT OF VENICE BEACH*

The Rollicking Bun—Home of the Epic Scone—is the center of
Suzanna Wolf's life. Part tea shop, part bookstore, part home, it's
everything she's ever wanted right on the Venice Beach boardwalk,
including partnership with her two best friends from high school,
Eric and Fernando. But with thirty-three just around the corner,
suddenly Suzanna wants something more—something strictly her
own. Salsa lessons, especially with a gorgeous instructor, seem like
a good start—a harmless secret, and just maybe the start of a fling.
But before she knows it, Suzanna is learning steps she never
imagined—and dancing her way into confusion.

"*The Merchant of Venice Beach* has a fresh, heartwarming voice
that will keep readers smiling as they dance through this charming
story by Celia Bonaduce."
—Jodi Thomas, *New York Times* bestselling author

A Lyrical e-book on sale now!

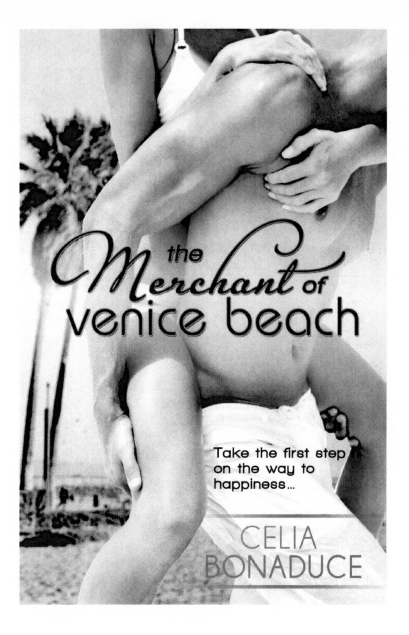

# the *Merchant* of
# venice beach

Take the first step
on the way to
happiness...

## CELIA
## BONADUCE

# CHAPTER 1

Suzanna knew she was out of her element as soon as she walked up to the dance studio. She couldn't help but compare the place to her own little run-down business on the other side of town. Her combination tea shop and bookstore was her pride and joy. Or the bane of her existence, depending on her mood. The place could have subbed as a location for *Fried Green Tomatoes: The Sequel*. A location scout had actually asked Suzanna about it. While the tea shop sat smack on the rundown boardwalk in Venice Beach, DIAG-NOSIS:Dance! was on more ritzy Main Street—uptown in every sense of the word. Maybe not as uptown as Santa Monica, but Main Street was the best Venice had to offer.

As she walked into the dance studio, the wooden floors gleamed at her and the disco balls suspended from the ceiling threw off sparks of promise. The mirrors—the endless walls and walls of mirrors—showed nary a ghost of a fingerprint. Suzanna sneaked a peek at her reflection because, in all honesty, there was no escaping her reflection. She became instantly aware of the little muffin top peeking out between her T-shirt and jeans.

*I look like someone who could use some dance lessons.*

She hovered in the back of the studio and checked out the dancers as casually as she could. Some of them were clearly professionals, but Suzanna was relieved to see there were others who seemed like regular people . . .just ordinary folks who'd decided they needed to dance. Except even the regular people were beautiful. Everybody was in shape. Everybody had perfect hair. Even the janitor and the staff were fabulous. She could feel her nerve ebbing away.

Suzanna eyed the front door.

*Too late for a graceful exit?*

She started to leave, but caught sight of the gorgeous dance instructor from the Wild Oats entering through her escape route. He took her breath away, and she doubled her resolve to become a dancer as he glided past. She inhaled his exotic cologne, an intoxicating blend of lavender, peppermint, roasted coffee, tonka bean, and chocolate. Being raised in Napa Valley and running a tea shop gave Suzanna an edge when it came to identifying scents. She tried to focus, looked around, and located the front desk. She was determined to speak to a Beautiful Person in person.

*This is going to be worse than signing up at a gym. That's not true. I don't think they are going to weigh me at the dance studio.*

Dancers were swirling around in gaspingly ethereal pairs as she beat a path to the front desk. She felt like a colossus bushwhacking her way through gracefully swaying weeping willows.

The Beautiful Person looked up from her computer, looked at Suzanna, and screamed.

No, she didn't. But Suzanna was braced for it, and when it didn't happen, she was grateful for the woman's tiny benevolence. The Beautiful Person was so fragile, she appeared to be made out of lace. She looked like a faerie.

Suzanna started to swell.

"May I help you?" the faerie inquired in a whisper.

"I'm thinking of taking some dance lessons," Suzanna whispered back, trying to keep her feet on the ground. She was swelling so much, she was sure her feet wouldn't stay there for long.

"Private or group?" the faerie continued. Her voice was so wraith-like that Suzanna could barely hear her, even though Suzanna reckoned her ears might be clogged from the swelling. She didn't know which.

The faerie tactfully ignored the fact that Suzanna appeared to be ingesting several canisters of helium. The studio was a business, and Suzanna guessed the girl had seen all kinds. Suzanna knew about that. She owned a business herself.

Suzanna tried to keep her eyes from squeezing shut—the pressure was awful. She felt as if she were about to tip sideways and float to the ceiling, a bouncing, bloated gargoyle looking down on the Beautiful People below.

She hated when this happened. Eric and Fernando always insisted that she wasn't really bloating and floating, but Suzanna thought they were probably just being polite.

The first time she had what she referred to as a "panic swell," she was in junior high school and madly in love with a boy named J. Jay. They had a drama class together and were cast opposite each other as the leads in *Romeo and Juliet*. In rehearsal one day, Suzanna was standing on a ladder that was serving as the balcony and looking down at J. Jay, with his blond hair and blue eyes. She poured her heart into the dialogue, trying to convey that this was not just Shakespeare talking, but her—Suzanna. She infused adolescent passion into every syllable:

> My bounty is as boundless as the sea,
> My love as deep; the more I give to thee,
> The more I have, for both are infinite . . .
> I hear some noise within. Dear love, adieu!

Wildly in character, she turned on the ladder to determine what noise she was hearing from within, and *bammo,* she bumped down the ladder and fell to the floor in a heap. A gasp rose, in unison, from the other kids. As soon as it was clear that she was not dead, this being junior high the gasp turned into suppressed giggles and predictable guffaws. This was not the end of her humiliation, however. A collective gasp once again filled the auditorium as she picked herself up off the floor. She looked around at all the kids laughing and pointing, and that's when she started her first panic swell.

It started, as always, in her ears. She could no longer hear the kids laughing, making it doubly hard to determine what was so hilarious. Then, her body started to expand as the kids continued to point and the full weight of what was going on became clear. . .

The straps of her training bra had somehow come loose on her descent into hell, and her bra was circling her waist. At this point, she had liftoff. Her toes could no longer stay on the ground. She floated to the ceiling and bounced along the tiles until she managed to pull her shirt over the offending undergarment. To add insult to injury, J. Jay was leading the pack in their hilarity. Suzanna prayed that she would be able to stay on the ceiling forever, but suddenly, *pop!*—she was back on the ground, pretending to find the whole thing hysterically funny.

Suzanna pretended to laugh. Then she pretended to laugh harder. In the kill-or-be-killed world of junior high, Suzanna came up with one of her lifelong survival skills. In times of severe humiliation and mortification, she would laugh so hard it looked like she was crying. That way, when she *was* crying, no one could tell that her heart had been broken into a million pieces. It was really very effective, not to mention a great cover. It was something that she used many, many times in her life.

She recommended this approach to Fernando, who took it with a grain of salt—he had no problem weeping copiously when he was unhappy—and to Eric, who disregarded it. Suzanna thought grimly that she'd had to use this strategy when it came to Eric more than once in her life and that perhaps things would have turned out differently if he hadn't ignored it.

Through swollen eyes, she looked around the studio and saw that the dancers all seemed to be having private sessions. She thought of the hot dance instructor and how much fun it would be to have his entire focus. Even though she would, of course, have to pay for his complete focus.

Would it feel like going to a dancing prostitute?

But dancing was a wholesome, healthful activity . . . she wouldn't really be a "john," would she? Another possible plus: a private lesson would lower the risk of public humiliation.

"Private or group?" the faerie inquired again, sounding a little less serene.

Suzanna tried to steady her voice so that she sounded normal; the panic swell brought an elevated timbre to her voice.

"Private . . . I guess."

"Great! They are $120 a lesson."

The faerie beamed up at Suzanna, and *pop!*—she was back on the ground.

"Did I say private? I meant group."

*What's a little more public humiliation anyway? I mean, after the bra incident, I'm a veteran.*

"Groups are great, too," squeaked the faerie. "We have several different classes. Salsa, ballroom, tap . . ."

"Wow . . . so much to choose from."

"Level?" the faerie asked, switching gears.

Suzanna was momentarily stumped, but noticed a small anteroom at the studio, where a class was being taught by her handsome dance instructor. He didn't notice her staring as he whirled on assured feet and with his alluring hips.

"Who is . . . what is that class?" Suzanna asked.

"That's beginning salsa."

Watching the dance instructor in action, Suzanna felt remarkably . . . inspired.

"I'm a beginner," she said. "And I am going to start with salsa."

Suzanna rummaged through her purse and pulled out a credit card. She held it out to the faerie and then snatched it back. Her roommate, co-worker and co-best friend, Eric, in the midst of earning his business degree, had made their method of paying for things so elaborate that she could never keep her credit cards straight. She pulled out another card and handed it over. Suzanna took her receipt and looked at it with pride. She was signed up for classes on Monday nights at seven thirty.

The faerie breathed, "You don't have to limit yourself to Monday evenings. You can come whenever you want. There are continuous salsa classes here and you can take any of them."

Suzanna felt all warm inside, as if the dance studio wanted to become her second home.

Classes were $15 a session (what a bargain!). The faerie told Suzanna to wear comfortable clothing and, if she were really serious about this, to get dance shoes. This sounded like sage advice: the faerie knitted her tiny brow when she said it. Suzanna stared mutely at her. Dance shoes. She should get dance shoes. But Suzanna had absolutely no idea what that meant.

*Shoes in which I will dance, perhaps?*

As Suzanna continued to ponder the mystery of dance shoes, the faerie slid a brochure toward her. Suzanna opened it. It was from a store called Dante's Dancewear, where she could buy dance shoes. She choked when she saw the prices. There was nothing in the catalog for less than $130! Maybe she'd see about buying them later, when she was more in the swing of things.

Suzanna thanked the faerie and let her know in no uncertain terms that she would see her Monday, lest she think Suzanna a quitter. She slipped the brochure into her purse and headed toward the door, where she collided with her dance instructor.

"Oh, hi," she said. "We always seem to be running into each other."

The dance instructor blinked languidly at her.

"I'm going to start taking salsa lessons with you," she added.

He looked at her feet.

"Bring the right shoes."

Quivering from her encounter, Suzanna left the studio and the beautiful dancers behind, happy and terrified that she and her new dance shoes—which were now definitely part of the agenda—would be joining their ranks in a few short days.

Suzanna had never been much of a shoe girl. Even during the *Sex and the City* years, she couldn't imagine hobbling along the mean streets in four-inch heels. Plus, an upbringing in Napa in the eighties and early nineties didn't really lend itself to shoe lust. Napa was a big jeans-and-T-shirt kind of valley. The only place more casual than Napa, as far as Suzanna knew, was Hawaii. She had a friend from there who said he wore flip-flops and shorts every day all the way through high school. The school made the students wear long pants and closed shoes for graduation. Suzanna wondered if they had ever even heard of dance shoes in Hawaii.

It was evening and Suzanna had the bench outside the little library on Main Street to herself. She pulled out her dance shoes catalog and smoothed it open on her lap. She had stopped at Coffee Bean and Tea Leaf, ordered a Moroccan Mint Tea Latte, and poured it carefully into her bright-red travel mug. She wasn't exactly hiding the fact that she drank tea from a corporate chain, but she knew that many of her own customers would be more than a little surprised—and judgmental—if they knew she patronized such a place when she owned a tea shop herself.

One of Suzanna's little rebellions (and secrets) was that she loved the Bean. Suzanna knew there was no way to whip up those chemical-infused concoctions in her traditional space, but it was always fun to slip off to the Bean and sample whatever new, weird thing was being offered. She hadn't been in love with the Strawberry Crème tea, but, honestly, this chocolate-mint concoction was delicious . . . and the pomegranate-blueberry latte was a keeper.

Suzanna thought about her other secret. She had never kept anything from the guys before, and deciding to keep these salsa lessons on the down-low made her feel both guilt-ridden and exhilarated. Sort of like Diane Lane in *Unfaithful*, when she'd slept with Olivier Martinez and was horrified and proud of herself at the same time.

Suzanna flushed. She knew just how Diane Lane's character felt. Powerful, for the first time in ages. Alive. Taking a chance, no matter what anybody thought. Ready for a change.

But too chicken to say it.

Taking a long, soothing sip, she thumbed through the dance shoes catalog, already feeling as if she'd been accepted into a secret club.

*I am one with the dance world . . . or I will be when I settle on some shoes.*

There was much to absorb. There were ballroom shoes, jazz shoes, tap shoes, and various rounded-toe versions of athletic shoes. Suzanna immediately discarded the jazz and tap shoes as they were footwear for avenues she was sure she was not (at this time) prepared to dance down. She was drawn to the athletic shoes, but something told her that these were not going to fly in the steamy world of Latin dancing. She didn't think athletic shoes were what the instructor had in mind when he sneered at her feet. Next, Suzanna rejected the ballroom shoes. They were too fancy, too high, too Beyoncé.

And then she saw them. A whole category called "character shoes." These were the perfect shoes for a woman in her thirties. A woman— grounded and with modest goals.

Well, if you called wanting to nail your new dance instructor a modest goal.

Currently a Field Producer on HGTV's *House Hunters*, Celia Bonaduce's TV credits cover a lot of ground—everything from field-producing ABC's *Extreme Makeover: Home Edition* to writing for many of Nickelodeon's animated series, including *Hey, Arnold* and *Chalkzone*.

An avid reader, entering the world of books was always a lifelong ambition of Celia's. Her debut novel *The Merchant of Venice Beach*, a Venice Beach romance, was first published by Kensington Publishing in August 2013. Two more books in the series followed, and the dream continues with the brand-new Fat Chance, Texas series.

You can visit Celia on the web at www.celiabonaduce.com.

Your best shot at love...

A *Comedy* OF *Erinn*

CELIA
BONADUCE

A VENICE BEACH ROMANCE

MUCH *Ado* ABOUT

*Mother*

*When it comes to life's
big questions, who knows best?*

CELIA
BONADUCE

CPSIA information can be obtained
at www.ICGtesting.com
Printed in the USA
FSOW02n1317020715
8490FS